# AWAKE UNTO ME

Visit us at www.boldstrokesbooks.com

# AWAKE UNTO ME

Kathleen Knowles

2012

# AWAKE UNTO ME

ISBN 13: 978-1-60282-589-5

This Trade Paperback Original Is Published By
Bold Strokes Books, Inc.
P.O. Box 249
Valley Falls, NY 12185

First Edition: January 2012

**Credits**
Editor: Victoria Oldham, Shelley Thrasher
Production Design: Stacia Seaman
Cover Design by Sheri (graphicartist2020@hotmail.com)

# Acknowledgments

Amanda Williford, archivist, Golden Gate National Recreation Area Archives, for her patient assistance to me in digging up historical facts about the Presidio and the beginnings of the Army Nurse Corps.

Stuart Lustig, MD, Langley Porter Psychiatric Institute, University of California, San Francisco, for sharing his expertise on child and adolescent sexual trauma.

Mark Kucharski, for sharing his views on restaurants and their workplace politics.

My beta readers: Joanie, Yvette, Karin, and Carol.

My very patient editor, Victoria Oldham.

Thanks to my supportive family: my sister, Karin, and my spouse, Jeanette.

Special thanks to Joanie VDB who said to me a long time ago, "You know, you really can write."

For Jeanette, whose love informs every word I write

# CHAPTER ONE

*The Barbary Coast*
*San Francisco, September 1888*

"Kerry! Go dump that pot out and rinse it at the pump," Rose shouted from the second floor of the Grey Dog Saloon.

Kerry knew better than to argue. If she kept quiet and did her chores, she could escape to the waterfront and no one would miss her. Rose called her a shadow as she came and went from the house on Jackson Street.

After her chores were done, Kerry scurried out the front door of the Grey Dog and raced to the waterfront a block away. The saloon was one of the oldest in the area and, like its neighbors, was home to a whorehouse upstairs. Kerry didn't think living there was odd; she'd lived there her whole life. Rose and Sally and the other whores had raised her after her mother died when she was born.

She shaded her eyes from the bright sun reflecting off San Francisco Bay and highlighting rocky Alcatraz Island. Rose said the Spanish explorers had named the island *La Isla de los Alcatraces,* "the island of the pelicans." Kerry couldn't see any pelicans, only the grim-looking military fort that took up most of the island and cast dark shadows on the peaceful blue waters of the San Francisco Bay, where a few small fishing boats trawled under the crystal-clear sky. The ever-present westerly breeze ruffled Kerry's hair.

Walking north past Jackson Street to Vallejo Street, she reached a weatherworn warehouse with several barrels in front and pulled some clothes from behind one. She'd traded Teddy Black, the son of the warehouseman, some underclothes she took from one of the whores for them, although she didn't know, or care, what he wanted with women's clothing. If Rose found the boys' clothes in her bedroom at the Grey Dog, she would take them away. Minny, also the daughter of one of the whores and Kerry's bunk mate, couldn't be trusted, not to keep a secret.

Tucking them under her arm she headed for the farthest pier. The tide was out and the smell of seaweed, dead fish, and the waste from the ships made her eyes water. She ducked under the pier, pulled off her faded cotton dress, and put on the shirt and corduroy pants with suspenders. After pulling a cap down low on her face, she walked back to the warehouse and hid the dress. She went off in search of Lucky Jack who, when he was in the right mood, sometimes behaved as her father, which he was. Otherwise he tended to ignore her.

A few hundred yards out from the docks, the cutter *Defiant* lay at anchor, in the day before from Boston. Jack would be looking to steal some of her hands for the *Rosalind*, since the captain of the *Rosalind*, Meeks, was always looking for men. He needed new crew every time he took *Rosalind* on runs up the coast, since most of his crew would either run away or jump ship. The attractions of the Barbary Coast were too hard to resist. Along with gambling, Jack had taken up crimping, the kidnapping of sailors, a couple years before because the money was good. There were so many gamblers on the coast, the competition was fierce, and Jack never seemed to get enough money from gambling alone. But there was never a shortage of ships in need of hands, nor of the unscrupulous captains who would pay for them, which was where the other part of his business came in. The big ships arriving in port would founder in the mud of the bay if they tried to make it to the docks, so the Whitehall boats, big rowboats, ferried their crews and goods back and forth. Lucky Jack was in cahoots with a couple of the boatmen from the Whitehall boats who made extra money by delivering the sailors into the hands of men like Jack, crimpers, who would get them drunk, take their money, then sell them for a good price to other ships. Other than drink and whores, it was the main industry of the Barbary Coast District of San Francisco and had greatly contributed to the area's reputation for danger.

Everyone said Jack was the best crimper on the Barbary Coast. He could spot his marks and get them drinking and spending in the Grey Dog before sunset. Leo, the Grey Dog bartender, was his partner, and the hapless sailors would pass out from the opium-spiked booze and wake up in ropes onboard the *Rosalind* or one of a dozen other ships. The pretty waiter girls who served the booze were whores who entertained the sailors before they were given their doses and dumped into the cellar below. Most of them aren't so pretty, Kerry thought, looking at the women wandering among the tables or leaning against the bar, but the sailors didn't care. The captain Jack had a deal with that particular night would come in the early morning and haul them away. Kerry had heard Jack and Leo laughing about the poor sailors who not only didn't get women, but woke up on a strange ship going somewhere they didn't want to go.

Kerry found Jack passing the time with Leo and some of the Grey Dog regulars, the way he usually did when he was waiting for a ship to release her crew to the diversions of the Barbary Coast. Kerry boldly walked up to him and pulled his sleeve.

"What do you want, boy?" he said roughly, without turning around. "My shoes are shiny enough."

Jack, they said, could see around corners and Kerry believed them. "The Whitehall's going out to the *Defiant*."

"What? Now?" Jack jumped off the bar stool and strode out the door with Kerry after him.

"Jack," she said, "it's me."

He squinted in the sunlight. "Aw, Christ, girl. What are you about?" He looked closer. "Are you crazy? What if someone spots you?"

"No one knows but you and maybe Leo. I want to help you."

"No. Never. You—"

"Let me, Jack. Please. I don't want to spend all day inside with the girls. I'd rather spend it with you."

"You want to learn the game, do you?" He smiled, seeing a little of her mother Molly in her and a lot of himself. She had a light dusting of freckles across her nose, dark brown eyes, and, like Molly, dark hair. She was slight but tough and quick. She had grown up a wharf rat and rarely smiled, so when she did it was extra special.

The take from gambling and crimping kept Jack well dressed, comfortably fed, and took care of young Kerry and whichever whore took his fancy at that moment. Jack wasn't sure how much Kerry knew about his work, and he usually tried to ignore her even as he made sure Rose had money to support her. Jack didn't know what he could do to keep her out of the whore's life as he'd promised Molly. He would never leave the Barbary Coast, not even to find a better life for Kerry, since he reckoned his skills didn't suit him for regular employment.

"I can't stand being in the house all day helping Rose with chores. And there's always some man who—"

"Stop, enough! I know the type." Jack furrowed his brows. She was right. Some of Rose's customers weren't avid for any of the pretty waiter girls because eighteen- or nineteen-year-olds were too old. His promise to Molly came back to him as he stood there contemplating his daughter. Kerry was reaching the age to be noticed and to start whoring. He shuddered.

"Right, then. Here's the drill. You bring me five boys off the *Defiant* and you'll get your cut, but look sharp. Old Tom's girl, Maggie, will be about and after the same marks. Don't let on who you are." Jack meant the owner of the boarding house down the street, a wily old drunk named Tom Harlin. He laughed. "She'd be better looking and more useful if she had any teeth."

"I won't. Maggie's not too smart that way. She only knows how to draw a dumb sailor in to get his head cracked."

Jack laughed again. "True. Old Tom makes the poor shanghaied sailors suffer knocks on their heads as well as the hangovers from whiskey and laudanum. At least I don't give them that."

Kerry shot from the saloon, intent on showing Jack she could do her part. Holding her cap to her head, she ran full tilt to the dock and waited, bouncing on her toes in anticipation.

The sailor boys of the *Defiant* tumbled off the Whitehall, shouting and laughing. They'd been round the Horn and mostly at sea for six months as they sailed from the East Coast to the West Coast. They had half their pay and were ready to taste the famous pleasures of the Barbary Coast. It had been forty years since the Gold Rush, but the legends of San Francisco's seafront had only grown. Sure enough, Kerry saw Maggie Harlin pull up alongside the youngest looking of the *Defiant* sailors and smile. She stayed back and watched.

"Howdy, sailor!" Maggie crowed with her toothless lisp. "I can show you a good time."

"Is that a fact?" the sailor said, suspiciously. "How do I know you won't rob me when I'm asleep?"

"Well, I never!" Maggie said primly. "I'll give you an honest fuck, I will, and send you on your way whistling."

"No, thanks, sister. I prefer women with teeth in their heads, not gap-toothed hags."

Maggie grinned wider. "You don't know what it feels like to get a suck from my mouth."

Kerry saw the sailor hesitate and she was at his side. "Mister, that whore's lying. They rob you blind, drug you, and next thing you know you're are on a whaler going back to the North Sea for a year."

The sailor looked hard at her, then back into the horrible toothless grin of the whore.

"Oh?" he said, raising an eyebrow. "What would you offer instead?"

Kerry smiled then. "I can show you to a good saloon with honest drinks and pretty waiter girls, if you want that. A good cheap bed for the night and breakfast to send you off in style the next morning." Kerry was surprised that lying came so easy to her.

"Sorry, girl. I believe the lad here, not you."

Maggie frowned and peered at Kerry, who had taken care to black her face here and there and put a cut above her nose. She tugged at the sailor's sleeve so he'd follow her.

"Hey, boys," the sailor called to his mates. "I have a guide here to take us to paradise. Or some version of it."

Kerry walked into the Grey Dog with all six of them—one over her quota. Her father and Leo looked on from the bar. Then Jack tossed her a silver dollar. "Be gone with you, lad. This is no place for a youngster."

Kerry stared at the silver coin in her palm.

"Gentlemen," Lucky Jack said, "welcome to San Francisco. Can I interest you in some card-playing along with your refreshment?"

❖

A week after she started working for Jack, Kerry grabbed Minny's hand and said, "Come on, I want to show you something." The fog had burned off and the mid-morning sun lit Meiggs Wharf, giving it a deceptively innocent and peaceful air. They looked much like a boy and his sister. Minny, a year younger and small for her size, looked up at Kerry worshipfully.

"Where we going?" she asked plaintively.

"You'll see." They scampered a couple of blocks down the wharf until they stood in front of a ramshackle building. The sign above the door said, Warner's Cobweb Palace and Saloon, and below, in smaller type, Oddities of Interest.

Kerry ranged freely about the wharf area of the waterfront district, looking for marks off the myriad ships docked in the San Francisco

Bay's biggest port, and had come upon Warner's Cobweb Palace early on. Minny and Kerry went inside and waited for their eyes to adjust, the sounds of animals assaulting their ears.

Minny clutched Kerry's arm fearfully. "What's that?"

"Shush," Kerry said. "You'll like this."

"No, I won't!" Minnie looked up and saw the thousands of spiderwebs adorning the rafters and screamed. Old man Warner would never kill a spider and over the years they had spun thousands of webs. Some of the spiderwebs had been there so long, Warner's saloon customers joked they would be there long after he bit the dust. He let the local kids in to see the spiderwebs and his animals during the day before the saloon got busy.

"Stay close to me!" Kerry figured Minny needed to get out more and away from Rose and Sally. It was funny how protective they were of her, considering the future she was likely to have. Kerry noticed the food stains on Minny's dress and the remnants of porridge on her face. Unlike Minny, however, Kerry was beyond their control. Rose had thrown up her hands after she found out Lucky Jack had set Kerry to luring marks for his crimping operation.

In the dim light, Minny and Kerry gazed at the huge cages with monkeys and kangaroos. When a huge blue parrot saw them, it screeched, "Puta! You loco!" and some gibberish old man Warner told Kerry was probably Chinese. The bird was half crazed from the whiskey the saloon customers fed it.

To Kerry the Cobweb Palace was by far the best and most interesting place on the wharf.

"Tell your pop the *Mary Lou* is in from Philadelphia," old man Warner said to Kerry. When the parrot heard his voice, it squawked, "Grandfather!" in a hoarse voice, making Minny jump and Kerry laugh.

Everyone knew Warner had a soft spot for kids, though he could curse a blue streak at anyone else and had a rough way with women. Thousands of pictures of women covered the walls of the Cobweb Palace from floor to ceiling, most barely visible in the dark and under all the cobwebs. When she wasn't looking at the animals, Kerry stared at the pictures everywhere. She had her favorites and would gaze for ages at Gertrude or Priscilla or Fay, trying to divine who they were and what they would be like in person. Some of them looked like real ladies. The only women Kerry knew were the waiter girls at the Grey Dog or other saloons in the Barbary Coast, and they sure didn't look like the women in the pictures. Giving in to Minny's insistent whining, she led them back outside.

"What do you want to do now?" Kerry asked.

"I don't know," Minny said, sucking her thumb. Just then, Kerry spotted her friend Teddy from Black's Warehouse.

"Hullo," he said.

"Hey. You was able to get away from your dad today?"

"Yeah. I was coming to find you. I've got to get away before the old man notices I'm gone. Want to go to downtown?"

"Only if we can go to Chinatown first."

Tommy made a face. "I don't like that place. All that strange stuff in the stores smells bad and them people are weird."

They had gone to Chinatown the month before and, while Kerry was fascinated by the Buddhist temples and the food markets with endless bins labeled in Chinese, Teddy was not. She was grateful that he kept it secret about her clothes instead of ratting her out. Boys could go places girls couldn't, and she wasn't about to let a skirt stand in the way of her adventures. He had told her she was more fun to be with than the boys on the Barbary Coast, who only wanted to pick fights.

"Pop said the Chinese will kidnap us and sell us into slavery."

Kerry rolled her eyes but decided to humor him. "So where do you want to go?"

"What about the Palace Hotel? I know a guy who works in the kitchen, Sam Reed. He can get us something to eat. Something good."

"Yeah. First I have to take Minny home."

"Well, be quick about it then. I'll wait here."

Kerry dragged Minny home, dropped her off, and waited until she'd curled up and fallen asleep almost instantly on the couch before running back to Teddy, who was throwing rocks at an abandoned building's windows. They made their way through the maze of streets until they stood in front of the Palace Hotel. They were on New Montgomery Street staring at a building larger than any ship they'd ever seen. It occupied an entire square block and was eight stories high.

"Come on. Let's go inside," Teddy said, and pulled her arm.

They entered the lobby. It was, if possible, even grander inside than out, with a giant central court with a ceiling of thousands of panes of glass and great marble columns. Kerry stood with her mouth open, feeling every bit of dirt under her nails and grime on her shoes. It was a universe removed from the grubby barrooms and music halls and dirty wharfs of the Barbary Coast.

"I could do that. I could work here," Teddy said softly as a bellboy pushed a cart full of cases past them.

"How much money could you make? Not much, I bet."

"Silly. It's not the money they pay you. It's the tips from all the rich people who stay here. Really, really high-class people come here, like them nobs that live up on the hill yonder."

Before Kerry could respond, they heard a sharp voice from nearby. "Hey! What are you two ragamuffins doing? Get out before I throw you out."

They ran back to the street.

"Come on." Teddy grabbed Kerry's hand and dragged her around to the alley behind the hotel. He stuck his head in the door and Kerry peered over his shoulder. He spotted Sam standing at a sink as big as a bathtub, piled high with dishes.

"Pssssst!" Teddy hissed.

"Hey, Teddy. We have to be quick. The cooks will be here soon for dinner service. Chef will have my head if he catches me on French leave." Kerry knew French leave meant fooling around, not doing your work. She'd heard Jack say it to the waiter girls more than once. She figured the French must not work at all.

They followed him into the kitchen and into a giant walk-in cooler crammed with food.

"Don't take too much," Sam said unnecessarily. The amazing quantity of food mesmerized Kerry. On one side she saw barrels of live lobsters and oysters and slabs of meat and whole chickens and ducks. On the other side lay crates of every kind of vegetable imaginable, boxes of potatoes, turnips, and squash. In yet another part of the cooler, Sam showed them the prepared food. Kerry and Teddy helped themselves to chicken legs and steak while Sam kept a lookout, stuffing their pockets with as much food as they could fit. Teddy even put a drumstick in his sock.

On their walk through the kitchen, their arms laden, Kerry stopped to gaze at the huge wooden work tables and the array of pots and utensils hanging from the ceiling. She saw racks of knives and four great stoves, each with six burners and a giant grill in the middle. It was after lunch and before supper so the fires were low. Even so, the kitchen was tremendously hot.

More than the food, the kitchen itself drew Kerry. She knew only the tiny kitchen in the Grey Dog where the women cooked their simple meals, and this was a different universe, a big, clean, magical one.

Teddy grabbed her arm again. "Come quick. We have to go, Kerry! We can't get Sam in trouble."

She stole one last look at the gleaming surfaces before she let Teddy pull her out of the kitchen and into the alley, where they sat to consume their stolen meal.

# CHAPTER TWO

*The Mission District*
*San Francisco, April 1891*

"Elizabeth, dear. Please run over to the Italian market and buy some carrots and cabbage for dinner."

Beth's father George looked up and frowned but didn't object. If her mother Frieda was busy, he allowed Beth to run quick errands as long as she came directly back to the store. Their busiest time was afternoons as the neighbors came home from work and stopped in to do their shopping at Hammonds Dry Goods.

The store stood on the corner of 17th and Valencia, about two blocks from the Mission District's chief landmark—the church and mission of St. Francis of Assisi. The Spanish priests had built it over two hundred years before, and it was still the biggest Catholic church in the neighborhood.

Its parishioners were the Italian and Irish immigrants who had come during the Gold Rush, and although they hadn't found any gold they found a place to settle. The Hammonds were a "mixed" couple. George was German and Frieda was Norwegian, which made their only daughter, Beth, not that different from the rest of the neighborhood melting pot.

The Mission District was sunny and placid, far different than crowded, noisy downtown San Francisco. It was a mere two miles away from the Barbary Coast, but other than a few businesses such as the Hammonds' store, it was purely residential and home to respectable working families.

Beth was relieved to get away from the constant tension at home.

Her father worried about the business, about what people might think—really about everything. The worry made him irritable.

She strolled down Guerrero Street and turned on 17th Street to Mission Street. It was April and the afternoon sun was warm. She looked up toward the twin hills in the distance and saw the fog approaching, as it almost always did at that time of day, although it wouldn't reach the Mission until nearly dark.

In the Rocco Produce store, at least one of the many Rocco children was always at work. Beth thought how different it would be if she had a brother or a sister to take some of her parents' attention and to help them. She walked slowly past the racks of vegetables and fruits, bursting with life and color. She ran her hand over thick-skinned cantaloupes, spiky artichokes, and glossy tomatoes. What would they taste like? Her family ate only a few different vegetables, none of them what her father called "exotic." The Roccos' vegetables seemed so alive and earthy compared to the beige barrels of rice, wheat, sugar, and the like in her parents' store. She chose a cabbage and the orangest carrots she could find and put them in a mesh bag.

Mama Rocco stood behind the counter, waiting on customers even though she spoke no English. A Rocco kid Beth didn't know stood next to her. The Rocco children were taught by the fathers at the Mission Dolores, and Beth went to the public grammar school. This was not the solemn-eyed boy who was usually at his mother's side but a girl of Beth's age, her natural coloring darkened by outdoor work.

She smiled brilliantly at Beth, who automatically smiled back. Mama Rocco spoke rapidly in Italian, likely instructing the girl to weigh and add up Beth's purchases. It's the same thing I do, Beth thought. But Mama Rocco was also smiling both at Beth and her daughter, whom she patted on the shoulder. Beth swallowed a sudden lump of emotion, knowing she could never expect such a gentle gesture from her own parents.

Beth walked home with their smiles on her mind.

As she was getting ready for school the next morning, Beth asked, "Mama? Do you need anything else at the Italian store? I could go there after school before I come home."

Frieda fixed her with a sharp look. "I suppose we need some more onions and turnips for the stew. Don't dawdle. Your father needs you directly so I can go home to prepare supper."

"Yes, Mama, I won't be long."

After school, Beth practically ran the three blocks to Rocco's

Produce. She was thrilled to see the girl from the day before standing behind the counter. Mama Rocco was busy elsewhere in the store and the girl smiled her radiant smile and asked, "What's your name?"

"Beth Hammond." She smiled shyly. "What's yours? What school do you go to?"

"My name is Theresa. I go to St Agnes. Where do you go?"

"Guerrero Primary. It's on Guerrero Street," Beth added, then felt foolish.

"That must be why it's called by that name then," Theresa said seriously, not as though she meant it in a nasty way.

Beth was silent, searching for something else to say. Theresa looked at her expectantly but when Beth said nothing, Theresa saved her by asking, "Are you shopping for your mama?"

"Yes. It's for supper tonight."

"I see. What are you having? We always have spaghetti or something like that."

"Uh-huh," Beth said, not knowing what exactly Theresa meant by spaghetti.

"What are you having?" Theresa asked again.

"Beef stew."

Before Theresa could say anything, Mama Rocco spoke sharply. Theresa glanced over Beth's shoulder at a man standing behind her. Beth didn't understand Italian but she recognized it was time to leave.

"Good-bye," Theresa said cheerfully. Beth gave Theresa another shy smile before she darted from the store.

❖

Several days passed before Beth had an excuse to go back to the produce store, but when she was able, she saw that Theresa was alone, and the thought of talking to her again made her giddy.

Theresa giggled as she added up Beth's purchases.

"What's so amusing?" Beth asked.

"Nothing." Theresa kept smiling to herself.

"Oh. Do tell me. It's not nice to keep a secret."

"It is just that you always buy the same thing. Don't you get bored with what you eat?"

"No. It's just what we eat." Feeling a sudden and inexplicable need to defend her family, she said, "It's what my father likes."

"Oh, I know. We eat what my papa likes, but he's easy. You could come over and eat with us some time."

Taken aback by the invitation, Beth immediately tried to think of how to persuade her parents, especially her father, to allow her to go to her new friend's home. Any little difference in routine could annoy him.

"I don't know if I can, but I'll ask."

"Mama is having her sister and my cousins to supper Thursday so she'll be making a great deal of food. You could come then."

❖

"Theresa asked me to supper with her family on Thursday. May I go, Mama? May I please?"

"Who are these people?" Frieda asked suspiciously.

"They own the produce store. You know them—the Rocco family."

Frieda nodded thoughtfully, putting away the groceries with her usual staccato movements. "I'll ask your father."

At the dinner table that night, Frieda said, "Beth has been invited to dinner with the Rocco family. You know of them. They own the produce store."

"Eh. The Italians. Why would they ask her?" George kept his eyes on his plate and kept eating.

"Their daughter, the second child, I believe, is the same age as our Beth."

George didn't look up. "I don't like Italians."

"They are well regarded. We would do well to be neighborly. Besides, it would be good for Beth to have a friend."

"She has friends."

"No one special. Please, dear. It's just for dinner."

"No," George said shortly. "We need her at home and I don't know them."

In the kitchen after supper as they cleaned the dishes, Frieda told Beth, "Don't worry, I'll speak to him." Beth nodded and went to her room when she finished her chores, disappointment making her feet heavy.

❖

Beth sat nervously at the huge table. She couldn't even count the number of people in the house, let alone remember their names. The Rocco family spent a good half hour before supper talking and kissing and hugging. It was altogether a strange and wonderful occasion.

When Theresa introduced Beth to Mama and Papa as her friend, they had startled her by kissing her soundly on both cheeks. Her own family would never do such a thing. Her mother occasionally pecked her cheek or gave her a small hug, but she certainly wouldn't have done it with a friend she'd brought home for dinner. She'd never been at a supper table with so many people and so much noise. And, most of all, they were happy.

The contrast between the Roccos and her drab and morosely silent parents struck her as everyone laughed and shouted and passed huge bowls of food around. The conversation went on in mixed Italian and English, and Theresa sat beside Beth and kept up a whispered translation. The food was odd too, but wonderful. Beth had a huge steaming plate of fragrant spaghetti, meatballs in a vibrant red sauce, and bread with spices on it. Theresa encouraged her to try everything.

"Insalata too," she said as she passed a huge plate of salad to Beth. Beth's family distrusted green, leafy vegetables and never had them, and as she ate them she thought she knew why. She found them bitter and foreign but ate politely.

Theresa and her brother Nicolo walked Beth home. Theresa hugged Beth and said, "Maybe you will come out to the farm with me sometime to bring in the goods for the store. Papa has asked me to come help in two weeks. It's south so we go out and stay the whole day."

Beth nodded. "I'll try," she said. She was buoyed by her success; not only had her father finally agreed to let her have the Roccos as friends, but she had made it through the occasion without making a fool of herself. The world suddenly felt a million times brighter, and she hadn't even known it was dull.

"Listen to me play this, dear, and read the notes," Frieda said. She and Beth were seated at the piano and George was in the armchair reading his newspaper. Beth read the title, "Für Elise." Frieda played the simple melody slowly, letting Beth hear each note. Then she moved to one side and Beth took over.

The piano was Frieda's pride and joy. Her mother had bought it in

Minneapolis and had laboriously carried it overland to San Francisco when she joined Grandpa Olaf there in 1852. Olaf had tried and failed to make his fortune in the gold fields, eventually giving up and settling for being a policeman instead. The piano was the family's only recreation, since George disliked or distrusted any other possible forms.

Besides the piano, reading pleased Beth the most. She did well in school and helped her father at the store because it would never occur to her to do otherwise, but her real joy was books: Dickens, Hardy, the Brontë sisters, the poetry of Emily Dickinson. She read two books a week because the Mission District had been recently blessed with its own branch of the library. Beth no longer had to go downtown to Kearny Street with her mother. Since it was close enough she could walk to the library by herself, even though she couldn't stay long because of her work at the store. Beth had to work all day on Saturday, but after dinner, if she could get her homework done, she could often cajole her parents into letting her go to the library. George grumbled but Frieda gently overrode his objections.

"She's the best girl in the world, dear. Give her at least this much privilege."

"Books are no good for girls."

"She only reads novels and poetry, dear. They won't harm her."

"The only book she needs is the Bible."

When Frieda mentioned Beth's request to go the Rocco farm, her father's face turned the color of the spaghetti sauce they served at their dinner, and Beth curled into herself and stared at her plate.

"No. I said, no. I need her at the store."

"All right, husband. As you wish." She turned to Beth, who was nearly in tears, and quietly said, "Don't be concerned. I'll ask him again later."

Beth returned to her room, disconsolate. She hoped her mother was correct. She very much wanted to go to the farm with Theresa and her family. Something about Theresa's smile, the way she laughed and fooled around, made Beth feel happy and that life was full of joy and possibility.

❖

Beth didn't know how her mother had done it, but when she got up, her father had told her to be careful and not be any trouble. She raced around getting ready, thanking her mother profusely as she ran from room to room. She ran to Theresa's shop and laughed at her stories and her sibling's silly torments all the way to the farm.

The Rocco family and their farm workers spent the morning in the field, then had a huge lunch under the grove of oak trees near the southern edge of the property. Papa Rocco's brother and his family lived at the farm full-time, and once again the crowd at lunch seemed enormous to Beth. Since everyone took a little wine at lunch along with all the food, they were drowsy, and Theresa took Beth over to the little stream about a mile from the fields.

"What do you think you'll be when you grow up?" Beth asked Theresa, who lay on her back with her eyes closed.

"Let me sleep," Theresa said. "I'm tired and you ask too many questions."

"I want to know."

"I'll work in the store until I get married. Then I'll have a family. What else would I do?"

"I don't know. I really hope I'm not going to be working in my parents' store my whole life."

Theresa turned on her side and looked at Beth. "But why ever not?"

"I don't know. I just don't want that. I don't know what I want. I don't want to get married either."

"Oh, goodness. Of course you do." Theresa again closed her eyes, as if the conversation was over.

Beth sat and looked at the stream and beyond it the sun shining over the vast fields of vegetables and the green hills in the distance. She was utterly at peace in one part of her mind and anxious in the other. *I only know what I truly don't want, not what I truly do want. How will I ever know?*

## Chapter Three

When there were no ships in and no opportunity for crimping, Lucky Jack started a card game. It took longer to make money but was more fun and less dangerous.

There was no such thing as a slow night at the Grey Dog. The waiter girls circulated constantly, flirting with the patrons and getting them to drink. There was always a mix of sailors, miners, and every variety of criminal known to the Barbary Coast. Jack stood at the bar for a while and looked around, talking off and on with Leo.

Jack sighed and swallowed his shot of whiskey. "I wish I could do something other than crimp or gamble—something honest. I could live respectable-like and give Kerry a better life."

"Eh?" Leo poured another glass and pushed it over to Jack. "You're not really fit for honest employment. You been down here since you was a kid. You ain't never had no regular job."

Jack laughed. "That's true. But I don't go in for robbery or murder. Running women isn't to my taste. That don't leave much."

"You're pretty good with the cards," Leo pointed out. "If there's a greenhorn to fleece, you do all right. You're Lucky Jack."

"That's 'cause I don't lose my shirt and no one gets mad enough to shoot me." Jack turned around and scanned the crowd.

He saw a man who, from his sober suit, looked to be a gentleman, sipping a whiskey and looking around expectantly.

"What's his story, you reckon?" Jack asked Leo. It was a game they played—guessing the wants of and/or background of the strangers who made their way to the Grey Dog.

"Banker."

"Nah. Too thin. Doesn't look greedy enough."

Leo laughed and they clicked glasses. "Then what's your guess, Jack?"

"Hmmmm. Let me see. He's not in business, I'd swear."

"Look now," Leo whispered.

Jack turned on his bar stool. One of the working girls, Sally, had sauntered over to the gentleman's table. Without being able to hear a word in the noisy saloon, Leo and Jack knew what she said.

Remarkably, though, the gentleman smiled and responded, but instead of settling in his lap, Sally flounced away with a frown. Jack and Leo rubbed their chins in bemusement.

"He's not here for the girls," Leo said. "He's not a drinking man, that's for sure. He's had that one whiskey for an hour."

"Well, that leaves just one thing."

Jack slid off his bar stool and strode over to the stranger's table. He decided to put on his best manners, having long ago learned what type of speech would do for each man. He would curse rough and raucously with the sailors, and he could sound dangerous enough for the hungriest murderer on Barbary Coast to leave him be. He could lull this one with politeness and lure him into a game where he could easily take him. The gentlemen were always like that.

"Good evening, sir. May I buy you a drink? My name is John O'Shea. Friends call me Lucky Jack."

"Good evening, Mr. O'Shea. A drink would be most welcome and some information would be even more welcome. Addison Grant, at your service."

Jack waved two fingers at Leo, who sent one of the girls over with two glasses of whiskey. "What brings you to this part of town? Not a lady's company, I take it?"

"Ah, no." The man smiled. "I was hoping to find a card game."

Jack smiled broadly. "Well then, sir. You've come to the right place. I believe I may be able to accommodate you. Your game, sir? Five-card draw?

"Blackjack."

Jack drew back, surprised but intrigued. He had learned the deceptively simple game from a fellow from Reno and had liked it because the odds were decent.

"Well, then, sir, let us get comfortable and begin. Do you want a bottle?"

"Indeed not, sir. I prefer to keep a clear head."

"Then I will as well," Jack said, disappointed that the fellow wasn't a drinker who would be reckless or become befuddled.

Jack pulled out his cards and shuffled. "Let's begin."

They dealt ten hands between them, and the stranger won every game. A crowd gathered and Leo spotted Jack two hundred. They'd done this before to good effect: the Grey Dog could make a profit and Jack took a healthy cut.

"Who's in?" Jack asked. Three besides Mr. Grant signaled and the four men started a game. Blackjack wasn't as well known in San Francisco as it was in Reno. They went another five rounds and the stranger won four and the house won one. The other players weren't skilled and were drinking heavily, so it was basically a duel between Jack and Grant. The others dropped out and Grant bet all he had one on one hand. It looked to be suicide, since the house had a nine showing and Jack had a ten as the hole card. Grant showed a two, a five. He signaled another hit. Jack dealt him a ten. They turned over. House showed twenty; Grant blackjacked. The crowd cheered.

Afterward, Grant bought Jack a drink and thanked him for the game as the crowd dispersed.

"Where are you from, mister, and how did you manage to play cards like that?"

"I'm matriculating at the University of California Department of Medicine. I'll graduate in June. I expect to practice medicine here. Although I come from Boston, the good city of San Francisco suits me. I learned to play cards when I was a freshman. I enjoy the diversion."

"You don't say. A doctor. I'll be damned. You're a hell of a card player, and although I don't think I want to play you anymore, we could do something for each other. Can you tell me how you play the game like that?"

Addison laughed. "I count cards. And I figure the odds. It's not foolproof but it is serviceable. I can tell after every hand what's left in the deck."

"Is that a fact?"

"It is, Mr. O'Shea, and I can show you. I must leave but I'll be back in two days. Thank you most kindly for the introduction, the drink, and the company." Dr. Grant slapped his bowler back on his head, waved genially to all present, and walked out of the saloon.

❖

Addison, as everyone called him thereafter, returned as he'd promised, and he and Jack sat playing for hours every weekend. One evening, Kerry came over to the table and stood next to Jack and observed the play.

"Who's this, then? I never expected to see children in these parts."

"This is my daughter, Kerry. She's ten."

"I see. Kerry? Would you like to learn to play cards with us?" Addison asked kindly.

Kerry nodded silently. Jack nodded to her and she sat down next to him and helped him with each hand.

"Does her mother know where she is and what she's doing?" Addison asked.

"Nah. Mother's dead. Doubt she cares now. Molly told me if nothing else, though, to not let Kerry go bad."

"And how will you do that?" Addison asked in a genuinely curious tone.

"I don't intend for her to be a whore."

Addison paled. "Good God, of course not."

"As long as she stays close to me, she's safe, I reckon. She's a smart kid."

"I can see that." Addison grinned at Kerry, who grinned back.

Jack was surprised that Addison got a smile out of Kerry. *She likes him. He's a good man.*

"Get upstairs, girl. Me and the doctor got to talk."

As Kerry nodded and walked away, Jack watched her. She'd grown taller in the last year, and her pants were too short and her shirt too small. He figured if she was going to dress as a boy, he might as well go ahead and give her money to get some clothes that fit. He turned back to Addison.

"Doc. I want you and me to do some business. You got that system you got and I can get you the marks. If there's a game going, you get more idiots than you can handle. They're all figuring to win some money. I know you're a respectable-like fellow but…" Jack looked at Addison. "I'll be the dealer, you'll be the ringer. We can clean up, I tell you. Split fifty-fifty."

"I'm your man, sir. We can have a go at it during the weekends. I have classes during the week. I'll use the money to pay back some of my educational debts."

"No worries." They shook hands.

Leo was skeptical when Jack told him their plans later. "It sounds like a winner, Jack, but too good to be true. They ain't all *that* stupid down here in the terrific Pacific." He used the Barbary Coast's nickname sarcastically.

"Ah, you're like an old woman sometimes, Leo. The doc looks like an honest gentleman who's ripe for the taking."

"Yeah, but word travels fast, Jack."

"We got it all figured, Leo."

The next year was lucrative for Jack and Addison. A seemingly endless stream of greenhorns and old hands wanted to take on the fine young doctor. Leo served him cold, strong tea so it would look like he was tossing down the whiskey, and he and Jack used signals to telegraph their strategy, leaving no one the wiser. They all went away shaking their heads, with empty pockets.

"I do believe, Jack, I've made enough to pay my parents back for both my baccalaureate and medical degrees, thanks to you."

"You're a clever fellow, Addison. I've made me so much money I started an account for Kerry at the Bank of California. I've never saved a penny before I met you. I don't know…if something ever happened to me…" Jack fell silent.

Addison sipped his drink.

"I never met anyone like you before. I never made so much money from cards as I have with you. And you make me think about things when we talk, you know? Things I never cared to think about before. You're a good man. One of the best I've met." Jack stopped again, trying to get up the courage to ask Addison what he wanted to.

"I want you to be a co-signer on the bank account so's you can help Kerry and get the money to her if…well, if something should happen."

"With pleasure, Mr. O'Shea." Addison shook Jack's hand tightly, and Jack knew he'd made the right decision. Grant would take care of Kerry and Kerry's money if he wasn't around to keep an eye on her anymore. He ground his teeth as the same sense of dread came over him as it had been doing for the last few days. He ignored it, like he always did, and swallowed past the lump in his throat when he watched Kerry laughing with some of the bar patrons. He couldn't imagine not being around to see what she might become one day. Slamming his glass on the table he stood abruptly. "What say we go find ourselves some games outside the Grey Dog, Addison?"

They went around to a few different bars and found themselves in one of the lowest of the many deadfalls on the Coast. The crowd was rougher than usual and hard drinking.

Addison won a couple a rounds and big tough stood up and said, flatly, "Yer cheatin' and I can prove it. Let me see the deck." Jack handed it over swiftly. The man couldn't prove a thing since it all resided in Addison's agile mind.

The hoodlum made Jack and Addison stand up and he searched but could find no cards on either of them, naturally. He growled and frowned and they went back to playing. Addison won again and then again.

The ruffian stood up, his face purple. "That's it! I don't know what yer game is but I've had enough." He pulled out a gun, causing all to dive for cover except Addison and Jack. Addison was taken by surprise, but Jack wasn't. He'd figured it might get ugly, since this wasn't the kind of place where men easily parted ways with their money.

"Easy there, pardner. You saw for yourself he's clean."

The hoodlum snarled and grabbed Addison's arm suddenly, got him in a headlock, and with the gun at his temple, looked straight at Jack and said, "I say he's a dirty rotten cheater and you give me back all my money or he gets a slug in the head that will spoil his nice looks."

Jack stood up slowly, his hands in the air. "We don't want no trouble, pard. I'll get your money. Just give me a moment."

Jack reached into his shoe and brought out a derringer, and as quick as could be he shot the hoodlum in the arm. The gunslinger howled in pain and let Addison go. This time Addison used his head and dropped to the floor.

Jack grabbed the ruffian's gun, and he and Addison got on either side and hauled the man outside and threw him in the shallow muddy water under the boardwalk. Jack hefted the man's gun and joked, "I'll give it Leo and add it to the collection!" He glanced at Addison when he didn't get a response.

"How're you doin, Doc? You're lookin' a little shook up."

Addison put his hands in his pockets, but not before Jack saw them shaking. "That was close," Addison said.

"It was bound to happen. This ain't Nob Hill with the swells, Doc. This is the Wild West. Let's us go back to the Grey Dog and get a drink to settle your nerves."

They walked down the Embarcadero. From melodeons they could hear the singing and the pianos. A couple of drunks staggered out of a saloon and nearly ran into them. Jack pushed them aside, shouting, "What's the matter, you can't see in the fog?" Jack laughed, but quieted when he noticed how pale and silent Addison was.

Back in the comparative safety of the Grey Dog, they sat and talked.

"I—I think I may have made all the money I need, Jack. Tonight made it clear to me that I should retire from the card business. If you ever need anything, Jack, you can find me easily. I'm taking a position as house staff at the City and County Hospital right after I graduate. I've come to consider you a friend."

"Well, I'm sorry to see you go but it was a great lark while it lasted," Jack said, sipping his whiskey and avoiding eye contact. He didn't want to seem soft to Addison so made sure he couldn't see the disappointment he knew would show in his eyes.

"It was indeed. Something to tell my children about if I should be so lucky to have any. Keep a close eye on Kerry, Jack."

"I sure will try, but sometime, some hoodlum might get me at last, and then Kerry will be alone." Jack contemplated his whiskey for a long moment and then leaned forward, looking Addison in the eye. "Could I ask you something, Doc? I ain't ever asked no one for a thing in my life. But you're a good man and the closest thing to a friend I've had next to Leo."

"Good God, man, you saved *my* life. Just ask."

"If something happens to me, I want Kerry to come to you. If I ain't around to protect her, I want her out of the Barbary. You're already a co-signer on that bank account I set up for her."

"Of course, Jack. Don't worry. I'd gladly take her in and look after her. It's the least I can do."

"Thanks, Doc. I ain't going to let her know. I don't want to worry the child, but I'll leave word with Leo so he knows what to tell her if it goes bad for me."

"Well done, Jack. You can depend on me. Take care of yourself and your girl."

"I will. God speed, Doctor."

Jack swirled his whiskey in his glass and stared into space long after the doctor had left. A chill crept up his spine but he shook it off. If someone did get him one day, Kerry would be safe. And even though he never would have thought he'd give a damn about anyone, he realized his daughter could be the only thing he'd ever do right. With a deep sigh, he downed the rest of his whiskey and motioned for another.

# Chapter Four

In the Grey Dog Saloon, no pretty waiter girl was more important to a party than Sally Jean Miller. She'd wandered into the place at sixteen after she was abandoned by her father, who had gone off to make his fortune in the Comstock Lode. Her mother had left long before she could remember. Rose gave her a place to stay. And work, of course. At twenty-nine she was still lovely: blond and plump and with a sharp wit, all of which made the customers think of her as a sweet, girl-next-door type, and virtually no one knew Minny was her daughter, they were so close in age.

It was her smile that gave away her true nature. When she smiled, it didn't reach her eyes, which were hard, and flat, and soulless. But it didn't matter to the Grey Dog customers. They wouldn't care if a girl's mother died or if her father had abandoned her. Her story didn't matter, just what little reprieve she could offer from a harsh reality. Sally was starting to drink more, and Rose had chastised her more than once for being drunk and sassy when she was talking up customers, saying it could get her killed. She would pretend to listen, but said she didn't have much to live for anyway, so she'd drink enough that pretending to be alive didn't feel like such a giant lie.

Sally was lazing in bed on a Sunday morning because, although the Barbary Coast deadfalls stayed open all week, the girls weren't required to work on Sundays since it was the only slow day of the week.

"Come on, girl, go downstairs and ask Leo for a glass of beer for me."

"Leo won't give me no glass of beer unless I pay for it," Kerry said irritably. Sally had always ordered her around like an impatient older sister, and usually she just put up with it, but her mind was elsewhere and she had no time for Sally's nonsense.

Sally was in her drawers, lying on the rickety single bed with one leg over the other and kicking her foot lazily. "Hey, Kerry-o, what's the matter?"

Kerry's back was to Sally as she pulled out the pieces of wood and added a few to the fire, but she turned around at the sound of Sally's voice. She was wondering if Jack was going to crimp some men off the *Bangor*, the whaling ship from Maine, and if she could get in on the action. Since Addison had gone, Jack was crimping more to make money. Ignoring Sally, she turned back to the firewood.

"Kerry, come over here, girl. Or should I say boy?" Sally giggled.

Kerry turned around and frowned at Sally. "You can think what you like, Sal," Kerry said. "I don't care."

"Oh, don't be so mean. You do care, don't you? Kerry, I'm sorry I teased you. C'mere and sit down."

Sighing loudly, Kerry dumped the rest of the wood in the bin and sat down in the rickety chair next to Sally's bed.

"Noooo, girl, sit here next to me." Sally patted the bed. Kerry glared at her, not sure why the reference to her clothing bothered her. She still wore trousers and a cap and passed as a boy; she'd gotten used to it and it was easier than having the men bother her all the time. But she didn't know how she thought of herself exactly. She was just who she was and Jack never mentioned anything. She couldn't make out what Sally was up to, but she decided to find out and sat down on the bed.

"That's better." Sally was smiling and Kerry noticed Sally still had a good set of teeth, even if she only brushed them once in a while. Being this close to Sally when she was in her drawers made Kerry unaccountably nervous, although it never had before.

"You're a good girl, aren't you?"

"I'm not a…" Kerry said, flushing and looking at her boots.

"You almost said, 'I'm not a girl,' didn't you?"

"No."

"Yes. You did and I'm here to tell you, Kerry O'Shea, that you are indeed a girl." Sally's tone was light and mocking, but she didn't sound as cruel as she was apt to be.

"It's time to start acting like a girl. You'll never make a good whore if you don't have at least some wiles."

"I ain't never going to be a whore," Kerry said, emphatically. The thought of lying with a man repelled her.

"You can't go on crimping with Jack forever. They'll know. You can't hide it."

"Yes, I can. The sailors are stupid and they get stupider when they get drunk."

"You're wrong. But let's not fight. I didn't call you over to fight." Sally kept smiling at Kerry and kicking her foot lazily up and down.

Kerry looked at her quizzically. Sally never did the littlest thing without thinking hard about what would be to her benefit. She leaned forward suddenly and kissed Kerry on the mouth.

"What you do that for?" Kerry demanded. She very nearly wiped her mouth but stopped her hand in time. Her lips tingled.

"Just 'cause. I knew you'd like it." She stared at Kerry and stroked her cheek with surprising gentleness. "You did like it, didn't you?"

Kerry nodded, afraid to say it out loud. She had, in fact, liked it very much, which thrilled her and scared her in equal measure.

"Be a dear and go downstairs and get me a glass of beer. Get one for yourself. There's some money on the dresser."

When Kerry returned with the beer, Sally said, "Lock the door." Kerry swallowed and did as she was told, knowing a locked door meant private business—the kind of business the whores did with the customers. She knew the mechanics of men and women and knew the girls sometimes were private with each other. She knew about their alliances and feuds, their pouting or complaining. It was all background noise.

Kerry didn't know what Sally had in mind, but she wanted very much to find out. She thought it might have to do with that closed-door business. She awakened in the night sometimes with her body on fire and her breath coming in gasps as she listened to the cries of passion through the walls. She knew the cries were fake because she heard the girls snicker about their acting abilities when no one was listening, but nevertheless she had discovered her own remedy for the feelings that wrapped around her body with each woman's moan. Sally's kiss had started a feeling in her very much like the ones that sometimes woke her up in the middle of the night.

Sally patted the side of the bed next to her and Kerry slowly sat down and swung her legs up, handing one of the glasses to Sally. They clinked glasses and Kerry took a giant gulp. She had had sips of beer before and didn't like the taste, but she knew somehow this was part of whatever Sally had planned and didn't want to balk at any of it lest Sally refuse to go on—and she *really* wanted Sally to go on.

"You're fifteen now, ain't you?" Sally asked. Her eyelids were lowered and she had a funny little smile on her face.

Kerry nodded.

"You like girls, I bet. Don't you?" She grinned when Kerry didn't say anything. "You used to only like boys. I always saw you with that ratty little guy—what's his name? Teddy?"

"Teddy's not—" Kerry started to protest, her ire up at the slight.

"Shush. I told you, girl. I didn't bring you in here to fight. I'm just sayin'."

Kerry fought to keep her temper. It was true she wasn't spending time with Teddy. He'd gotten a bellhop job at the Palace so he wasn't around much. When Kerry wasn't helping Jack, she would wander over to the Cobweb Palace and saunter through the dark, gazing at the pictures of girls like they had when they were children. Like the cobwebs, the pictures had multiplied over the years. Kerry would stare at one and try to imagine what the girl would be like in real life, what she would feel like, smell like. She liked to think that the portraits in the Cobweb Palace were of nice girls, good girls.

"Yeah," Kerry said finally. "Maybe I like girls."

Sally lowered her eyelids again and asked, "Would you like to touch me?"

Kerry had about drained her glass of beer and she was feeling pretty good. Sally was being nicer than ever and looked pretty in her drawers. The tops of her plump, pale breasts peeked out from the yellowed ruffle of her chemise. Kelly looked at them longingly and Sally burst out laughing.

"It's plain as day what you want, Kerry-o. C'mere."

Sally pulled her into an embrace and they kissed again. The sensation of their tongues together almost sent Kerry into a swoon. Sally pushed Kerry's head down to her breasts and Kerry kissed Sally's chest and the tops of her breasts, and without any prompting she reached up to squeeze them, her hands trembling as she felt Sally's nipples harden under her fingertips. Sally's reaction astonished her when she threw her head back and groaned.

"Oh, girl, you're going to slay me with those lips, you are. Come on."

With that she unbuttoned her chemise and pulled it over her head, ripped off her drawers, and looked at Kerry with challenge in her eyes. "Take your clothes off."

Kerry obeyed as though she were a puppet with Sally pulling her taut strings. The room was dim but not full dark, since it was twelve noon, but with the old shade pulled the light was a sickly orange. The beer and Sally's eyes and Sally's kisses were altogether overwhelming to Kerry. She was light-headed because even though she'd seen Sally naked before she'd never felt this way—all warm and tingling and aching to touch her. Sally was a little plump and so very soft. Kerry lay down next to her and ran her small, slim, tanned hand from Sally's throat down to her crotch.

Sally trembled and murmured, "Mmmm. That sure feels good. You can make me feel even better. Do what I show you."

With that, she pulled Kerry's head to her breast, gripping her dark brown hair. Kerry knew without being told what to do and licked the shiny pink nipple offered to her lips, reveling in the feel of the soft but wonderfully hard flesh as she ran her tongue over it and sucked it into her mouth. Sally was moving all over and moaning loudly. She guided Kerry's fingers none too gently to where she wanted them between her legs. Kerry had an odd feeling of familiarity since she had her own body as a reference. She knew what Sally felt, but feeling Sally around her fingers, so soft, and hot, and wet, made her nearly cry out with her own pleasure as her rich, dark scent filled her nose.

In a moment or two, Sally's hand gripped her wrist hard, her breathing shallow and fast, her moaning taking on a shrill, desperate tone. "Faster," she gasped. Kerry obeyed. She realized suddenly what kind of power she could wield and she liked it. She liked seeing Sally all helpless and pleading. It all ended suddenly as Sally heaved, uttering one sharp cry, and pressed her legs together hard, her wetness filling Kerry's hand as her back arched before she collapsed back onto the bed.

"Oooee. Girl. You done me right. I knew you would." Her breasts were going up and down, and they were rosy and had a little coating of sweat. Kerry lay quietly just looking at her in wonderment, trying to decide if it would be rude to lick the sweat from Sally's beautiful breasts.

Sally was a lot of things but tender wasn't one of them. But, for some reason, her hand on Kerry's cheek seemed tender. Caring, even. Whatever just happened to her at least made her a little grateful or something, Kerry thought, feeling eight feet tall and ten years older to have been the cause of it.

She smiled shyly and Sally laughed. "You're something, you are. I don't think I ever got it as good as that. C'mere." Those two little words were exerting a powerful effect on Kerry, and she was readier than anything to heed the call.

Sally cradled Kerry in her arms, hugging her small, slim body tight. Kerry was about to smother in her breasts, but she thought, This is a fine way to go. Sally started stroking her all over on her breasts and back and backside, squeezing her now and then. She whispered into Kerry's ear, "I reckon I get to show you what for now. I'll treat you reallll nice. 'Cause that's how you treated me. I don't forget that."

Kerry jumped a foot, though, when Sally pinched her nipples a little too hard.

"Oh, sorry, sweetie. I didn't know you were like glass. I'll be nicer. In fact, I'll be so nice you'll think you died and gone to heaven." Sally's hands were everywhere, and everywhere her hands went, her lips followed. Kerry squirmed, half from discomfort and half from arousal. She didn't know exactly what she wanted, but she knew she needed it. Now. The sensations of Sally's hands and tongue on her heated skin were driving her crazy.

"Do you touch yourself?" Sally asked suddenly.

Kerry nodded. Her ability to speak had somehow fled. Sally was looking at her closely and insinuating her fingers in those places where no one but Kerry herself had been. Her fingers were clever and insistent, and Kerry had to shut her eyes. She couldn't stand the feeling but she also couldn't stand the thought of it stopping. She was concentrating hard and she was shocked when the fingers stopped. Before she could fully absorb that, she felt her legs pushed apart and the brush of hair on her thigh, and then a warm, wet mouth covered her most private, most sensitive place. She gasped and started to shove Sally away.

Sally raised her head. "Shhhhh!" she ordered, and went back to her task, wrapping her arms firmly around Kerry's thighs.

When it was over, Sally propped herself up on her elbow and gently tweaked Kerry's nipple. "Now you know what else to do. How about you show me what you learned."

❖

Kerry came looking for Sally a few weeks later to say hello and steal a kiss or two before Sally went down to the saloon for the night. She found Sally in her room with little Minny sitting at the mirror. Sally was painting her face.

Kerry stopped short in the doorway. "What are you doing?"

"Time she went to work," Sally said shortly, not looking at Kerry. Kerry had always treated Sally's daughter like a little sister and protected her, and the thought of her starting in as a whore enraged her.

"She's too young. She ain't ready yet."

"She's not and you ain't got nothing to say about it no how. Not all's as lucky as you to be a crimper with Jack."

"Sally, you can't do this yet."

"You can just shut up 'cause you ain't her mother. *I* am, and I'll take care of her."

Kerry usually went up to bed early if she wasn't working with Jack, but she stayed in the Grey Dog that night. She couldn't believe Sally was going to do what she said, but sure enough she had Minny next to her, looking ridiculous in face paint like she was twenty and not thirteen.

They went upstairs with a man and Kerry followed. When she burst into the room, she saw Minny laying on the bed, Sally sitting there smoking a cigarette as calm as could be, and the man just unbuttoning his pants. Kerry flew at him and threw herself on him, pummeling him with her fists. It was like hitting a brick wall. He roared and threw her to the side. Sally grabbed her by the shirt, and as she heaved her out the door, Kerry heard Minny scream.

She stayed away from Sally for a few days because she was so mad, but Sally came into her room early one evening to talk. She was ready to go to work, but she sat down on the bed and spoke to Kerry quietly. "Kerry honey. I know you're mad at me but there ain't no other way. Minny's got to earn her keep and there ain't but one way for her to do that. Maybe it's not the life I woulda chose for her, but I am looking out for her. She'll be fine."

Kerry kept her face turned away. "No, she won't," she growled. But Sally was right. Minny was born to a whore and born to *be* a whore, and that was that.

"Don't let no one beat her up. She's so small," Kerry finally said.

"I told you, honey. I'm her ma, remember? I'll look after her." Sally patted Kerry's shoulder and leaned over and whispered. "If you're done being sore at me, how's about coming up to my room about noon tomorrow?"

Sally whispering in her ear made her shiver. She nodded. She'd go because she wasn't able to stay away.

## CHAPTER FIVE

George Hammond stood straighter when he saw the minister, the Reverend Egon Svenhard from their church, St. Francis Lutheran, enter the store. The reverend was a fat, sweaty man. He was unctuous and imperious, but he was known to ensure that his parishioners patronized businesses he favored. Those who crossed him could find themselves without customers. It was all done very subtly and George was anxious to keep on Reverend Svenhard's good side. He needed the reverend to back him for a loan from the reverend's brother Eric.

"Good afternoon, Reverend Svenhard."

The reverend's hard, glittering eyes roved over the interior of the store, George, the shelves of dry goods, and finally came to rest upon Beth, standing quietly at her father's side.

"Ah, George, I stopped by to speak with you. Eric told me you have applied for a loan. As his brother and your pastoral counselor, I am duty bound to advise him as I see fit."

"Yes, of course, Reverend."

"How large is your debt?" Reverend Svenhard asked.

George rubbed his hands together nervously and blinked. "Five hundred, sir."

The reverend questioned George on the details while Beth waited on other customers and listened covertly.

At supper that night, George told Frieda about his talk with the Reverend Svenhard.

Beth listened to her father but watched her mother's face and noticed she said nothing. Beth sensed her mother didn't like or trust the reverend but would never say so directly to George and start an argument.

"Theresa told me that Mr. Giannini at the Bank of Italy will lend you money. He's lent money to her father for good interest," Beth said without thinking.

George turned and frowned at her. "Quiet, child, this is none of your affair and—"

"George. She's only trying to help."

"I would not borrow money from an Italian," George said with finality.

Frieda bowed her head and said no more.

A few days later, Frieda was minding the store, and George was meeting with Reverend Svenhard. "Beth?" her father called. "Please come here." Beth put down the book she was reading and obeyed. George rested his hand paternally on her shoulder and said to the reverend, "She's our only child, but she is a very good girl, obedient and does well in school."

As her father spoke, Beth felt the reverend's beady eyes staring at her and noticed that he seemed a bit nervous. He licked his lips and blinked. He was sweating though the day was mild.

George said to her, "The, ah, reverend wants you to come to him for private Bible study."

Beth said nothing.

George cleared his throat. "Come, girl, speak up."

"If that's what you wish, Father." Reverend Svenhard repelled her though she couldn't say why. Beth usually fidgeted or daydreamed through the reverend's sermons on sin and salvation because she found them both boring and frightening.

❖

On the following Sunday, George spoke to Reverend Svenhard quietly after church.

"Very good, it's settled," Reverend Svenhard said. "I will inform Eric you are an excellent loan prospect."

Two days later, Beth walked into the reverend's study to begin her private Bible study with him, her stomach unsettled and her palms sweating, even though it seemed like it should be simple enough.

"Please have a seat here," Reverend Svenhard told Beth, who tried to seat herself comfortably in the hard cane chair. She had been fetched with a very fine carriage that had exchanged its passenger, a Negro maid, with Beth. Svenhard had, for some reason, offered his maid's services on the days that Beth would be at Bible study.

Beth waited silently for the reverend to turn around. He was fussing with something on his desk, but all she could see was a large expanse of black wool. Heat radiated from him; the room was warmish from afternoon sun coming in through the large bay window.

The reverend turned around and handed her a Bible. "Open it."

She obeyed wordlessly. On the flyleaf, Reverend Svenhard had written an inscription:

> *To Miss Elizabeth Hammond:*
>
> *May you find peace, knowledge, and comfort from this book now and for the remainder of your life. It is my privilege to teach you the lessons of our great Lord and Savior, Jesus Christ, and of his heavenly father, almighty God.*
>
> *Yours very sincerely,*
> *Egon Leif Svenhard*
> *28 April 1891*

"Treasure this with all your heart, Miss Elizabeth. Keep it by you and read it every day. It's a well that never runs dry."

She swallowed and remembered her manners. "Thank you, sir."

"You are welcome, child. Now open to Romans 1, verse 20, and let me hear you read aloud."

She complied and though the reverend appeared to be merely attentive to her voice, she felt his eyes on her, as though he was studying her, probing her. He had an air of expectation that she didn't understand.

They would repeat this pattern for many weeks. She would read while he listened. He would talk to her about the passage, then tell her to write out her thoughts to bring with her the next week. He would read them aloud and mostly he would murmur approvingly; rarely did he have any criticism. In spite of her discomfort in the reverend's presence, Beth glowed with pride at his praise. For the first time she felt like she was good at something.

❖

The major harvest in the year occurred in October, and the Rocco family spent several weeks at the farm. They harvested grapes, apples, hay, pumpkins, and many other things. The family's children, it was understood, would be absent from school to help, and Theresa invited Beth to come for a few days. It took some persuasion, but Frieda managed to induce George to let Beth go with them. He had successfully gotten the loan from Eric Svenhard, and Reverend Svenhard would always speak to them after church in a friendly fashion and praise Beth's reading and attentiveness. George would beam and thank the reverend warmly, but Frieda was more reserved.

Beth was wildly excited at the opportunity to join the Rocco family for the harvest. Her shyness was long gone; she felt at home with the family. Theresa's brothers teased her as they did Theresa, but more gently. They extravagantly admired her long blond hair and light greenish-hazel eyes. She was exotic to them, which was an interesting, and not unwelcome, feeling for Beth.

It was a warm day and Beth and Theresa joined the farm workers and two of Theresa's brothers in the apple orchard. Theresa competed with her exuberant brothers for how many apples they could grab in the least amount of time. Theresa, determined and nimble, made Beth drag the tallest ladder over to one of the big apple trees and told Beth to steady it.

"We will win. Pietro is afraid of heights so he does not like to pick up high."

She called to him, a few trees down the road. "Pietro, look at me! Pietro, *spavento!*" she taunted him. For Beth's benefit, she said, "Scared." She laughed merrily.

Beth grabbed the apples Theresa threw down as fast as she could, tossed them in her basket, and soon had all within reach. Theresa climbed to the very top step of the ladder.

"Theresa, it's too high!"

"Just hold steady, Beth. It will only take a moment." She stretched to reach two big apples and lost her balance. She tumbled to the ground with a cry, the apples flying every which way.

Beth ran to her and saw with terror that Theresa had struck her head on a rock and was bleeding profusely.

"Pietro," Beth screamed. "Help."

Pietro came running over, followed by two of the farm hands. They all started to jabber in Italian.

Pietro's eyes were huge. "I will get Papa," he gasped, and raced off, running toward the other end of the orchard.

Beth clamped her hand on Theresa's head wound, not knowing what else to do. She wept and pleaded with Theresa to wake up. Theresa lay still; she was pale but she seemed to be breathing. The blood trickled from under Beth's hand and into Theresa's hair, but the flow had slowed down.

It was an eternity, but finally Pietro came back with Papa Rocco puffing at his heels.

Papa threw himself on the ground and picked up Theresa in his arms. She moaned and her eyes opened, although they were unfocused. Papa bellowed, "Get some water and a cloth!"

Beth sat back on her heels and watched as Papa cleaned Theresa's head of blood and whispered to her in Italian. Theresa slowly returned to consciousness and started crying while her father rocked her in his arms.

As he cradled Theresa, Papa looked over at Beth. "Lizbetta," he said, using their nickname for her. "You did well. My foolish son did not know what to do but scream for his Papa. These farm boys are dumb. Don't worry. The blood is a lot but not so bad. From the scalp it bleeds much but it's not dangerous. She got a crack on her head but she's fine. You did well to put pressure on it. Thank you."

Along with her relief, Beth felt something else—a kind of pride. *I knew what to do.*

❖

Beth opened her Bible and read the passage the reverend indicated. Reverend Svenhard stared out the window, hands clasped behind his back. Beth glanced at him every so often; he was usually attentive to her reading. When she reached the end, he turned to her. He seemed, if possible, even more sweaty. He tugged at his collar and cleared his throat.

"Was it not a good reading, sir?" Beth asked.

"No. No. Ahem. Of course not, it was fine. You did very well." Reverend Svenhard closed his mouth. Beth waited for him to say more, puzzled that he seemed distracted and hesitant.

"Beth, ah, from time to time, it's often the case that a man such as myself finds himself in a quandary."

"Sir?"

"Beth, I have become very fond of you as a teacher is apt to become fond of a pupil."

"Yes sir."

"I have become so fond of you, I fear I may lose my mind if you do not feel the same."

"I don't know what I feel, Rev—"

"Ohhh." He exhaled and clasped her close to him. She tried to back away but he held her tight and his breath rasped in her ear. His hand fumbled between their bodies as he struggled to open his trouser buttons. Beth realized what he was doing and closed her eyes. He fumbled in his pocket, murmuring, "Mustn't leave evidence—they'll know.

"Hold this, please!" he said in a hoarse, gasping whisper.

She opened her eyes enough to see it was his handkerchief. She was shaking as though she was in a cold wind, the handkerchief trembling from her fingertips. He took care of himself in several quick, hard jerks between their bodies. Beth stood still, afraid to move, afraid to breathe. Reverend Svenhard let her go and sat down in his desk chair with his back to her. He stayed silent, and she realized that she was expected to leave. She picked up her Bible and walked out the door, sick to her stomach and terribly confused.

❖

The pattern had altered. It was a matter first of a short, uninteresting Bible reading, then Svenhard would grasp one of her barely visible breasts and perform the ritual into the handkerchief she held. Beth would simply close her eyes and imagine she was reading a book or lying in the apple orchard talking with Theresa.

He said to her one day, "It is not necessary to tell anyone of this. It is between us. You understand?" She nodded dumbly, having grasped what he meant. It was clear—no one would believe a respected minister of the Lutheran church was abusing an eleven-year-old parishioner, and she knew her father needed the reverend's good word for his business. She knew he would not impregnate her; he was not so addled as that. She was grateful that he only seemed to need to touch some part of her body as he performed his horrible actions upon himself. There came the day, though, when he grabbed her hand and led it to his body.

"I want to stop the Bible lessons," Beth told her mother that night.

"Why?" Frieda asked, concentrating on cutting the potatoes.

"I don't want to go see Reverend Svenhard anymore."

"Don't be silly, girl. Your father wants you to go. It's good for you to receive such a fine education from such a man as Reverend Svenhard. It's an honor."

Beth knew her mother well enough to hear what Frieda hadn't said. She wouldn't try to persuade George. Only one adult offered possible solace. In the middle of the night, she packed a few clothes and some books and crept downstairs and out of the house.

She threw pebbles at Theresa's window until Theresa appeared. She raised the sash and stuck her head out. "Shhhhhh! You'll wake Maria. What's the matter?" Maria was the youngest Rocco child, and she shared a room with Theresa.

"I can't tell you. Just let me in, please."

Theresa and Beth huddled in Theresa's bed. Beth shook and cried but Theresa couldn't persuade her to say what was wrong.

The next morning, Beth stood before Mama Rocco, who in the last year had been making a bigger effort to learn English because of their growing business and was often eager to converse with Beth.

"So, Lizbetta. What is the matter you should come to us in the middle of the night? Your Mama will be worried. I have the boys walk you home. Lizbetta?" Mama raised Beth's downcast face and peered into her eyes. "Theresa, please go help Papa in the store."

"But—"

"Theresa, leave us. Please go help Papa in the store."

"But—"

"Theresa, not now. Go, please. I must speak to Lizbetta privately."

Theresa reluctantly left them.

"Lizbetta, come over and sit down, child." Mama Rocco gave her a glass of milk and waited.

"Will you tell me what is the matter?" She brushed a tear from Beth's cheek.

"Reverend Svenhard," she whispered.

"Who?" Mama asked, mystified. "What?"

Beth looked at Mama's face, her kind black eyes, the dark mole next to her nose. She finally had to try to say something. "The reverend.

Of our church. He—" She began to cry then and couldn't bring herself to say the words out loud.

Mama took Beth over to the davenport and sat her down. She sat down next to her and put an arm around her. "Is this reverend—" Mama clearly searched for the right words, her brow furrowed as she struggled. "Look at me, child."

Beth reluctantly met her eyes.

"Is this man doing something to you he should not?"

Beth looked at her a long time, then nodded.

Mama let loose a stream of Italian curses, words Beth had learned from the men in the fields during the harvest. "Come, child."

At the Hammonds' flat, Mama asked to speak alone to Frieda. Beth waited in her room, going back and forth between relief that the truth was coming out and terrified at what Mama Rocco would say to her mother and what her mother would think.

They had dinner and Frieda sent Beth to her room right after. Beth was upset they wouldn't play the piano, but some part of her knew that she could not be part of the conversation between her parents.

After a long while, Frieda came into Beth's room and sat down on the bed. She was pale and sad.

"Your father says you are to go and apologize to Mrs. Rocco for telling such a terrible lie."

"Mother, I didn't lie. It's true."

"It can't be true. You are mistaken. Furthermore, after you have apologized, you will make your farewells. You will not visit the Rocco family again."

Nothing more was said. Beth returned to her lessons with Reverend Svenhard. George got another loan at a very good interest from Eric Svenhard and their store prospered. George complained about her silence and melancholy, but Frieda would simply excuse it as childish moodiness. "Growing pains," she told George.

If she saw Theresa when she was out doing chores, she avoided her out of a deep sense of shame. She hated that Theresa thought she had abandoned her. When she went to the store, she felt Mama Rocco's eyes on her but she never said a word. She was afraid it would get back to her parents.

Beth learned a valuable lesson about trust: there was no reason to have any, especially not in the people closest to her.

## Chapter Six

When Beth was fifteen she received word that she would not be going to Reverend Svenhard's house anymore for Bible lessons because he was ill. It was some four years after she had started, and she had rarely missed a week. She'd become inured to it since she had no other choice. She received the news of his illness with no emotion. On Sundays, his assistant minister took over the Sunday services and George, out of respect, paid a call to Mrs. Svenhard to express his concern.

"Allow me to send Beth over to help," he pleaded. "She was so close to him. It is a great disappointment that she must discontinue her study with him." Beth had grown even quieter over the years, as if to speak at all would break something inside her.

Mrs. Svenhard agreed and so Beth came to their home, not for Bible study but to assist the private nurse they had engaged to take care of the ailing reverend. It was cancer of the stomach, they said. Beth absorbed the news dispassionately.

Beth entered the bedroom on the heels of Nurse Jennings, a silent, severe woman. She glided about the sick room, speaking only when absolutely necessary.

Svenhard's eyes still followed Beth whenever she was in his sickroom and he watched her closely, but he was helpless and she was beyond his reach. She felt nothing at all—not anger, not pity. Nothing.

Beth assisted Nurse Jennings at her tasks. "You may call me Jane," she told Beth. Jane was gentle but firm, and not quite as forbidding as she had seemed at first. She was kind in her way; it was only with the Svenhard family that she was frosty. She treated her patient as though he were an errant twelve-year-old.

"Reverend, you are not allowed to have whiskey. The doctor has spoken." Beth found it gratifying over time that the man who once gave orders to everyone now had to take them whether he wished to or not. Beth asked Jane her reasons for doing everything and Jane always answered patiently. Beth found that comforting and was emboldened to ask more questions.

"Doctor Graham prescribes the medicinal dose. I am to give it twice a day as a tincture. See here. It is mixed with alcohol." The medicine was laudanum, to reduce his pain, Jane said, and the dosing was strict; otherwise it could kill him. Jane showed Beth how to take his temperature and how to prevent bedsores. Together, they even bathed the reverend. Jane was, of course, detached. Beth was beyond even disgust at having to help Jane perform this task. She cared only about the knowledge she was gaining, not about the reverend or his pain.

Jane had a different way of speaking with the reverend than she spoke with his family. Jane was respectful, even subservient with Mrs. Svenhard, who treated her as something better than a maid but not quite as an equal. When the doctor came once a week to examine his patient and confer with the family, he also would speak at length with Jane. She would listen to him intently and report at length on her observations. Beth could see the doctor needed Jane to tell him about the reverend's condition, and he was serious with her. Beth saw that though he gave her orders, they were orders he had formulated with information she gave him. She liked the amount of power Jane had, even though it was subtle.

Jane went out on a rare errand one day and ordered Beth to stay and watch the reverend. His wife had gone somewhere as well.

"I am trusting you with this. It is not usual for a nurse to leave for any reason. But we are almost out of laudanum, and he has to have it."

Reverend Svenhard was quite ill then and could no longer leave his bed at all.

Beth stood at the side of the bed and looked down at the reverend. He said nothing, but his watery, glazed eyes still followed her every move. It seemed to her as though he might have been asking her to forgive him. She picked up the bottle of laudanum. *I could kill him. No one would know.* He stared at her, his eyes shiny with pain. He had lost most of his weight and was skeletal. She looked at him, twirling the bottle of tincture of laudanum in her hand. No, she concluded. *It's better he is alive and can be reminded by seeing me every day what he's done.*

"Please," he croaked. "I am in so much pain. Have pity. I…"

Beth looked at him closely. *You won't say it. You don't think you did anything wrong.*

"Nurse has gone out. She must bring more laudanum. You cannot have any."

He had often whimpered and whined after their activities. He seemed to believe her very presence had led him to his actions. "You do this to me. You have the most terrible effect on me," he would whisper.

Perhaps she *was* the guilty one. She often remembered her mother's face after she talked to Mrs. Rocco and how her mother had never spoken of it again after the conversation with her father. In her parents' view, she was clearly guilty, Beth was sure. Otherwise they wouldn't have done what they did, forcing her to keep seeing the reverend, never speaking to her about what she had said. When Beth read *The Scarlet Letter*, she knew then she might not have to wear a letter, but she was every bit as branded as Hester Prynne and would pay as Hester did for the rest of her life.

Jane had said, "It is our duty to prolong life and to relieve suffering." Beth thought, We're allowing him to live, but I'm glad he's suffering and doubly so every time he looks at me.

When Jane wasn't looking, Beth would purposefully undermix the reverend's pain medication. She would smile when he pleaded with Jane to give him more painkiller, and she would refuse, saying she must follow the doctor's orders. For Beth it was more satisfying than overdosing and killing him. Her anger rose to the surface, and she let it stay there.

❖

"I want to go to nurse's training. Jane will help me," Beth announced to her parents. "I want to start as soon as I graduate from high school." She stood silently and listened to her parents argue.

George said, "No. Never. I will need her at the store. That is her future."

It was the only time Beth ever saw her mother stand up to her father. "He's dead," Frieda said to George. "We're free. You will let her go."

George fumed, but in the end, he agreed.

It was a great satisfaction to Beth that she was required to live in the student nurses' dormitory at the hospital. She was never once homesick, as some of the other students were. She recognized the feeling as relief. *Svenhard is dead. I am no longer his prisoner nor must I bow to my parents' wishes nor anyone else's any more. I am free.*

## CHAPTER SEVEN

L ucky Jack was standing at the bar bemoaning the poor state of the crimping business to Leo. Kerry, having nothing better to do, was listening, although she would have rather spent every second with Sally, but Sally shooed her away, saying, "I got to make some money, girl, and I only know one way to do that."

So Kerry was forced to find something else to do with her spare time besides hang around Meiggs's Wharf. Teddy was at the Palace Hotel most of the time, still working as a bellhop. She hadn't made any other friends, nor did she want to.

Jack said, "That ugly monster Big Moe is getting the lion's share now. He's bribed all the captains and everyone's scared to death of him."

"You ought to go back to gambling, Jack. It's not quite as dirty a business."

"Nah. It's no good without Dr. Addison. I never could get the hang of his system."

Leo shook his head again.

Kerry caught the name, Big Moe, and it started a train of thought. She'd heard Sally talk about who she wouldn't take on as customers— he was one of them. Kerry would've rather not had her doing any whore business, but she knew there was no chance of that. Rose would kick her out of the house if she didn't pull her weight, and Sally, if nothing else, was a realist. Kerry could entreat all she wanted but Sally wouldn't budge.

"You're a lovesick little fool, you are." Sally had scoffed at her. "I thought you was tough. I was wrong." She'd given Kerry's hair a yank or her nipple a tweak.

But listening to Leo and Jack talk, Kerry had a germ of an idea. She resolved to talk to Teddy about it.

❖

Kerry had her time with Sally in the afternoons after she woke up. She would bring Sally her wake-up glass of beer and get in bed with her.

"Ugh. You didn't wash before you went to sleep?" Kerry asked. She'd started touching Sally right away, but the moisture on Sally's thighs wasn't Sally's.

Sally yawned. "I was too tired. Leave me be then."

Kerry rolled over and lay on her back and stared at the ceiling, grinning when Sally rolled out of bed a second later without saying a word and went to take a bath. Before she could talk to Jack, she had to get all her plans together. She didn't want to fight with Sally since she was an important part of the plan.

When she'd gone to him, Teddy had said, "It's the truth. Big Moe's got all the captains from every whaling ship and most of the others in his pocket. It's the boatmen who do most of his dirty work. You have to bribe them better than he does."

"I can manage that if you lead me to the right ones," Kerry said.

"Oh, jeezus. You can't be thinking of pulling one over on Big Moe, Kerry. That's suicide."

"No, see, I got it worked out. Just listen."

Teddy was dubious but finally said yes, because he'd never known Kerry to be wrong about much.

Now she had to convince Sal. *For money, it shouldn't be a problem.*

She lay in bed and thought out what she would say when Sally came back. *Well. After we get a little fun.*

"Here I am, Kerry-o. All ready for you." Sally jumped into bed and rolled over on Kerry and rubbed their breasts together and Kerry stopped thinking of anything. When Sally got her started, that was all she cared about, though, truthfully, Sally's charms were getting a mite thin. Kerry was getting disgusted by the drinking and the men. When they were done and Sally was blowing smoke rings up at the ceiling from the little cigars she favored, Kerry kept up a light teasing touch all over her body to distract her and soften her up.

"Sal. You feel like makin' some money you don't have to split with Rose?"

Sally exhaled and said, "How you figure?"

"I got a plan. I gotta get Jack some more crimping and I need your help."

"So what do you want me to do?"

"You know that thug, Big Moe. Well, I want you—"

"No. I ain't fucking him."

"Easy. I think you can make him think you will, but you won't have to."

Sally sat up then and looked at Kerry. "What are you talking about?"

"I need you to entertain him for a while while we get his marks off the next big ship."

"You want me to do what?"

"Just string him along. I'll give you the laudanum to spike his whiskey. You just have to keep him by you for the night."

"That's it?"

"That's all."

Sally stared at the ceiling, her eyes narrowed in thought as she puffed away on her little cigar. "Okay, Kerry. You got yerself a deal. How long do I get to keep that piece of crap in my bed overnight?"

"I'll make sure you get a fair cut, even if I have to take it out of my own."

Sliding her fingers inside Kerry, Sally grinned wickedly. "Oh, I'm sure I'll get mine, sweet girl."

❖

Teddy gave Kerry the word a week later. The gossip at Black's said a big shipment was coming in. Kerry had convinced Jack that the scheme would work, and although he was reluctant he gave in to Kerry's certainty. They would offer the Whitehall boatman a good price and tell him that Big Moe was indisposed for the evening. Jack looked hard at Kerry and asked, "What do you mean indisposed?"

"He'll be with Sally."

"Oh, Christ."

"She's gonna give him a dose of laudanum just like we give the sailors. He won't remember a thing. He'll go to her thinking he can have her for a while and then be ready to meet the longboats when they come in. I know which one he'll go for."

"You have it all worked out, I guess."

"I do, Jack. Just give me some money."

It worked perfectly. Jack got six able-bodied sailors for the captain of the *Leeward On*. Sally told Kerry that Big Moe was almost chivalrous to her when he came around, but after his one glass of whiskey, he went down like a buffalo that had been shot, and when he woke the next morning, she'd been kind to him and told him all sorts of lies about how wonderful he'd been. He left her with a pounding headache and not remembering a thing, which bothered him no end, seeing as how his not remembering included anything that happened to Sally. He went away puzzled and hung over.

Kerry went around to Black's and found Teddy where he could always be found when he wasn't bellhopping.

"Big Moe might not be as dumb as we thought," he said, his voice fearful. "He's been askin' a lot of questions. No one says nothing, of course. They ain't crazy."

That night, Kerry raced upstairs to Sally's room to find out if Big Moe had come back around.

Sally was sitting at her dressing table, brushing her hair. She looked up and met Kerry's desperate eyes in the mirror. "What's your hurry, girl?" she said, her tone dismissive. "It's time for me to go to work. You can hear them all down there." She tossed her head to indicate the noise from the saloon that filtered up through the floor.

Kerry took a breath and forced herself to speak calmly. "Big Moe might come back around to talk to you. Just play dumb, will you?"

"Don't worry about me, lover. Look after yourself."

Kerry knelt and put her arms around Sally's waist. "I just don't want nothing to happen to you." She buried her face in Sally's side.

Sally kept brushing her hair. "It's fine, darling. It's going to be fine. Now let me loose. I have to get ready."

Kerry reluctantly let her go, stood up, and bent to give her a long deep kiss. She wasn't sure, but she thought Sally didn't return the kiss as warmly as she usually did.

❖

Leo shook Kerry awake roughly. She looked into his face. It was a stolid mask.

"What time is it?" She rubbed her eyes.

"Four a.m. Come on."

"What's wrong?"

"Get dressed quick. We need to go."

In a dank basement in police headquarters, Leo and Kerry stood with a policeman next to a grim-faced man in a heavy apron. At the sergeant's nod, the morgue keeper pulled back the sheet. It was Jack, his head bashed in. Kerry stared for a long moment, then turned and buried her face in Leo's waistcoat and wept.

"I guess you got your answer then," Leo told the sergeant. "Send the burial fee to me."

Back at the Grey Dog, Leo shoved a shot of whiskey across the bar to Kerry. "It was Big Moe. I guess you know that," he said, his voice dull with grief.

She nodded, unable to speak. She tossed down the whiskey, welcoming it as it seared her throat, crashed into her stomach, and a moment later caused her head to spin and her mind to dull. Leo watched her for a moment, then poured another shot. She drank it. And another. The room pitched and she went with it, cracking her head on the floor before darkness hit.

❖

Kerry woke up in the early evening, her mouth foul and her head pounding. Neither was enough to distract her from her first thought. *Jack's dead. My fault.*

Rose poked her head in the door and said, "You up? Hungry, I expect. Stay still and I'll bring you something."

"You all right?" Rose asked when she came back with some bread and soup. Kerry didn't answer.

"It woulda happened sooner or later, child. He knew that."

Kerry said nothing. She ate the food mechanically, *Jack's dead. My fault* running a noisy loop in her head.

"You can stay here, you know that. He woulda wanted you to. We can always find a place—"

"Shut up. Just shut up," Kerry said emotionlessly. The food was making her head feel better. Being sober, though, was letting her mind work again.

She found Sally in her room, making up for her night's work. Sally wouldn't meet her eyes.

"I heard about Jack. I'm sorry, girl. You come by tomorrow around noon, and after I get some sleep and clean up, we'll have us some fun. I can make you feel better."

"You told Moe, didn't you?"

Sally flinched and looked away.

Kerry grabbed her by the shoulders and shook her.

Sally started crying. "He was gonna beat the life out of me. He's a mean SOB, you know that. I had to tell him. He was suspicious of me entertaining him after I told him no so many times. Then he couldn't remember anything."

"You got Jack killed," Kerry said tonelessly.

"Well. It was your idea. It ain't my fault if Big Moe is smarter than we thought."

"Yeah. It was my idea." Kerry let go and stepped back, staring out the dirty window. "But the truth came outta your mouth. I ain't never sleepin' with you again."

"Kerry! Honey. I'm sorry."

Kerry left.

Down at the bar, Leo didn't slide another glass of whiskey to her. Instead he handed her an envelope.

"Read it to me," she said. "You know I can't read."

> *Leo's writing this for me. I told him to give it to you if something happened to me. You can't stay here on the BC, Kerry. I'm gone, no one is going to protect you, and I don't want you to try and make your living here. It's no place for a bright girl like you. It's nothing but drunks, murderers, thieves, and whores. Not you. Go find Dr. Addison Grant. He promised me if you or I ever needed him, to just come find him. He's out to the big county hospital in the Western Addition part of town. He'll take care of you. I want you to make something of yourself. I love you, girl. I always have. You're the best thing I ever done.*
>
> *Your father,*
> *John Aloysius O'Shea*

Kerry made Leo read it a couple more times. She listened intently and nodded. She was silently speaking the words from the letter to herself, memorizing them. *Aloysius? I never knew that. Huh.* Leo handed her another envelope. It had some bank notes in it and a savings book.

Leo cleared his throat. "He left this for you too. I don't know how but old Jack managed to save some money."

She looked blankly at the items for a long time.

Leo said, "You should take it and go. Like he said, there's nothing for you here." He gestured around the bar.

Automatically, Kerry looked. She saw the pretty waiter girls and the customers drinking. She heard the noise. She smelled beer, whiskey, and smoke. *Jack's gone.* She felt sick to her stomach.

She picked up the envelope. She counted it all, stuffed into her pockets. She went upstairs and begged a carpetbag off one of the whores and packed what few clothes and belongings she had. She found Rose, who stared at the suitcase instead of Kerry's face. Kerry ignored the unshed tears. Rose had given her a place to live, food to eat, and some occasional money for clothes in return for Kerry doing work around the building. But she had never gotten so much as a hug from the woman, and suddenly it just didn't matter that she would be leaving her behind.

"Tell Sally I said good-bye."

Rose nodded and Kerry hefted the suitcase, put on a cap, and walked the four blocks to the Ferry Building to catch a cable car uptown.

## Chapter Eight

A n hour or so later, she stood at the reception desk at the City and County Hospital feeling very young and very lost. She'd kept asking conductors which car to take until she got to the one that served the hospital.

The nurse on duty looked up and peered into her face suspiciously. "Help you, son?"

Kerry got a nice little stab of satisfaction that her clothes could fool the likes of an old battle-ax like this one. "Ma'am. I'm looking for Dr. Addison Grant."

"Do you have an appointment?"

"Uh, no, ma'am."

"Whom shall I say?"

Kerry gave her name and the nurse instructed her to wait. She sat down on the hard bench near the door and, after a short time, fell asleep on her suitcase.

She had another abrupt awakening, but this time, she didn't see Leo or Rose, but a tall man with kind brown eyes and a deep voice.

"Kerry. Sorry to wake you. This is a surprise. It's me, Addison."

She remembered his voice more than anything else. He'd only had a mustache before, but now he had full sideburns and a beard. His hair was fuller as well. He wore a white coat over his suit and had a stethoscope in his pocket.

"Addison?" Her memory was working a little. It was the man who'd been around her father for a year or so when she was only eleven and then was gone as suddenly as he arrived.

"Nurse Brett!" he called sharply.

A young woman in a white dress and cap came over. "Doctor?"

"Take this young lady to my office. Make her comfortable, and give her tea or lemon water. Whatever she wishes." He turned back to Kerry and rested a hand on her shoulder. "I'll be with you presently. I have to finish rounds. Please make yourself comfortable." His smile was kind and the knot in Kerry's chest eased a bit. "The fact that you're here tells me something has happened to Jack."

Kerry nodded dumbly and then walked off with Nurse Brett, who gave her curious, sidelong looks. They arrived at a cramped office and Kerry sat down on the straight-back wooden chair. Nurse Brett asked, without a trace of sympathy, "Do you need anything?"

"No, nothing, I'm fine. Thank you."

The last forty-eight hours had been terribly disorienting. She wanted to be alone until the doctor came back. His presence and manner reassured her even if her memory of him was imperfect.

She fidgeted and looked around. She'd lived her entire life on the Barbary Coast except for her and Teddy's forays into other areas of the city nearby. She was as unfamiliar with an office as she would be with a king's palace. In spite of the hard chair, she fell asleep, her dreams tortured by the image of Jack in the morgue.

Addison shook her shoulder gently. She sat up, blinking and confused.

"We'll be going now. Is that all you have with you?" He pointed to the small suitcase.

Kerry nodded, somehow embarrassed. On the carriage ride home, she told Addison about Jack, leaving out the unnecessary and sordid details of Sally's involvement. Addison listened without comment.

Then he put his arm around Kerry and said, "I always feared Jack would come to an untimely end. He asked me if anything ever happened to him if he could send you to me. You will reside with us as long as you like. Even if Jack hadn't entertained and enriched me, I owe him my life." He told her about the card game and the ruffian who wanted to murder them both.

Kerry listened, smiling sadly at the scene she could picture so vividly. She closed her eyes tight against tears.

"You must be still in shock. No matter. Just come home and rest. Laura will look after you."

"Laura?" Kerry asked, mystified. For some reason it hadn't occurred to her Addison would have anyone else in his life.

"My wife, Laura," he said.

Kerry felt a stab of unease and was quiet for the rest of their ride.

Addison stopped in front of a large wooden house with tall bay windows. "Wait here. I have to stable the horses just down the street."

Kerry stood by the house with her bag, feeling more forlorn than ever.

Addison strode back, then stopped in front of her and touched her shoulder briefly. "Just a moment, I'll come out and fetch you." He seemed a little nervous and it was several moments before he reappeared on the porch and said, "Kerry, please come in."

Kerry mounted the steps and walked past Addison into the entryway. A woman with blond hair pulled back into a severe bun stood at the foot of the stairs.

"Laura. This is Kerry O'Shea, the daughter of an old friend. She'll be staying with us for the time being. Kerry, my wife, Laura."

Kerry shook hands gravely with the pretty young woman before her. In the last few hours, I've met two women who aren't whores, she thought with a kind of wonderment. I'm in a regular house in a quiet neighborhood. Adding that displacement to the emotional disjointedness she felt from Jack's death, Kerry had to struggle to keep a sense of self. She gazed at Laura, who looked back at her doubtfully, as though she were some exotic animal for which Laura had no idea how to care. Maybe that was true.

Addison, clearly conscious of having sprung a surprise on Laura, rubbed his hands together. "Here we are then. Laura, I think for tonight you can give Kerry her supper in the spare room. We won't want to try her with too much company until she gets settled." He went on to give more instructions to Laura regarding bed linen and night clothes and washing things.

His anxious stream of orders embarrassed Kerry and clearly angered Laura, who stood rigidly nodding her assent at his instructions. But she nonetheless went swiftly about the tasks of "settling" Kerry.

When Kerry was lodged in the guest room with the door closed, Laura and Addison sat down to dinner together, and Laura wasted no time speaking her mind. "Addison. I'm aware of your charitable impulses. But bringing someone home and with no warning?"

"I do apologize, my dear Laura, for her unannounced appearance, but this is a special case." Addison assumed his wife would go along without question with his ideas and whims and plans and opinions. Laura did so but reserved the right to direct the displeasure she couldn't display to her husband in other directions. She wasn't the least aware of her unconscious resentments. She was only thirty but in five years of marriage to Addison had acquired an irritable habit of pursing her lips when she was displeased and had succeeded in training her mouth to remain in that configuration. Addison pretended not to notice.

"I made a promise to her father many years ago, and I won't turn a young woman out on the street, regardless of her background. Thank you for being kind to her."

And with that, Addison closed the discussion of whether or not Kerry would be staying with them.

❖

A few days later, Kerry sat in Addison's study. "You can't read?" Addison exclaimed. "Well. I'm sorry. Don't be alarmed. I mean you no harm. I'm just surprised. I shall teach you, no matter. It won't be difficult." He had taken the letter from Kerry, surprised when she requested that he read it out loud because she liked hearing it, although she couldn't read it herself.

Kerry tried to relax in the spare room, where she lay in a bed far more comfortable and luxurious than any she had ever experienced. She felt as though she had been transported to another planet.

It wasn't as though she wasn't grateful to Dr. Grant. She understood he was kind and well meaning and had had great regard for her father. When she showed him the bankbook, he was very serious.

"He has left you a bit of money. I hope you'll be able to put it to good use. But we'll have to teach you numbers as well as letters."

"I could take it and go live somewhere else, couldn't I?"

"Tut. Don't speak of that. You're only fifteen and…you aren't recovered from Jack's death. You need some time." He'd finished somewhat lamely.

"I guess I have plenty of time," Kerry said, refusing to let the tears fall as she stared past Addison at the trees outside.

"I promise, the pain will ease eventually, Kerry, and I think you'll learn to like it here, if you give it, us, a chance."

"I don't think your wife likes me, Addison," Kerry said bluntly, staring at him. "She looks at me like I'm something off her shoe."

"No, no, Kerry, nothing like that. She just doesn't like surprises, that's all. When she gets to know you, I'm sure you'll be the greatest of friends."

"I don't have friends, but Jack trusted you and thought this is where I should go, so I'll stay, at least till I figure out what else to do. Deal?"

Addison blinked, obviously unused to a young woman being so forthright. "Yes, we have a deal, Kerry. Just promise me you'll be patient." He smiled, patted her knee, and left the room, closing the door softly behind him.

Sighing, Kerry curled on her side and finally cried. Would her Barbary Coast tears stain the pure white linen under her cheek? As she fell asleep, she wondered if Laura would be able to accept her. *I guess I can go back to the Barbary if it comes to that.*

# CHAPTER NINE

I can't do a thing with her. I took her to a dressmaker and had her fitted. She spent all of one hour in the dress and then changed back into trousers, saying the dress tripped her. She demanded I take her to a barber to get her hair cut! When I refused, she tried to cut it herself so that I was forced to give in. Her language is disgraceful. She is like a cat that's spent his life outside and is now shut up in the house. She will *not* listen to me." Laura paced the length of the living room, punctuating her frustration with dramatic flourishes.

"Laura, darling, I would hope you could open your heart and your mind. She's an orphan with no place to go. Think of it as an opportunity. She needs the help of a woman like you."

"She grew up in a whorehouse, Addison, with a criminal for a father. I fear it's too late to do anything with her. Mark my words, you'll regret this charitable impulse of yours, when she disappears one day with my mother's silver."

"I don't believe that will happen. Please try to be patient, my dear. She'll come around eventually. It's just that her background is so out of your experience. Try to give her time to adjust."

Addison gave Laura his best smile and patted her shoulder. Laura simply pursed her mouth, turned on her heel, and left the room. He hoped things would settle down eventually. Laura wasn't worldly. She'd grown up in a genteel home in Kansas City and they'd met when her father had come to San Francisco for a medical meeting and brought his family along to see the "Paris of the West."

Addison knew the San Franciscans had made up the concept purely to feed their own civic pride, but Laura embraced it wholeheartedly and had indeed convinced her skeptical parents that San Francisco and Addison were her destiny. San Francisco, Addison thought, just as

Jack had told him long before, was really the wildest of the Wild West. Laura would never know anything of that, of course. She was, Addison realized, being exposed through Kerry to a side of San Francisco she had no idea existed. Addison hoped she would come to accept Kerry and that Kerry would, in time, become more civilized.

❖

After she left Addison, Laura went to the kitchen, feeling put upon and misunderstood. Everything about Kerry was contrary to her experience, her upbringing, and her wishes. Addison was trying to smooth matters over, but he seemed to have no appreciation for the position he'd put her in.

He'd said, "She'll come to see your way eventually after she's settled in. She'll notice other respectable young women and will want to attract the attentions of a young man. She'll want to emulate you and listen to your counsel."

Laura sighed and figured she might as well give in on the matter of Kerry's clothes and appearance. She only hoped it wouldn't prove embarrassing to Addison.

She started chopping vegetables for their dinner stew and sensed someone behind her. It was Kerry, standing in the door of the kitchen, shyly and quietly. She was clad as usual in boots, rough wool trousers, and a collarless shirt. Mindful of Addison's admonition to be patient, Laura didn't remark on Kerry's appearance, although every time she saw her she felt like gnashing her teeth.

Much to Laura's astonishment, Kerry said, "May I help you?" She smiled shyly, and that tiny smile made Laura's tension ease slightly.

"Of course you may. I'd welcome that." They spent a relatively pleasant few hours making the stew and a couple of loaves of bread. Laura was charmed by Kerry's attentiveness and serious questions, and, for a while, the awkwardness and hostility disappeared as they worked together.

After that day, it became a habit for Kerry to join Laura in the kitchen every day, and she quickly mastered basic cooking skills. Laura, not content to have reached a *détente* and to have acquired a very competent kitchen helper, still couldn't quite keep her feelings under control.

One afternoon, a couple of months after her talk with Addison, they were working together on several pies that Laura had agreed to make for the church social. Laura was pleased that Kerry was so willing help cook, but it irritated her that when it came to all other female accomplishments and skills, Kerry wholeheartedly resisted Laura's attempts to teach her.

"You're becoming quite a cook. It's an art all women must master. Someday you'll be married and cooking for yourself and your husband. It's a shame you don't take to the other homemaking arts as well."

Kerry looked up from the pie crust she was carefully shaping and scoring. "I'm not getting married," she said flatly. Her eyes had darkened and her brows furrowed.

"Oh, but of course you will," Laura said lightly, feeling her temper rise.

"No. I will not."

"Young lady." Laura faced her, infuriated. "If you think we're going to look after you for the rest of your life, you're sadly mistaken. Although," she gave Kerry a scathing up-and-down look, "I can't think what man would have you."

Kerry threw her fork down, untied her apron, strode out the kitchen door, and started upstairs to her room. Laura went after her and stood at the bottom of the stairs, gripping the newel post, her chest heaving.

Several months of repressed anger surfaced and she let it have free rein. "You come back here this instant, you little guttersnipe. I'm speaking to you and you will listen. You're a disgrace. You're disgusting. It's only because of my husband that you're even in this house." She ran up the stairs and into Kerry's room and began wildly slapping Kerry's head, face, and shoulders. Laura grabbed Kerry's arm to keep her still but Kerry slipped away easily. As angry as she was, Laura knew she was no match physically for the wiry adolescent. She screamed, "I'll have you gone or I'll know the reason why. Don't think you can always run to Addison."

While Laura ranted, Kerry gathered a few things and threw them into her shabby old carpetbag. She snapped it together and ran down the stairs with Laura following shouting at her, her fury unabated. Kerry threw on a cap and a jacket. She'd grown a few inches and had become even lankier and looked even more like a boy, Laura noticed, which further angered her.

"Where are you going?" Laura screeched. "Stop."

Kerry stopped long enough to stare at Laura for a long moment. "Since you don't want me here, why are you trying to stop me?" She walked out the door, leaving Laura speechless.

❖

Kerry remembered the way and it didn't take all that long. She walked into the Grey Dog and the first person she saw was Sally, facing away from her and looking at herself in the mirror as she smoked a cigarette, puffing out the smoke theatrically. Cigarettes were the new thing for women like Sally. She belatedly saw Kerry standing behind her. She grinned and turned around and rested her elbows on the bar.

"Well. I never. Look what the cat done dragged in. Kerry-o, I'm glad to see you."

For a reply, Kerry dropped her bag and pulled Sally into her arms and kissed her until they were both gasping. The customers burst into applause. Sally looked into her eyes for a long moment when they broke the kiss, then tugged her arm and Kerry followed her upstairs.

Sally went to find Rose. "I'm not workin' tonight and don't try to get me out." She dragged Kerry into her room and locked the door, then stood against it breathing hard and spoke to Kerry, who was across the room taking off her coat and cap. "C'mere." They fell on the rickety bed laughing and trying to take off their clothes between kisses. Kerry got her head between Sally's legs right away, and the whole bar full of pretty waiter girls and drinkers downstairs heard Sally scream.

"I thought you hated me," Sally said softly, tracing a finger down Kerry's cheek and over her collarbone and breast.

Kerry lay with her head on her arms, looking at the cracked and grimy ceiling, thinking she ought to feel better than she did. She heard Sally's voice from a distance. Sally poked her in the side and she looked at her.

"I did, for a time, but I know it wasn't your fault our scheme went bad. Moe woulda killed you if you hadn't told him."

Sally snuggled in close. "I missed you so much, girl. Ooee."

She and Kerry stayed in her room all night making love.

❖

Laura borrowed a neighbor's carriage, rode to the hospital, and demanded Addison be called. He was quite out of humor when he finally reached the main desk.

Laura said without preamble, "Your little charity case has left and I'm happy about it." She was perversely pleased to see Addison struggle to keep his temper.

"Laura, you don't know what you're saying. I'll be home in a few hours and we'll discuss it then."

Much later, when Addison came home, he drew Laura to sit down on the sofa. "Did she say where she was going?"

"No, Addison, she didn't say. And, frankly, good riddance."

Addison scrutinized her for a long moment and said, "You're overwrought, Laura, and you don't mean that."

"Yes, I do! I mean every word of it. You don't know what this is like."

"Laura, the only thing that poor girl is doing is not listening to you. You must be easier. She hasn't had the life you've had. You mus—"

"I must? I must? I must what? Addison Grant, you're a selfish, selfish man. You bring this strange girl into our house and I have to be the one to take care of her. You're at your hospital all day and you don't know what it's like."

"Laura," Add said sternly, "the only thing I can see is she doesn't fit your idea of a respectable young woman. Give her time. Don't try to force this. She hasn't done you any harm. You've upset her and now she's run away. I'm going to find her. I believe I know where she is."

❖

Leo recognized Addison when he walked into the Grey Dog. "She's here but I don't know just where right at the moment. Have a drink." Leo didn't reckon he wanted to send Addison upstairs to knock on Sally's door.

Addison had one drink to be polite, and then he wrote Kerry a note he left with Leo.

❖

The next morning, Kerry came downstairs and Leo motioned her over and handed her a note. She read it slowly, using all the work she'd done with Addison.

Then she looked around the Grey Dog. *Same old same old. Laura talks about* me *being disgusting. She has no idea. There's old Toby moppin' the puke off the floor so they can reopen and start the whole*

*thing over again. I think Sally's put on some weight and she smells like*
*a brewery. She'll be back to whorin' pretty quick. I think I better go*
*back to Addison's house and try to make amends and get along with*
*Laura somehow, though I don't see how.*

Sally seemed neither surprised nor angry when Kerry packed up and prepared to leave. She sat on her bed just like always, resting her ankle on her knee and kicking up and down lazily. Kerry wouldn't meet her eyes.

"I guess you're just too good for the likes of us now. But happy to oblige you for free, anytime you feel like slumming." She was smoking another cigarette and her eyes were hard and glittering.

"Sorry, Sal. Guess you're right and I got to head back to the swells. It's been nice seeing you." Kerry put a heavy emphasis on the word "see." After their first frenzy, it wasn't good like it used to be. Too much had changed, even in such a short time. Sally looked run-down from too much booze and too much time on her back. But then, maybe that's how she'd always looked, and Kerry just hadn't seen it through the haze of lust.

Kerry made her way back to Addison's house; she couldn't bring herself to call it home. The visit with Sally left her feeling more dislocated than ever. She knew she couldn't go back to the Barbary Coast, but she had to do something to get her out of the house and away from Laura. Of that she was very sure.

When Kerry returned to the Grants, she went straight to her room without a word to Laura and waited for Addison to come home. He called her into his study to hear her side. She knew it was painful for him to hear, but she told him truthfully what happened.

"Addison, I got to have somethin' to do, somewheres to go during the day." Kerry sighed. *To get away from Laura.*

"By all means, I think that would be for the best."

That evening, the three members of the unlikely and unhappy family sat in the parlor and talked. It was more of Addison talking and Kerry and Laura listening.

"I'm at my wit's end with the both of you," Addison said sadly. "We must have peace, for all our sakes. Laura, please refrain from insulting Kerry and most assuredly do not hit her. Kerry, I beg you, please, to respect Laura and try to get along. Both of you must come to me with your troubles instead of quarrelling."

She and Laura wouldn't look at each other. They nodded their assent, and all three of them chose to ignore the thick tension in the air.

❖

Her old friend Teddy Black finally saved Kerry from her long, boring days at home with Laura. She ventured downtown to the Palace in search of him, hoping he was still there and still remembered her after the many months that had passed.

He greeted her with enthusiasm. He cut a suave figure in his uniform and cap with gold braid. "Can you beat it? The place where we used to sneak in and steal food. I heard you left the Barbary Coast. Sorry about Jack."

Kerry looked away and said nothing; it was still painful to think about his death, and her recent visit with Sally hadn't improved her mood very much. "Can you get me work in the kitchen?"

"I can get you in the kitchen but not as a cook. The competition for that's fierce, I'm telling you. They can't keep dishwashers, though. It's a brutal job and nasty, too, with all them dirty dishes and the giant pots and pans. My Lord! That's why no one lasts doing it!"

"I don't care. Just get me in. I'll do the rest."

The head chef, Henri, fixed her with a skeptical eye. He was a stern, mustachioed Frenchman. "Eh. You are a girl? You might have fooled me. You want to wash dishes? Well, then, that is your choice. I am not going to baby you, though, *mademoiselle*. You will make your own way, and if you are not up to the job you will be told to leave."

"Just give me a chance," Kerry said.

It was horribly hard work. Kerry spent hours washing dishes that never stopped piling up. She would wipe the sweat off her face and grimly remind herself that it was better than being at home all day with Laura and her theatrical sighing and her nasty little remarks she tried to dress up as advice. Plus, she was making money honestly, and it gave her a measure of pride to have coins in her pocket no one could take from her.

"You need an occupation, I don't question that," Addison said, "but surely something better than a dishwasher?"

"Well, I'd rather cook but they don't have a position there at the moment." In truth, Kerry knew, she could gain a cook's position only by the sheerest chance. She was very lucky to be a dishwasher.

At the beginning of her employment, Teddy said, "It's odd you washing dishes and all. Some of the boys," he meant the other bellhops, "ask me if you're my girl and why you wear men's clothes. I told them to shove off, it was none of their business, but still…" He'd looked so anxious, Kerry almost decided to quit, but the talk had died down.

## Chapter Ten

At six a.m. on a dull, rainy San Francisco autumn morning, the probationary students for the class of 1898 met at the Women's Ward One of City and County Hospital. Their instructor for the day, Nurse Bennett, eyed her class critically.

"Nurses. Each of you will collect your supplies from the wardroom. We have some cleaning to do."

The probationers scurried away and returned with their buckets, mops, and sponges.

"Cleanliness is the first principle. The ward must be spotless by six thirty a.m."

They made their way among the beds of the patients. Beth wondered how the sleeping patients felt about the nurses' early morning cleaning. The smell of carbolic cleanser wafted up as they laboriously scrubbed the floors.

Nurse Bennett followed each nurse to check her work. She had sharp, beady, dark eyes and the demeanor of a crow. "Hammond. You are missing half the floor."

"I—" Bennett's expression silenced Beth, who was on her knees. She resumed scrubbing vigorously. When Bennett moved on, Beth whispered to the young woman next to her, "I suppose she'll check on us to be sure we don't leave a drop of water behind. Is this really nursing? We've been here for more than a month and haven't touched a patient. They treat us like a lot of scullery maids."

Beth's companion, a redhead named Virginia, snorted. "My favorite task is bed making. How in the world could it possibly matter to a sick person if the corners of their sheets are squared strict military style?"

Beth shrugged. It was, it seemed, a price of admission to the profession of nursing to be able to perform menial cleaning duties perfectly and cheerfully.

Later, Beth sat in one of their nightly medical lectures and yawned. It was a trial to learn anything after twelve hours in the ward, but she fortified herself with black coffee at dinner. Many of the girls would nod off and Beth was determined not to. They were taught several subjects, including, anatomy, physiology, hygiene, surgical technique, and diet. She loved all the lectures, but her favorite were the ones on infectious diseases with Dr. Grant.

She and Virginia were two of five girls who managed to survive their first few months.

On her rare day off, she would go home and sleep for the entire day, which perplexed her parents. It had taken an enormous amount of cajoling, begging, and arguing to get her father to agree to nursing school, and her days spent sleeping allowed him to voice his doubts every time. She ignored his complaints and slept.

The patients made the difference in Beth's life. When a sick woman or child looked up with gratitude after Beth had administered a healing bath or a soothing medicine, she felt instantly better. All the nurses she encountered, from the probationers like herself up to the school superintendent, seemed to be either one of two types—the healing angel or the exacting taskmaster. Some of them seemed to believe discipline was the secret ingredient needed to recover from sickness or injury.

*They frown on sentimentality: the hospital is not a place for the soft-hearted. There is no room for independent thought. Apparently, we're all to be stamped from the same mold.*

The discipline of nursing school extended to the complete control of what little personal time the students possessed. It was left over from the days when the earliest nurses were in religious orders. A nurse was expected to be almost the equal to a sister in chastity, obedience, and devotion.

Most of the girls fretted under the restriction of their personal lives. Virginia joked, "I may never meet a husband unless he be recovering from a broken leg or some hideous malady."

Beth was unconcerned with meeting anyone. She focused wholly on the work, which wasn't mentally exacting but was certainly grueling, and she didn't see how anyone could have any energy left over for social obligations. Beth preferred to spend her free time reading either for pleasure or from a medical text she borrowed from one of the doctors.

She ignored the other nursing students, who talked among themselves about their odd classmate.

❖

A controversy among the students' mentors relieved the tedium of ward work. Dr. Grant and Nurse Sand had petitioned Superintendent Henry to allow the first-year students some time working in the men's wards. Only second-year students were permitted to work there because of some vague moral tenet, i.e., first-years weren't sufficiently mature. Nurse Sand was the head nurse of the men's ward, and she believed it would hasten the instruction of the students to care for male patients, who were more numerous and more variously afflicted. Dr. Grant concurred and the two of them were locked in polite battle with Superintendent Henry.

"It's not proper!" the superintendent asserted.

"Begging your pardon, ma'am," Nurse Sand said, glancing at Dr. Grant. "I do not see how it is a harm to advance this instruction one year. I believe the first-years are able to master the necessary detachment."

"I do not want a gaggle of giggling girls performing this procedure with our poor patients."

Dr. Grant cleared his throat and Superintendent Henry gave him her full attention. She clearly resented any encroachment upon her sphere, especially her direction of nurses' training, but she was nevertheless required to respect doctors at all times.

"Nurse Sand, Madam Superintendent. We are, at present, quite shorthanded in the men's wards. We need to get some help for the number of patients who are currently in our care. It is the duty of the nurse to treat male patients. They are, to their nurses, like little children. The first-year students are a sober and alert bunch. I beg you to please reconsider."

"Very well," she said with a sigh, obviously defeated. She stomped down the hallway in her flat nursing shoes, her ankles jiggling under the bunched material of her cotton stockings. Dr. Addison and Nurse Sand nodded at the nursing students to continue their work and walked away, speaking to one another quietly.

"I wasn't allowed to care for any men other than to give medication until I was a second-year. I don't see why you firsties are being allowed." The second-year student, Nurse Matthews, was speaking to

Beth, Virginia, and their classmate Rebecca over the still body of a male patient the following day.

"Let's get on with it then," Virginia said acerbically. "It's not going to get any better for the patient the longer we delay." They were gathered around the patient's bed. He was in for an appendectomy and had been given chloroform. At that moment, he was out cold.

"I don't think he's going to feel it," Beth observed.

"You don't know that," Rebecca said. She was wide-eyed and reminded Beth of a field mouse.

"Quiet!" Matthews ordered. "To insert a catheter, you must be quick but gentle."

They grew quiet as Nurse Reynolds showed them how to lubricate the tip with petrolatum.

She lowered the patient's cover and lifted his gown. They were dead quiet. Rebecca did look as though she would burst into giggles at any moment, but Matthews fixed her with a look.

"What did you think?" Virginia asked her afterward. Beth narrowed her eyes, not understanding the question.

"About, you *know*. Most women don't get their first look until they get married. Unless they're fallen women. We'll be handling them routinely." She shook her head in amazement.

Beth shrugged. "It's of no consequence except that we're to take care of more patients. That can only be good. Don't you think?"

❖

Near the end of her second year, Beth nearly got dismissed, not for being incompetent, but for being too competent.

She was in the typhoid ward under Dr. Grant. The head nurse of the ward was Nurse Smith. She was sugary to the patients, obsequious to the doctors, and a holy terror to her underlings. She wasn't terribly bright either, but she took orders well until they received a patient who was uncommonly charming and handsome. He had never had any problems until he got typhoid, and he was well on the mend. Dr. Grant issued his usual order though—broth only for another thirty-six hours. Solid food too quickly could rupture a typhoid patient's gut and kill him.

Their patient, Mr. Simms, was wheedling Nurse Smith unmercifully, and she seemed just as happy to go along with his flirting. Beth shook her head and turned away at his fourth request. Smith came over and Beth watched with horror as she fed him a large piece of bread and handed him more before returning to another patient. Beth went to him and put out her hand. "Spit it out."

He rolled his eyes and tried to look innocent, swallowing quickly.

"That other one, she said it was fine."

"Give it to me," Beth said, evenly.

"I don't know what you mean," Simms said slyly. He caught sight of Nurse Smith.

"Nurse!" he called, and waved her over. "This nurse thinks I can't have food."

"Hammond. What are you about? I have seen to this patient. Go tend to the others."

"Dr. Grant said no food yet. And—"

"Be quiet. It's none of your concern."

Beth was nonplussed. She knew Nurse Smith was countermanding the doctor's orders and it was potentially dangerous, but she was the underling and Superintendent Henry was strict in her requirements that all observe the pecking order. *Well*, she mentally shrugged, *if he doesn't sicken, it's not my business. Smith should know.*

It so happened that Beth had night duty and it fell to her to summon the doctor to see to Simms. He had woken with gut pain.

"He had some bread earlier," Beth reported dispassionately. "No, I do not know how he came by it."

"Well, Nurse, I should think you would know by now what this means. We will have to take him to surgery and hope his intestine is not too badly damaged, causing him to die of peritonitis. Thanks to you."

Beth opened her mouth and closed it again. It would do no good to start pointing fingers.

After Simms's surgery, Dr. Grant came to find Beth, who sat quietly at the nurses' desk sipping cold coffee and marking patient charts.

"Nurse Hammond. Simms will survive. We were able to patch the intestine after we removed the bread. No infection, I believe."

"That is good to hear, Doctor."

"I wager you did not commit the basely stupid act of giving him food? It would be entirely unlike you."

Beth looked at him but said nothing.

"I am going to take it up with Superintendent Henry."

"Doctor! Please. It's not important. The patient will recover, you said."

"Why in God's name didn't you say something, Nurse Hammond?" Addison spoke sharply.

Beth stared at her cold coffee, unwilling to be a tattletale.

"Never mind. I'll deal with it myself." He stalked off and Beth watched him with trepidation. Sighing, she got to her feet and went to check on patients.

"You needn't have told her, you know," Smith hissed into Beth's ear later as Beth was trying to get a little sleep before the day shift began.

Beth was unable to sleep as it was. She sat up and straightened her clothes and looked Nurse Smith in the eye. "I didn't tell her, Nurse Smith. Dr. Grant told her."

"But it's none of your business."

"I agree, but since we're speaking of it, you let him take the food and you knew it was risky. So it's not my fault if Superintendent Henry is displeased with you. I didn't tell her though."

The superintendent reprimanded Beth for both allowing the patient to eat and for contradicting her senior nurse. If I'm ever in charge of a ward, I'm going to treat my employees with a lot more care, Beth thought. I'd prefer private service if this is what it's like.

Private service, she knew, was more common than ward work. The hospital made money from sending its nurses to the homes of the wealthy, who could afford not to have to go to the hospital. Beth was never sent, probably because Dr. Grant deplored exploitation of student nurses. He also always requested her for his cases. It was, she thought, one very handy outgrowth of the preeminence of the doctors, if the doctor in question was Addison Grant.

# Chapter Eleven

Beth sat with the rest of her class listening to Dr. Grant's final lecture on bacteriology. It was eight o'clock in the evening. They had spent a ten-hour day on the wards already, with only a couple of meal breaks. It was, Beth reflected, a clear indication of what the school thought was important: eleven hours with patients and one hour learning medicine.

She stifled a yawn and tried again to get comfortable in the hard wooden chair. She wished she had more energy for the medical lectures, which were fascinating. The priorities were so rigid, however, that the staff nurses thought nothing of pulling a student out of a lecture to care for a patient if they deemed it necessary or were too lazy to do it themselves.

Unlike most of the other doctors, Dr. Grant didn't behave as though it was beneath him to teach student nurses. As an expert in infectious diseases he took them into the disease wards to discuss the symptoms of each illness, just as he would medical students. Most of the girls loved him for his smile and his wavy brown hair. He always came out on top when they discussed the doctors. Unmoved by the others' glowing praise of his appearance, Beth very much appreciated the way he treated them.

Addison cleared his throat. He stood still, looking into the middle distance. "I think, before we dive into our last lecture on *Clostridium tetani*, I would like to take a few moments to share some thoughts with you. Your superintendent may say my sentiments would properly be communicated by her and I have no wish to supersede her, but let me add my voice in support of her exhortations to you."

He paused, then, making eye contact with the students. "In two weeks you will graduate, armed, I believe, with sufficient technical knowledge. But what is most important, what will serve you best in the course of your careers, is not something I can impart to you. I would venture to say that most of you will not make nursing your life's work. You will marry and raise families. But some of you, I hope, will persevere, and I speak to those of you who will take that path of a lifelong profession. Some might compare it to the calling of the church, since many of your predecessors were sisters, but I want to distinguish between a calling and a profession. The time is coming when a woman will not be considered odd or out of place if she pursues a profession such as nursing or even medicine. Do not tell Superintendent Henry I told you, but two of my classmates at the University of California were of the fairer sex and did very well." He scanned the class and focused on Beth.

"Nurses must be professional. Oh, I know, it is professional to receive money for one's labors, but it is much more than that. The field hand and the carpenter receive money for their work as well. But that work, however important—and I heartily agree, honest toil is important—does not attain the status of a profession. As nurses, you work with your hands as well as your heart, but you must also work with your minds. Without those three parts operating in harmony and without consistent integrity, responsibility, and attention, you will not be fulfilling your calling, so to speak, or your profession. Character is what I refer to, ladies. Nurses must be of the highest character, if for no other reason than to be able to endure the egomania of doctors."

After waiting for their laughter to subside, he said, "The character of a nurse must be unimpeachable and her ethics and morals without question. I realize we have all endeavored to convey this to you in many ways, but I wished to make it explicit. But I will not take up any more of your time. Shall we proceed with our final subject?"

And with that, he began his lecture.

At the conclusion of the hour, Addison said, "Before you go— formal invitations will be forthcoming—but I wish to personally invite you to a farewell reception at my home next Friday evening."

Afterward, Beth approached Addison at his lectern. "Ah, Nurse Hammond. What can I do for you?"

"Dr. Grant. I was wondering…?"

"Yes, I was addressing those comments to you."

Beth was stunned. Did he really think she was lacking in morals or ethics? Or that she would be one of those who would marry and give up the profession? Her stomach dropped and she felt slightly faint.

"Ms. Hammond?"

"I only, um, wished to know if you could provide me with a recommendation when I apply for a post."

"With the utmost pleasure, Nurse Hammond. I would be honored. You are by far one of the best students."

"Thank you, Doctor." She nodded and walked away, confusion and relief warring in her mind.

Kerry and Laura predictably clashed over the food for Addison's reception.

When Kerry proposed the menu—cold honeyed ham, potato salad, and several cakes and pies—Laura said, "This isn't dinner bell for cowboys on a wagon train. I would rather we have tea sandwiches and petit fours."

"People'll be hungry," Kerry said. "We need to set out a good bit of food. No one ought to go away hungry from a party."

Laura flounced off to talk to Addison, who was in his office absorbed in a medical text. After she told him her trouble, he leaned back and pinched the bridge of his nose as though he had a headache. The squabbles never ended. Laura came to him nearly every day. She would agree to his entreaties to attempt to get along but would still find some reason to complain, though Kerry never said a word to him. He cursed his good nature and his inability to be a stern husband and discipline his household. He hated the conflict between his wife and the strange but oddly compelling young woman whom he felt bound to protect, but he felt powerless to stop it. He had hoped it would subside over time, but if anything it had gotten worse as Kerry grew older.

He shook his head and said, "Dear, it doesn't matter. Let Kerry take care of it. It's to save you trouble." He returned to his book, letting her know she had been dismissed.

Laura gritted her teeth and left.

Friday evening, Addison was on edge at the party, as it was his first time to host the graduates' reception. It was generally Dr. Bucknell's task. He wanted to make the right impression, and the infighting between his wife and charge wouldn't help.

He studied Kerry as she looked at the buffet critically. *She is handsome, to be sure, but without an iota of feminine charm. She's intelligent but rough.*

Kerry wasn't tall but her carriage gave her the appearance of height. She was broad-shouldered and more wiry than slender. Addison remembered what she had looked like five years previously when she had shown up at his front door tired, dirty, and terrified. The wariness was still there in her dark brown eyes and perhaps always would be. She had worn her hair cropped as a youngster and never gave up the style in spite of Laura's entreaties. The front doorbell chimed, jolting him out of his reverie. He went to greet his guests.

Laura stood beside Addison as the stream of guests flowed into their house. They lived in a newish neighborhood known as the Western Addition, as it was west of downtown San Francisco. It wasn't nearly as grand as Nob Hill or Rincon Hill, but Laura made the best of it, using whatever money Addison gave her to fix up their home. And if Addison didn't give her the money, she wheedled it out of her father. Addison was proud to have Laura as his wife. She was beautiful and gracious, the perfect hostess. He wondered briefly how to make life easier for her, but Beth's arrival soon captured his attention.

Beth managed a shy smile as Addison introduced her to Laura as his "best student" and said, "She lives right here in the city. Her parents have a store on Valencia Street."

"Shopkeepers. How quaint," Laura said with a sugary smile before taking his arm and moving him toward another group.

Beth went to the buffet, hoping to occupy herself with getting food and then with eating it. She had never been to a buffet party like this and was unsure exactly how to manage eating without sitting at a table, though the delicious food was fairly easy to eat without utensils. She foolishly poured a cup of coffee before she put food on her plate. Someone jogged her arm and the coffee spilled down the front of her dress. Mortified, she knelt and used her napkin to dab the coffee staining the carpet.

"Here, let me take care of that." Beth saw a hand on her arm and turned toward the voice. A dark-eyed young person held her gaze as she lifted her to her feet. It took a Beth a moment to realize her savior was female. She had short dark hair and wore trousers and a shirt with an apron over them.

"Come to the kitchen with me."

Beth was too stunned to protest. The young woman took her arm, led her to the kitchen sink, and mopped the front of her dress with a kitchen rag.

"You're making it worse," Beth said, her embarrassment making her speak more sharply than she meant to. "You must just blot it, like this." She stilled the woman's hand. Their eyes met again, and the woman nodded and stopped.

Beth took the rag from the young woman's hand and looked into her blazing eyes.

"Thank you. I can take care of this. Really. I'm grateful for your assistance but—"

"All right." The woman seized another rag, wet it at the tap, and returned to the dining room to clean the carpet.

Beth came up behind her. "I'm sorry for making such a mess."

The woman didn't look up from her kneeling position and said, "Please don't worry yourself. It's nothing."

"Here! What's this?" Laura said, keeping her voice low.

"Mrs. Grant, I do apologize. I spilled some coffee and—" Beth said, contrite. She realized she didn't know the dark-haired girl's name, but Laura helpfully supplied it.

"Well, then, we'll leave Kerry to it." She grasped Beth's arm firmly and led her away.

Laura kept Beth busy talking with the other guests, but finally she made her way back to the kitchen before she left the party. Beth vaguely wondered why Laura seemed to be keeping her away from Kerry, but she was embarrassed and felt she owed the strange young woman an apology.

"I wanted to thank you," Beth said. "I didn't get a chance to before. I'm sorry I spoke to you that way. I know you were only trying to help."

Kerry was silent. She didn't know what to say. In truth she wanted to beg the taller, serious-looking girl to stay and talk to her. She presumed she was a nursing student. She looked too young and too sweet to be anything else.

"What's your name?"

"Elizabeth Hammond."

"Do you have a nickname?" Kerry asked, with the hint of a smile.

"Usually people call me Beth."

"Then that's what I'll call you." They both paused awkwardly.

"You'll be done soon with training?" Kerry asked.

"Yes, in a few weeks we shall have exams."

"Where will you go then?" Kerry asked, silently praying it wouldn't be very far away.

"I'm not sure. I want a post in one of the hospitals here in the city. Of course it depends on if I pass my exams and upon the good opinion of the charge nurses at County Hospital."

"I'm positive you'll do fine," Kerry said firmly.

Beth blushed. Very pretty, Kerry thought, struggling with what and how to say what she wanted to. She didn't want Beth to walk out of the house and never see her again. She wanted to know her.

"Would you—I mean, do you? Uh…" She faltered and stared at her shoes. Beth looked at her curiously.

"I usually go to Golden Gate Park on Sunday afternoons," Kerry said, and paused.

Beth waited.

Kerry cleared her throat and asked softly, "Would you like to go with me sometime?"

"Oh, I'm afraid I can't. I must study for my exams. That's my only free afternoon."

Kerry's spirits plummeted.

"But I suppose the fresh air would do me good."

Beth smiled then and Kerry's heart leapt for joy. "It would, I think," Kerry assured her, nodding emphatically, still afraid she might change her mind. "I'll come by with the carriage around one this Sunday."

❖

Every spare moment Kerry had, she observed the kitchen routine and watched the chef, the *sous*-chefs, and the cooks produce the French haute cuisine for which the Palace was famous.

After meeting Beth, however, she kept to the sinks and the dishes, needing the time to think. She said Beth's name over and over again in her mind and silently formed it with her mouth: *Beth.* She formed the image of Beth behind her closed eyes and practiced what she'd say. She recalled reading *Romeo and Juliet* with Addison during their English lessons. She knew what she felt; she wondered what Beth felt. Did she feel the spark between them?

Beth, although she seemed mature, gave off a whiff of naïveté.

*That would be expected. She's no Barbary Coast pretty waiter girl. She's a good girl, a quiet, soberly employed girl who would know nothing of love or of a person like me, the orphan daughter of a gambler and a whore. She wouldn't likely want to have me as a friend even, let alone a lover.*

## CHAPTER TWELVE

Kerry silently gave thanks that the day was sunny and mild. Weather could be variable in the spring in San Francisco; storms could roll in off the Pacific with almost no warning. She'd been visiting Golden Gate Park from the moment Addison had trained her well enough to handle the horse carriage herself. They would drive out every weekend without Laura to accompany them; she was "at home" receiving visitors.

The park had become a refuge for Kerry. It was so different compared to where she'd grown up. She found the silence soothing when she came to the park during the week. It was more crowded on Sundays.

On the ride over, Kerry could see that Beth was ill at ease. She unconsciously picked at her dress and had trouble making eye contact. Kerry asked her questions about nursing, and by the time they made their way from the hospital to the park, Beth seemed more relaxed and Kerry felt relieved. After their unlikely meeting the week before, she was unsure of what to make of Beth; she only knew that she wanted to see her and to know her better.

"How is it that I never knew of this place?" Beth exclaimed. "It's so beautiful." She gazed around, taking in the scenery. They entered through the Fulton Street gate, past the two grand pillars, and down a small hill and around the Conservatory of Flowers to the main promenade.

"It's not so old, I heard. They started the planting only twenty years ago. It was all sand dunes. You can still see them," Kerry said as she watched Beth looking around with great interest. As they drove along the promenade, they could see, looking west, clear out to the ocean.

"You know of its history then?" Beth sounded surprised. She turned slightly toward Kerry, who faced forward to watch the road ahead as she drove. Kerry felt Beth scrutinize her, which was both welcome but unnerving. She tried to not let it bother her much, but it made her ears and cheeks feel warm. What would Beth's judgment be?

"Yes. When I like something, I make it my business to learn about it."

Beth's eyebrows came up and she looked slightly skeptical.

"Mr. Olmstead, who designed the Central Park of New York, helped plan it." Kerry looked away, suddenly embarrassed at her desire to sound smart. She focused on finding a place to stop and tied up the carriage horses near the Stow Lake boathouse in the middle of the park.

Beth took in her strong profile and her hands confidently holding the reins. She ignored the flutter of nerves in her stomach, attributing it to being out with a stranger.

She was content to have Kerry take charge of obtaining their boat, seating her in the bow, and rowing out to the middle of the lake. Boaters would make their way around an island, in the middle of which was Strawberry Hill, crowned by an observatory.

"We could come out some night to see the stars if you like," Kerry said.

Beth held her straw hat against the westward breeze that had started up and watched Kerry row the boat steadily. She was strong and sure, her lightly muscled arms pulling against the shirt as she rowed, her expression serious and watchful. When she turned to look at Beth, she smiled and Beth liked the way her face lit up, making her glow.

"Stop here!" Beth commanded.

Kerry obeyed with a nod and pulled into shore near a stone bridge.

"I want to feed the ducks," Beth said. They obtained some bread from a vendor, and Beth broke it into bits and tossed it into the water. Ducks circled the bread and flapped and squabbled.

"They'll get fat and won't fly if they're not left to fend for themselves and find their own food."

"I'm not feeding them that much," Beth replied, a little stung. In the wards, she wasn't used to getting questions from her patients, and the constant strict obedience she had to render the senior nurses chafed her.

"I didn't mean to upset you," Kerry said defensively. "I was just making a general comment. I meant no criticism."

"Shall we continue, then?" Beth asked. "Continue rowing, I mean." The slight disagreement and her reaction made her feel uneasy again.

"Yes, of course." They got back in their boat and paddled for a while. Beth was quiet and looked around at the other boaters. Many were engaged just as she and Kerry were, but almost without exception a gentleman rowed each boat and his passenger was either a single lady or perhaps a lady with a small child. Beth suddenly felt self-conscious without knowing why.

"May we return the boat now?"

Kerry nodded and they returned to the boathouse.

"Let's just walk for a bit," Beth said. They strolled around the lake to the stone bridge and walked out on it and leaned over the side. Beth felt Kerry's eyes on her. *She's waiting for me to say something.*

"I'm sorry. I was unkind to you."

"It's no matter," Kerry said quietly.

"No, I'm not very good with people who aren't sick." Beth laughed a little. "I don't have many friends."

"No? Why's that?"

"I suppose I'm too busy now. I have my schoolwork and we work in the hospital most days of the week."

"What about when you were young?"

"Ah, well, I was working then too, in my parents' store, or I was going to school and doing schoolwork. I had one friend. Theresa."

"Where is she now?" Kerry asked, seeming curious.

Beth shook her head.

"What of you?" Beth asked suddenly.

"My best friend is Addison."

"He is? But isn't he your father?"

"Well, he is my guardian, I suppose, and he is older. That's true. But he's not my father. My father's dead."

Beth waited but Kerry said no more until suddenly she asked, "Would you like a cup of tea?"

"Yes, thank you."

They strolled over to the Tea Garden. In the middle of Golden Gate Park a Japanese family, the Hagiwaras, had recreated a traditional Japanese garden for the Midwinter Fair of 1894, and it had proved so popular, the park kept it. With their cups of tea, Kerry and Beth ate the small almond-flavored cookies served with the tiny teacups.

"Echgh." Beth choked slightly and pulled a small piece of paper out of her mouth.

"What is this?" she asked, uncrumpling and reading it.

"Don't bite into your cookie, break it," she advised Kerry, reading the tiny paper.

"What does it say?" Kerry asked.

Beth looked up then, puzzled. "It says, 'Don't let opportunity pass you by.'"

"Good advice," Kerry said, and again, it seemed to Beth, some other meaning lurked behind her words.

"What does yours say?" Beth asked, allowing a hint of a challenge in her voice.

Kerry smiled as she broke the cookie and read the paper. "'You have what you're longing for, if only you recognize it.'"

They looked at each other without speaking, then sat in the pavilion, sipping their tea until it got too cold.

"I'd best get back to the hospital," Beth said. "It's getting late." She shivered. The evening breeze was chilly and she hadn't expected to be out so late.

Kerry settled her in the seat and put a carriage blanket around her legs. Beth was again struck by the sense that she was being cared for in an unusual way. *It's almost as if a young man is courting me. An odd feeling, but I like it.* They drove slowly out of the park and back on Fulton Avenue to the county hospital. They pulled up outside the entrance. Their outing had ended.

Kerry took a deep breath and said, "May I call for you next Sunday?"

Beth turned and looked at her steadily for a moment. She started to say no, but instead she surprised herself. "Yes, please. I'd like that very much."

❖

Kerry returned home to have dinner with the Grants. She was always quiet, but she was even more so that evening. She helped Laura with the cleaning and then excused herself. She wanted to be alone with her thoughts.

Beth's face swam into focus behind her eyes. She saw her soft, pretty face, her dark blond hair tied back, and her slightly aquiline nose. In the boat in the park, when she took off her straw hat, the sunlight behind had filtered through stray tendrils of that light hair. Kerry shuddered. *I do want to be a friend but I'm sure I already feel more. I can't let this happen. I'm respectable now—Dr. Grant's ward. That's who I am. What would Beth think of me if she knew the truth?* She fell into a restless sleep, replaying the afternoon with Beth.

The next week, as soon as they were settled into the carriage and on their way to the park, Beth took a deep breath. She had turned it over in her mind many times and finally decided that the best way was to just ask. "Why do you wear men's clothes?"

Kerry turned sharply and looked at Beth for a long moment. She was silent for so long, Beth feared she wouldn't answer.

"I always have, since I was small."

"I see. Why is that?"

"It's handy when I'm at work in the Palace Hotel kitchen."

"You work in a kitchen?" Beth was very surprised. That news distracted her from probing Kerry more thoroughly. Kerry went on to describe her employment as a dishwasher and her aspirations to be a cook, leaving Beth still uninformed as to the "why" of the men's clothes.

They again took out a rowboat on the lake. Beth's thoughts traveled back and forth between watching and admiring Kerry and feeling slightly self-conscious. She made the decision to let Kerry tell her in her own time why she flouted convention so completely.

For the next three weeks, they went to Golden Gate Park every Sunday afternoon. Sometimes they visited the children's carousel; sometimes they watched the people drive by in their fine carriages. They liked to watch the people riding on the bicycle path glide past. They were mostly men, but a few women in skirts gamely navigated the unwieldy vehicles.

"Would you try that sometime?" Kerry asked, her eyes shining and eager.

"Oh, I couldn't. I would fall."

"But you could get right up and start again."

"I suppose," Beth said vaguely. "But what if I got hurt?"

"Well, if you did, I'd be there," Kerry said, solemnly. "I'd put you in the carriage and take you to Addison right away."

"You're very gallant. Why is that?" Beth asked, startling Kerry and rendering her momentarily speechless.

"I, I—er…wouldn't like to see you hurt."

"Well, that's clear, but I've never had a friend quite like you."

"Well, you told me that you don't have many friends."

"I don't."

"You haven't told me *anything* about your childhood."

"There isn't much to tell. And you have told me nothing of yours," Beth retorted.

"So we're even. Shall I l take you back to the hospital?"

"Please don't be angry. I'll tell you next week. Are we coming to the park next week?" The plea in Beth's voice caught Kerry's attention.

"Yes, of course we will." The thought of not seeing Beth again made her feel ill.

❖

The next time they went to the park, Kerry took them to a quiet area with a few benches. They could see the ocean in the distance since the fledgling trees were not well grown. The western breeze felt fresh and kind on their faces. Beth looked in the distance for a while, thinking back to the past and how much she wanted to share.

"I had a very simple childhood," Beth said, breaking the silence. "My parents owned a store in the district by the old Catholic mission."

"I don't know where that is."

"You've lived in San Francisco all your life, haven't you?"

"Well, yes, but…"

"Well, then, you know the Spaniards founded their missions everywhere and one of the oldest was here."

"Huh."

"Where I grew up was named for the Mission Dolores. It's a lovely district, truly. Quiet and sunny."

"Quiet and sunny," Kerry repeated, looking into the distance, and Beth could tell she was thinking.

"So," Beth shoved Kerry lightly with her shoulder and caused her to jump from the touch. She smiled into her eyes. "Tell me something of yourself."

"My mother died when she had me. My father died when I was fifteen and I came to live with Addison and Laura." She stopped. Beth waited and it became clear that was all Kerry was going to say. Beth, used to silence as she was to anything, decided not to press her, although her curiosity was immense. She concluded it would just take time and decided not to examine why it was so important for her to find out about Kerry. Beth had been supremely content with the most superficial of friendships during her high-school years and at nursing school. At the hospital, work consumed her. She couldn't quite escape the gossip and chatter and intrigue of the other students, but she didn't participate, and after a while they stopped trying to draw her in.

Being with Kerry was different in so many ways. They talked and laughed, but she'd never felt so comfortable and secure in the silence as she did with Kerry. Some days they could just sit and enjoy the scenery, and the quiet never felt awkward. Kerry was kind and always attentive. She was comfortable in silence but would also chatter happily about all sorts of things—except her past. If it came up, she would always change the subject. Beth couldn't quite let it go, though she stopped asking. She was content that they were together every week and didn't question why she felt the way she did. She simply felt good having a friend.

The park's main road had a train stop near the entrance where a good many people dressed in their Sunday finest congregated to see and be seen. Beth and Kerry happened to walk by during one of their regular Sunday visits. The trains came out from downtown and went back and, in that democratic way of trains, brought all sorts of folk. There was always a good-sized crowd at the train station.

It seemed natural to Beth that she keep her hand on Kerry's arm during their walks. Kerry would glance down at Beth's hand every so often, and every once in a while, she would catch Beth watching her. Beth would smile but say nothing.

A well-dressed young couple stood on the train platform. The young lady carried a parasol and her beau was soberly dressed. The jarring element in the picture was the presence of a dirty and disreputable-looking man who was either entreating or menacing them; it was hard to tell. As Kerry and Beth approached, they could hear the man babbling.

"Ah now, pardner. This is a fine day to be in the park and with a pretty girl. Doesn't it just put you in a good-enough mood to give me a nickel?"

The young man was trying to ignore the drunken oaf, but he was clearly nervous. The girl with the parasol stared into space with a perfectly blank expression, as though not acknowledging him would make him disappear.

The dirty drunk staggered and nearly ran into the girl. That roused the young man, who turned and, with a burst of hostility, said, "What do you think you're doing? Get away from us, you, or I shall call the police!"

"Aahhhh. The hell with you then." The drunk staggered back a bit, then he unsteadily turned and said, "How about the young lady? Give a poor man a nickel for a drink?" He swayed so close to her he nearly fell into her.

Kerry dropped Beth's hand and strode over to them in a flash. She placed herself between the drunk and the young couple. Beth followed her and was close enough to hear what she said. It was the tone and cadence Kerry adopted that startled her the most. Her even, unaccented voice took on a lilt Beth recognized as Irish.

Kerry spoke in a low, insinuating growl with an unmistakable hardness, as though she was speaking through gritted teeth.

"Off with you, Bob. Now, or there'll be hell to pay, y'know? Not from the police but from me, and I can get some others, remember? Now git and stop pesterin' these two."

Surprised, the drunk had to focus on Kerry. He backed up and she took a step toward him.

"I'm a-goin, I'm a-goin. I don't want no trouble with no hoodlums." He staggered off. He had clearly not realized that Kerry was a woman.

The couple stared at Kerry for a long moment before the man said, "Thank you. That was very helpful." He was clearly embarrassed, and the young woman nodded. It was clear to Beth that they didn't know if they were addressing a man or woman. They left as soon as possible, evidently mystified.

Beth and Kerry walked on. Beth waited but Kerry didn't say anything.

"You spoke to him in such an odd way. But he seemed to understand you."

"It's nothing."

"You're a surprising person. I wouldn't have recognized you when you spoke if I didn't know what you look like and how you sound most of the time. There's a story here." Beth was challenging Kerry again.

"No, Beth. There's no story."

"Why do you wear men's clothes? Why do you work in a kitchen? Why aren't you married?"

Kerry kept her eyes ahead but colored slightly. "Because I'm more comfortable this way."

Beth persisted. "But why?"

"It's who I've always been."

"You won't say more than that?"

"There's nothing more to say." Kerry sounded defensive, and Beth decided to let her questions go unanswered, yet again.

"I believe there is," Beth said at length, sighing in frustration, "and I hope someday to hear it from you."

## Chapter Thirteen

I am happy you and Miss Hammond have become such great friends. I'd be pleased if you would attend the nursing-school graduation with us next week, and I know she would be pleased as well."

Kerry grinned. "Beth asked me already and I hoped to go with you."

Addison grinned back and patted her on the shoulder.

Laura was nonplussed when she heard the news. It was, of course, Addison's way to include Kerry in their social life. But it was one thing when they were entertaining at home. No one of special consequence came to visit, mostly just Addison's colleagues, who were all earnest doctors or sometimes nurses who didn't care about Addison's odd charge. Addison didn't pay attention to the tradition of social separation of doctors and nurses.

The women he worked with set Laura's teeth on edge. Many were the type Laura's mother would have called "strong-minded women" and "not content with their places." She had warned Laura not to become one of this sort if she knew what was good for her. It seemed to Laura that Kerry was a younger version of this type of woman. She showed no interest in a female profession of any kind but was independent and masculine nonetheless, and Laura despaired of ever getting her married off. How the hospital's graduation ceremony was of interest to Kerry was simply beyond her. *She must have asked Addison, and of course he said yes.*

On the morning of the graduation, as Laura and Addison were having breakfast, Kerry entered the kitchen. She had bought a nice wool coat and vest and sparkling white shirt. She didn't feel like going quite as far as wearing a tie, but she felt clean and dressed up and very pleased with herself. As she poured herself a cup of coffee, she heard Laura's voice behind her.

"Good gracious, you cannot seriously be thinking of going to this event dressed like that?" Kerry turned around, and Laura was no longer looking at her but at Addison.

"Addison? Say something!"

Addison colored slightly. He cleared his throat and tugged his tie uncomfortably. "Ah Laura, it's of no consequence. Please don't trouble yourself. Kerry is fine."

Kerry looked back and forth between the two of them. Laura's eyes narrowed and she set her mouth in a prim line. Kerry knew that Laura would only push Addison so far. No matter how upset he made her, she always stopped short of outright rebellion. It was hard enough to endure Laura's attitude, but the fact that she rarely got her way made it mostly worthwhile. Their carriage ride over to the hospital was silent and tense, and anyone looking at them during the ceremony would have thought them strangers.

At the conclusion of the ceremony, Beth and Kerry stood facing each other. Tongue-tied by shyness in this alien environment, they struggled to find the right words. Kerry was impressed and charmed by the sight of Beth in her white uniform and cap, nearly bursting with pride when they read her name and handed her the certificate. On her snowy white bodice was a gold pin denoting she had graduated from the Hospital of the City and County of San Francisco. When Kerry looked at Beth she didn't see the "angel of mercy" of popular sentiment, but rather a supremely confident woman. She was anxious though, now that Beth had graduated, about what would happen next. There was no time to try to ask any questions, though, as Beth took her arm and said, "Come meet my parents." She walked them over to where a couple stood apart from the crowd.

Beth made introductions, and Kerry couldn't manage more than a mumbled hello. George and Frieda looked at her curiously but made no attempt to engage her in conversation, though George clearly gaped at her attire. They seemed ill at ease with their own daughter, Kerry thought. Frieda patted Beth's shoulder and nodded at her without saying anything. George cleared his throat and mumbled something about his being glad she was through her course of study. Then he looked at Frieda and said, "Better we get back to the store."

They left after giving Beth perfunctory hugs but saying nothing more to Kerry. Beth and Kerry were alone again. Kerry relaxed a little but said nothing. She watched Beth's face and waited for her to speak.

"I'm going to have to move back home with my mother and father," Beth said after a long silence.

"Why?"

Beth laughed. "Dearest Kerry, they don't allow the graduates to remain in the hospital living quarters. We have to make way for a new class. It's a relief in a way because of how regimented they kept us. Living with mother and father will be freedom, after a fashion."

Kerry didn't hear any of the rest after "Dearest Kerry." That lovely phrase rendered what followed irrelevant.

"I've asked Dr. Grant to write me a letter of recommendation for a private post," Beth whispered.

"That's wonderful."

Kerry was in a hopeless quandary. The past several weeks had convinced her she was in the grip of something she'd never felt before. She felt trapped between two impossible choices. On the one hand, she wanted to tell Beth everything about her childhood and her feelings. But if she did that, it would end their friendship. She was practiced at keeping secrets and, rather than lose Beth, she chose silence.

*If she knew what I really am, where I really come from, that would be the end of it. She might never speak to me again.*

"I could ask Addison if you could come live with us," Kerry said, before she could even think about what she was saying.

"Oh, dear, that would be too much of an imposition."

"Not at all. You could stay in my room and we could go to the park every Sunday."

"Oh, Kerry. If I manage to get a position, I'll live full-time at the home if the patient is convalescing. I have to be present day and night."

That news deflated Kerry a bit but she took a breath and persevered. "Of course. But you don't want to go back home to your parents, do you?"

That question clearly startled Beth. "No. No, I don't," Beth said in a quiet but emphatic voice. "That's why I hope to get a private posting soon."

❖

Beth sat stiffly in the living room of a fine home near, but not quite on, Nob Hill. She was interviewing with the lady of the house for a post as private nurse for the family grandfather, who was diagnosed with cancer and needed twenty-four-hour care. Beth folded her hands in what she hoped was an attitude that looked calm and trustworthy.

Mrs. Greenaway peered at Beth as though she could discern something just by looking at her. She read the paper in her hand and looked at Beth, then read some more. "Miss Hammond…"

Beth cleared her throat. "Mrs. Greenaway. It is customary to address nurses as Nurse." She spoke in as respectful a tone as possible. She wanted the job, but one needed to establish a tone right from the start. Some of the other nurses had advised her that families were apt to take all sorts of liberties.

Mrs. Greenaway looked flustered for just a moment. "Ah. To be sure. You come highly recommended. Dr., eh, Grant speaks highly of your skills."

Beth remained silent.

"As does Superintendent Henry."

Beth bent her head in what she hoped was modest agreement.

"I, however, have concerns other than your, ah, nursing skills."

Beth waited.

"You will be necessarily left alone with old Mr. Greenaway—that is, your patient—for hours at a time while my husband is at work and I must go out. I have a very busy social calendar."

Which is likely why you don't have time to care for your father-in-law, Beth thought.

"Under no circumstances are you to entertain any young men while we are not here."

"No, ma'am. I wouldn't dream of it." *That was probably Mrs. Greenaway's deepest fear—scandal.* Beth struggled to keep from laughing. Men were the last thing on her mind.

"Very well then. We will require you to be on duty twenty-four hours a day. You may take a half day off every other Sunday."

Beth nodded again. It was a standard arrangement, so she'd just have to sleep when she could. She briefly flashed on how limited her time with Kerry would be, but shoved it firmly from her mind. Work had to come first.

❖

Beth and Kerry sat in one of their usual spots in the park, a bench in front of the Conservatory of Flowers. The horse and carriage were tied up nearby. They talked as they watched the parade of Sunday park visitors. Beth told Kerry about the Greenaways and their sick father.

"He's a sweet man," she said. "I don't think he's going to live long though. Dr. Wright isn't very optimistic, but he puts on a brave face before the family. He was surprised how much I knew about the progress and prognosis of lung cancer."

Kerry was looking intently at Beth's profile as she spoke and waiting for the moment when Beth would turn her calm hazel-eyed look at her. Their eyes would meet and Beth would smile sometimes, but otherwise she contained her emotions. Sometimes questions worked and Beth would reveal a bit more. Kerry wanted Beth's attention, her full attention, because it made her feel like the most worthy person in the world, for that moment, anyway.

"Would you be able to come out to the park with me on your day off?"

"I'd like to, but I may be so tired I can only sleep and wouldn't be much company for you."

"Oh, I wouldn't mind that." *I only want to see you and spend a little time with you.*

"Perhaps you could come and visit me," Beth said.

"Truly?" Kerry was surprised.

"Oh, yes! Mrs. Greenaway was only concerned that I not have gentlemen calling for me. I can't think she would mind if you stopped by for tea."

Kerry nodded, dumbfounded with happiness. Would there be gentleman callers? Beth had never once mentioned any man's name except for Addison's, and he didn't count. It gave Kerry hope.

*Perhaps it's only a question of getting her to understand whom and what she wants. She's fond of me, that I know.* It wasn't clear, however, *how* fond or what sort of "fond." Kerry thought, I don't know any more now than I did the first time we met. It was so much easier with Sally and her fluttering eyelashes, rocking foot, and saucy "C'mere." *Beth is a good girl, a naïve girl. I don't have the first idea what to do or say.*

A couple weeks later during their Sunday visit, between yawns,

Beth told Kerry, "Madam goes out every Thursday afternoon between one and four. Some sort of club meeting. Why don't you call then?"

"I'm done with the luncheon service at two. I could walk there in about forty-five minutes. We could have an hour." Beth was writing her short, friendly letters every few days, but it was painful not to see her every week.

"Well, then. Come after."

"I will. What shall we do now?"

It was late June and an unusually warm day. They were lazily driving through the park.

"May we just do this for a bit?"

"Of course." Kerry could see Beth's cheeks were pale and her eyes dark with fatigue.

They rode in silence and soon Beth fell asleep. Kerry tenderly covered her with the carriage blanket. Beth's eyelids fluttered but she didn't waken. Kerry stopped the carriage under an oak tree and watched her sleep until it was time to take her back to her employer's home.

❖

Beth let Kerry in the front door. She had been watching because she didn't want the knock to reach old Mr. Greenaway's ears. In her weeks of service at the Greenaway home, she'd managed to learn quite a bit about the way the household worked. The maid, a talkative sort, had relayed some of the conversation she overheard between Mr. and Mrs. Greenaway. She told Beth that the madam had a high opinion of her own ability to judge character.

"She told Mister that you had better watch your manners because you ain't much above a maid." The maid smiled grimly. Beth took in the information and decided she would have to be discreet, but she was still determined to have Kerry come for a visit. *It's not as though I'm violating her "no gentleman callers" rule.* Beth didn't question her unusual defiance. She'd been forced as a child into strict obedience and fell into the discipline of nursing quite easily. When it came to Kerry, however, she was naturally inclined to do as she wanted, even though she knew she might be bending the rules.

She drew Kerry inside with her finger to her lips and a mischievous smile. She felt quite wicked having an unauthorized visitor. *Almost as if I were entertaining a young man and Mrs. Greenaway would be livid if she knew.* She hadn't wanted to examine her motives too closely. As far as Beth was concerned, she didn't question her wish to see Kerry and be with her to the exclusion of anyone else. There *was* no one else unless she counted her parents, with whom she had little contact. Now she had an excellent excuse not to see them since she was posted as a private nurse with virtually no time of her own. What time she did have she devoted to Kerry who, in her cook's white uniform, was hesitantly following her through the Greenaway house.

"Holy cow," Kerry exclaimed, albeit in a whisper. "These folks are rich."

"Shhh!" Beth reproved her. "They have to be to afford me and their maid and their cook and everything else. Not that they pay me much. The maid is off today, by the way, and the cook takes a nap every afternoon after lunch. I think she's fond of brandy." Beth actually giggled and Kerry giggled with her.

"Oh, come into the parlor. I want to show you something." She took Kerry's hand and led her down the long front hallway, past a formal drawing room. They reached a room near the back of the house, dominated by a huge grand piano.

"Look," Beth whispered. She sat down on the bench and motioned Kerry to sit next to her.

She raised the cover of the keyboard reverently, conscious of Kerry watching her every move. Beth shuffled the sheet music on the stand and settled a book open to its first page.

"Turn the pages for me. I'll nod, like this," she nodded just slightly, "when it's time."

Kerry read the title of the music aloud. "Nearer, My God, to Thee."

By the words, she could tell it was a hymn. Of course, she didn't go to church. It was much different, however, to watch Beth play the piano and listen to a hymn the way Beth played it. Her face took on a stillness and her eyes closed. Her fingers glided over the keys. Kerry had never heard the piano played like that. There was a cranky old upright in the Grey Dog that people occasionally pounded out music hall tunes on, usually accompanied by drunken singing, but this wasn't a saloon entertainment—it was far different. Kerry had only gone to church once when she first lived with the Grants. Laura had insisted on it, but she disliked it so vehemently, Addison refused to make her go. He would have gotten out of it too if he could have, but that wouldn't do with Laura.

When she finished, Beth rested her hands in her lap and looked down. Kerry didn't know what to say.

"Please play something else," she said finally. She could have remained there listening and watching Beth for the remainder of her life and been content. Beth pulled a small pamphlet of a few pages out and opened it. The title read "Nocturne in E flat" by Fredrik Chopin.

Beth played, the notes flowing from her fingers. It was a slow, haunting tune with a few passages of rapid notes. Something about the melancholy yearning of the music seemed so perfectly suited to both of them and to the moment. This time Kerry looked hard at Beth's face. She seemed to have gone into another world. As beautiful as the music was, Beth's beauty moved Kerry more. If possible, she grew more beautiful as she played. Kerry stared; she couldn't stop herself and her throat went dry. She focused on Beth's lips. She closed her eyes and imagined kissing them.

As Beth played the last notes, she bowed her head and this time left her hands resting on the keys. Kerry moved as though she was under water. She put her hand on Beth's cheek, turned her head so they were face to face, and kissed her. It was neither a short kiss nor a long one; it was gentle and not especially passionate, but it was unmistakably a lover's kiss. Kerry was sure she felt Beth kiss her back before abruptly breaking away and closing the piano.

"You should go. It's getting late."

Kerry said nothing. She was too shocked by what she had done to say anything. She took her coat and shrugged it on. Beth walked down the long hallway and Kerry followed her automatically. Beth's stiff posture frightened her.

"Shall I come by for you on Sunday?" Kerry asked, ready to fall to her knees and plead if necessary.

"Yes, of course." Beth's smile seemed a bit forced, and she didn't look at Kerry. Her cheeks were a little pink.

Kerry nodded in relief. Beth closed the door with a muttered good-bye, leaving Kerry on the porch. She ran off quickly, unwilling to give Beth a chance to change her mind. *I did it. I kissed her.* She pressed her fingers to her lips and grinned.

❖

Beth climbed the stairs and went back to Mr. Greenaway's room to check on him. He was sleeping and she welcomed the chance to sit down and be with her thoughts. The room was dark, and the heavy drapes didn't let in much light or much air. In the warm, close atmosphere, Beth, short of sleep as usual, nodded off a little. Her thoughts bounced around. It seemed as though her lips tingled slightly where Kerry had pressed them with her own lips for that brief moment.

*I could come right out and ask her directly. She would answer. Then I would know. Do I want to know? What then? What do I feel?* She had accepted and returned the kiss at first because it felt real and normal and inevitable. But hard on the heels of those feelings was an urge to run and to deny. But she was clear about not wanting to hurt Kerry, who every time they met looked more bereft. *Well, not bereft exactly, but hungry. Part of me wants to find out what she hungers for. It seems to involve me. It seems I am being courted, but what does that mean?*

Beth had listened to the other nursing students prattle endlessly about their beaus or even patients they considered eligible. Beth knew she had no interest in young men and accepted that, but here was a young woman, albeit a unique one, courting her and claiming attentions normally given to a young man. Kerry's very appearance aroused interest. Beth had noticed looks whenever they were out together in the park, as her clothes and mien were that of a young man. *Yet, she is not. She is gentle, as women are.* Beth shook her head unconsciously, unable and really unwilling to reconcile Kerry's contradictions. She drowsed until the family returned home.

The day before her cherished day out with Kerry, Mr. Greenaway passed away in his sleep, and Beth had to write a hurried note to Kerry, since she couldn't leave the family until the arrangements had been made. Pausing to gather her thoughts, and debating the many things she wanted to write, she settled for something quick and simple.

> *Mr. Greenaway passed. May God rest his soul. I have returned to Mother and Father's. Will I see you next Sunday?*
> *My fondest and sincerest regards,*
> *Beth*

After asking the maid to give the note to Kerry when she arrived the following afternoon, she wanted to take it back. It seemed overly formal and didn't begin to convey her thoughts. Then again, Beth had no idea what her real thoughts were. She was unsure of what Kerry was after, though up until the day of the kiss, it had seemed to Beth that friendship was what she was being offered. She was no longer sure it was that simple, and she was even more unsure what she felt about, and for, her unusual friend.

❖

Addison came home from work in a state of excitement. "It's the war in the Philippines," he told Laura and Kerry. "The recruits are pouring into the Presidio of San Francisco and they have called for civilian doctors to help! The hospital has given me leave to go and I'll report there for duty in a week."

Laura clung to his coat and cried, and Kerry looked on in disdain. *He's not going to war. He's going across town to do what he always does—doctor people. Laura's such a fool.* She was uninterested, in any case, because she was thinking about her outing with Beth and what they would say to one another. Or, more precisely, if Beth would mention the kiss.

In the hot, fetid hotel kitchen, Kerry washed the mountains of filthy crusted dishes and turned over the moment of the kiss in her mind. While she always looked forward to her stolen time with Beth, part of her dreaded their next meeting. Would Beth be angry with her or think ill of her? Could there be any hope that Beth had enjoyed the kiss as much as she had? *It's so impossible to tell what she's thinking.*

❖

When Kerry came to call, Beth leapt into the carriage. "Get me away quickly!"

Kerry whipped the horses into a gallop, and Beth grabbed the broad-brimmed straw hat she wore and swirled it over her head and whooped.

Kerry spared a glance at her. Her eyes were alight and her mouth was slightly open and seldom had she looked more desirable. They tore through the Mission's placid streets until Kerry finally pulled the horses up and set them to a walking pace.

"Don't stop now! Don't stop until we're far, far away!"

Kerry laughed. "But I mustn't drive them too hard. Addison would be unhappy."

"I see. Well, I suppose we're far enough away." She settled back in her seat and then turned and grinned at Kerry. "Thank you for rescuing me. I thought I should die of boredom. I thought it would be a relief to be finally off duty, but I was wrong. Father waited for exactly two days before pleading with me to come work in the store. I couldn't say no, but after nursing, storekeeping is positively mind-numbing." She went on in that vein, and Kerry waited impatiently for the moment when Beth would bring up the kiss.

They ambled along the promenade with half of San Francisco milling around them, little noticing the blue sky and green grass, and the eucalyptus trees that swayed in the gentle breeze. Beth slipped her hand around Kerry's arm, as always, and they were complicit in their silent agreement to speak only of inconsequential things.

"Will you come take supper with us tonight?" Kerry asked abruptly.

Startled, Beth looked back at her, trying to discern from her face what she was thinking.

"I shouldn't. My parents are so happy to see me. They need me at home and—"

Kerry took Beth's hand and said in a low voice, "I'd like it very much. I've missed you."

Her brown eyes were so soulful and pleading, Beth relented. "I suppose—"

"Addison would love to talk to you, I'm sure."

"We just must stop and tell Mother and Father."

❖

Laura, though too well-bred to say so, was vexed at Kerry bringing Beth home for supper. It was just another instance of Kerry acting as though it was her home, although, of course, Addison had insisted it was hers, and that he would enjoy speaking with his former student. Granted, she had never brought any other friends home, but it was still rude to spring someone on the household at the last minute. She was especially annoyed since Addison's new post at Camp Merritt in the Presidio or army post was taking even more of his time than the hospital did.

Kerry left Beth to rest in the parlor and went to help Laura prepare supper.

"Is something wrong?" Kerry asked as Laura tossed silverware and banged pots in a flurry of displaced emotion.

"You have taken advantage of our hospitality."

"Is there not enough to eat?" Kerry asked.

"Well, no, of course not. You know I couldn't say no."

"Well. Addison always says anyone is welcome."

"That's fine for him, but for you…" She clamped her lips together, trying to keep her temper. "This is not your house," she hissed, glad to see Kerry blanch slightly.

Before she could respond, they heard Addison's voice from the parlor. "Nurse Hammond. What a distinct pleasure."

Laura knew he wouldn't even remove his hat and coat before shaking Beth's hand warmly. She could hear Beth's quieter greeting. Throwing a disgusted look at Kerry, she tossed the spoon into the sink and went to greet her husband. Let the silly girl cook herself, if she wanted company for dinner so badly.

❖

"It is, I tell you, a thorough mess of confusion and inefficiency! The army has called for recruits from all parts of the country to come immediately, and they are woefully unprepared. There are not enough tents, not enough food, grossly inadequate sanitation. The whole place is snarled in bureaucracy, and the army officers don't like to listen to their own surgeons, let alone civilian doctors." He laughed.

"But it's a challenge. I never can resist that sort of call, as you know, my dear." He smiled at Laura, who nodded and said, "Not in the least, dear Addison. You're never happier than when you can swoop in and take charge."

"Ah, if only that were true. I'm obliged to report to the military surgeon, who's a good fellow but harried beyond belief and hamstrung by the chain of command. And Nurse Hammond, I tell you, they have a sore need for good nursing help, but the army won't hear of female nurses. They rely upon their hospital corps, which is made up mostly of the very worst privates—incompetent louts who can't shoot straight or master the least detail of soldiering. So the army, in its wisdom, dispatches them to care for the sick and wounded soldiers." He rolled his eyes.

They listened to Addison speak at length of his experience, and Beth listened with rapt attention and seemed not to notice Kerry's frequent looks. At the end of the evening, they quietly drove home in the carriage.

"Beth?" Kerry said finally, as they sat outside of the Hammond Dry Goods Store. "I, er. I—um—" She didn't know how to ask her question.

"I want you to be at ease," Beth said firmly. "The kiss was… interesting. Thank you. I take it you were emotionally overcome by the music?" she asked, quietly.

"Ah, yes. That's true." Kerry actually seized upon that as a plausible explanation. *Well, I was overcome by your beauty as you were playing the music. I'm sure I'm falling in love with you. No, I am in love with you and was from the first moment I met you. The instant I looked into your eyes, I was lost.*

"Well, good, then. We are clear. Good night, Kerry, dearest." Beth squeezed her arm and jumped out of the carriage before Kerry could come around and help her down, as was her custom. Kerry turned the carriage around and dejectedly made her way home back to the Western Addition through the dark, quiet streets.

## CHAPTER FOURTEEN

I t was going to be another hectic luncheon service at the Palace's restaurant. The hotel was busier than usual even for summer; the war in the Philippines had brought many more visitors and workers to town. Kerry was kept occupied with the dishes, but she was always on the lookout for a chance to catch Chef Henri's attention and get put on a grill or even a prep station. Chef Henri made it clear he didn't think women belonged in the kitchen, but Kerry knew her perseverance at dishwashing and refusal to be intimidated hadn't escaped his notice. She desperately wanted an opportunity to prove to herself she was in the right place. All she needed was the chance, and she'd show him what she could do.

It was ten forty-five a.m. and the kitchen had been in full swing since eight in the morning. Although she wasn't due for her shift until noon, Kerry always came in a little early just in case someone didn't show up and she could convince Chef to let her cook. She tidied the sinks up and made sure the evening dishwasher hadn't taken her favorite scrub brushes. Like all denizens of a big restaurant kitchen, she was particular about her tools of the trade and woe to anyone who messed with them.

The cooks were lined up and firing their grills, laughing and teasing a skinny, pockmarked boy named Danny, who was in charge of the fish station. He had a wickedly painful hangover and was going about his setup with glacial slowness. It was all the usual chaos and the kitchen began to heat up as the stove fires were stoked. Chef Henri was marching around yelling orders about the food that needed to be brought out, and the *maître d'hôtel* was in the kitchen discussing the menu.

"Ho, Danny boy. How's your head, lad? Does it feel like General Merritt's army is marching across your brain?"

"Shut up, Mac," Danny said sourly. "You try doing this with your head fit to split."

"Oh, I have, boy, I have," Mac said with a sadistic grin as he poured oil into a hot pan.

Suddenly Chef Henri stormed into the stove area and thrust a pan of bad onions under Danny's nose. Whenever Chef discovered bad food in the cold storage, he unerringly knew to whom to bring it and how to present it for the maximum negative effect upon the culprit.

"You, Hanlan. I thought I told you to throw this out?" The onions had gone very bad. The pan was liquefied, odorous goo.

Danny looked down and gagged before bending over and throwing up on the floor.

"Agggh. You are a worthless piece of shit! Leave my kitchen. Sammy, clean this up. Kerry. You come, take this idiot's place. Hanlan, come back, I have changed my mind. You will sober up by washing dishes. See! I have given the girl your place. Idiot!" Chef Henri stalked out of the kitchen, and Kerry hurriedly grabbed an apron.

The sous-chef looked at her, his beefy arms folded over his chest. "Let's see if you can take it, split tail."

Kerry faced the sous-chef and looked him in the eye. She had been called worse, and growing up on the Barbary Coast had given her a thick skin. "Just be sure you call out the orders loud enough so's I can hear you. You tend to mumble."

The cooks hooted and catcalled, this time at the expense of the sous-chef, a sour-faced rascal named Jim who didn't cook nearly as well as he thought he did and played the petty tyrant with the other cooks while kissing the chef's ass.

Kerry scrambled to her station. By the end of the service, she had executed forty pieces of sole or steak nearly perfectly. Chef Henri's mustaches twitched and he ordered Danny demoted to dishwasher. She had her chance.

❖

Beth went to dinner at the Grants' house as often as she could politely get away from her parents. Though they no longer reacted much to her lack of attention to them, she felt guilty. She helped out in the store and with housework so they didn't complain. Kerry issued a standing invitation and she gladly took her up on it, although she always felt slightly ill at ease if left alone with Laura, who looked at her like she was a bit of fluff attached to the furniture.

"Please call me Beth," she said to Addison one evening early in the summer. She had been shy with Addison at first, since he was the only doctor she had ever seen socially, but he worked at putting her at ease by asking her questions and treating her as though her opinions mattered.

"With pleasure." Addison grinned. "If you're sitting at my table, I don't see why we should stand on formality, eh, Laura? By all means, please call me Addison. If we ever work together in a hospital again, we shall revert to the standard form." It was unprecedented for a doctor to be so informal, but Addison, as Beth knew, was quite unusual. "I'm entirely happy to have you become Kerry's friend. I was concerned at her lack of them. She knows no one but Laura and me, and she was in sore need of company. I can't think the various employees of the Palace's kitchen look upon her with anything but resentment. Although she's never mentioned anything or named anyone particular, I imagine it's not a welcoming environment for her. She's quite determined to stick it out though."

Laura pushed the food around on her plate silently, and Kerry gave Beth an amused and tender smile, which sent her stomach to doing flips. Beth quickly returned her attention to Addison's story, afraid someone might notice the sudden flush she felt creep up her cheeks.

Addison returned to his tales of the Presidio. "It's more crowded than ever. Waves of fresh troops arrive every day and there's no place for them. The army can't keep up with the demand for supplies. The army medical officers are at their wits' end with fully one-third of the troops on sick call at any one time. I believe the army may be reaching a level of desperation where they may be ready to entertain the idea of female nurses. I'll speak to Major Owen this week. Beth, if I should manage to persuade the major where his salvation lies, I invite you to come apply and I shall offer my strongest recommendation on your suitability and industry."

Beth felt a twinge of hope and returned Kerry's encouraging smile, thinking that working with Addison also meant she would be able to see Kerry more often. As it happened, they had planned a day out together to the Sutro Baths, and she couldn't wait.

❖

Along with what seemed like half of San Francisco, Kerry and Beth rode the train out to the Sutro Baths. Adolph Sutro, millionaire lumber baron, sometime mayor of San Francisco, and full-time entrepreneur, had built his palace of pleasure at the end of the San Francisco peninsula. He also made sure to build the means to bring the crowds to it. The Land's End railroad ran from downtown all the way out to the northeast corner of San Francisco. After leaving the downtown depot, the tracks wound through sand dunes along the Bay and finally climbed up the cliffs facing the Golden Gate—the great entrance to San Francisco Bay—so named by the explorer Fremont after the beginning of the Gold Rush. An amusement park stood right next to the Sutro Baths since Sutro was never a man to pass up a chance to make money.

"Do you know how to swim?" Beth asked Kerry on the train ride.

"Yes, I learned when I was a kid—in the Bay. We used to dive off the wharfs."

"Oh, dear. I never did. There was no water anywhere close in the Mission neighborhood."

"What did you do for fun?"

"I went to the library and I played the piano."

"That's all?" Kerry asked.

Beth fixed her with a stern eye. "I was going to school or I was helping at the store. That's all I had time for. What did *you* do besides swim in that cold, probably filthy, water?"

Kerry was uncomfortable. "Welllll. I didn't go to school. I don't know exactly. We went to downtown San Francisco or to Chinatown, but we stayed around home, mostly."

"Who is 'we' and where was home? You still haven't told me." Beth sounded plaintive rather than angry, and Kerry was at a loss to explain her upbringing, but then they arrived at the end of the line.

"Oh, look. Here we are," she said, brightly.

Beth filed her curiosity away, resolving to try again at another time. They debarked from the train and walked past a row of businesses designed to attract the bathgoers to spend still more money. Down the hill, they could see a large imposing building nestled against the cliff and beyond the huge Cliff House Hotel facing the restless Pacific Ocean.

Beth and Kerry stood open-mouthed in front of the entrance flanked by towering Greek columns. It was said Sutro wanted his baths to replicate those of the Roman emperors in size and splendor. They walked in through the imposing entrance and stopped just inside the door. They were a couple of floors above the huge swimming pools. Through the windows to the west, they could see the waves crashing on the Seal Rocks.

Beth swallowed nervously. She had looked forward for days to this outing, but the full significance of what they were about to do was just dawning on her.

They followed the signs downstairs to the ladies' changing rooms. A woman in a little booth gave them two worn-out swimsuits. Sutro required his bathhouse patrons to rent their swimwear from him, under the guise of it being healthier than allowing patrons to bring their own.

"Ladies' changing room that way," the woman said, "unless you want a private room. That'll be twenty-five cents more."

Beth and Kerry looked at each other and back at the bathhouse clerk. Beth said, "Yes, we do." She handed over the two-bit coin.

The woman gave them two wire baskets for their things and a key to a dressing room.

Beth realized with a combination of anticipation and an attack of nerves they were going to be in a room together alone, and they were going to have to take off their clothes. She didn't understand why this unnerved her so, but she was determined not to let her feelings show. Not only that, but she would have to get into the swimming pool and had never been in one. She braced herself, unwilling to do anything that would make Kerry think less of her.

Beth followed Kerry down the walkway and waited while Kerry unlocked the door. They entered a tiny bare room with a cold cement floor and one wooden bench.

Beth sat on the bench and removed her shoes. She wore a plain, light green dress that buttoned up to her neck and turned away from Kerry to unbutton it. The quicker she got through the changing process the better.

We're going to have to go through the entire process again later, Beth thought as she swiftly took off the rest of her clothes and got into the bathing costume, her back turned to Kerry. It was slightly ragged and an unpleasant grayish-blue. When she finally turned around, she saw that Kerry was already clad in her bathing suit and looking at her with an unreadable expression.

"Where shall we go?" Kerry asked, leading the way down the

hallway toward the pools "You choose. This is the biggest pool, the cold seawater one, and it has most of the toys—the rings, the slide, the ropes, and so on. Shall we start here?" She motioned to it and they stepped in together, gasping at the cold as it hit their legs.

Beth looked on and cheered from the steps as Kerry tried each silly pool toy, one after the other. Then Kerry hoisted herself up the side and sat next to Beth, dripping and panting.

"How about a swimming lesson?" Kerry asked, her eyes shining and the light from the huge western-facing windows reflecting on her wet hair.

Beth's stomach flipped over and she forced herself to take a steadying breath. "Oh, I couldn't."

"So you've come all the way out here, put on a bathing costume, and you won't even get in the water?"

Beth's temper flared at the implied slight to her courage. "Of course not! Very well. Just please don't let me drown."

"No, I'd never do that."

They stood in waist-high water.

"I don't want to put my face in," Beth said firmly.

"But you can't swim unless you do. Come on. I'll do it with you. Hold my hand, and when I count to three, hold your breath, close your eyes, and we'll duck under water for just a moment."

In spite of her anxiety, Beth couldn't help but be convinced by Kerry's certainty. She put her hand in Kerry's and nodded.

"Ready? One, two, three!"

Kerry almost had to drag her down and they surfaced immediately. Beth sputtered and wiped the water from her eyes.

"Close your eyes!" Kerry reminded her jovially. They did it several more times, and Beth got used to the sensation of being underwater. It wasn't so bad. Kerry's firm grip on her hand reassured her.

"Now I can show you how to stroke. Watch me." Kerry swam a little way away and then came back. She looked like a fish with arms and legs.

"Oh, no, I can't do that," Beth said.

"Of course you can. I'm going to hold you. Here. Lay back in the water. I've got you."

Beth leaned back slowly and forced herself to relax on Kerry's arms. Kerry slid her other arm underneath Beth's knees, cradling her. "See? Not so bad."

Beth looked up at Kerry's face. She was grinning, and it seemed to Beth that Kerry's expression contained an element of tenderness. She was so clearly anxious that Beth should feel secure and be happy that it was touching. And something else—the feel of Kerry supporting her in the water did help her nerves, but it gave her another feeling, one she couldn't name but was making her feel warm in unexpected places.

Beth grinned suddenly and Kerry laughed. "Now, turn over and do as I did. Turn your face to the side and breathe, then put your face in the water and exhale. Your arms are like this." They practiced for another half hour.

Then, without Beth even noticing, Kerry let her go and off she swam for a few feet on her own. Then she stopped and gave a cry of alarm. Kerry rushed to her and embraced her. Beth went limp against her.

"I got frightened when you were no longer holding me," Beth said. They stood together in the water. Kerry didn't relinquish her hold and saw that Beth didn't try to move away.

"Shhh," Kerry murmured. "All's well. You swam on your own."

Beth leaned back and looked at her silently for a moment before moving away from her arms. "Perhaps we better stop."

They went to warm up in one of the heated pools and sat there quietly, enjoying the hot water and steam swirling through the air. Kerry watched as Beth rested her head on the cement side, water drops on her eyelashes making her look like a water nymph from some old wives' tale. Kerry resisted the urge to stroke the damp hair from Beth's forehead and kiss her wet cheeks. She desperately wanted to taste the salt on Beth's skin, to feel her shiver under her hands like she had in the cold pool, but not because she was cold. Beth opened her eyes suddenly and they stared at one another for a long moment.

Beth looked away first and said, "I think I would like to go home."

Kerry nodded silently. Nothing she wanted to say could be said without scaring Beth away, no matter how much she wanted it to be otherwise. She shivered in spite of the warmth of the pool. The old worn-out bathing suit clinging to every inch of Beth's body showed Kerry the outline of her shape in considerable detail. She resolutely tamped down her feelings and took Beth's hand to help her out of the pool.

## CHAPTER FIFTEEN

Addison's superior, Major Owen, had no quarters for patients, inadequate supplies, and no fully trained hospital corpsmen. In the army, the hospital steward and the corpsmen functioned in the same capacity as civilian nurses. That was how the army had always done it and they didn't intend to change. Major Owen had heard, however, in the East, a woman doctor named McGee, newly hired as an acting assistant surgeon general, had begun to recruit civilian female nurses, and he reluctantly acknowledged that he had to do the same. Addison was one of the first of the volunteer civilian doctors, and so Major Owen appealed to him when it came time to take the first step.

Addison eagerly encouraged him. "It's a disorganized mess, sir!" he exclaimed. He had had to learn to always use the honorific, as he wasn't considered the major's equal although they had the same number of years of experience. The army way won every time. "These men are suffering and we must do something about it."

"I am aware of that, Grant. You don't have to convince me."

"The Red Cross is doing very good work but they are volunteers only. So are the Ursuline Sisters. You need a number of competent professional nurses."

"As soon as I can get the army to allocate me some money, I shall call upon your help to recruit. In the meantime, we have a dozen cases of typhoid, six cases of dysentery, and desperately need to get the hospital corpsmen into some kind of shape." Major Owen went off to the Ferry Building to meet the next incoming troop ship and arrange for transport of men who arrived there from all parts of the country and were already ill.

The following week, Addison and Beth drove the carriage out to the Presidio. "I fear to describe too much detail of the camp conditions, especially at the dinner table. It's too disgusting, but as a nurse, you're trained to cope, so I'll tell you now, Beth, it's horrendous. I don't see how we can keep anyone well and how we'll heal them when they're sick. These young men are raw recruits. They have no experienced officers to teach them proper camp sanitation. They dig privies right away, but they're inadequate and so horrible the men won't use them. The dunes near their tents are covered in waste and the whole area stinks. They don't wash their hands properly and are getting dysentery right and left.

"We have no proper hospital. We have a few tents the Red Cross set up and some that Major Owen has managed to wrangle out of the quartermaster. We may get a set of barracks soon to outfit as a hospital, but for now, it's a matter of making the best of it. The San Francisco summer weather makes it impossible for the men to be comfortable. The winds blow through their tents and chill them to the bone. The sand drifts everywhere. What is worse are the hospital corpsmen. They are the very dregs of their units. They are unlikely to make good soldiers so they are detailed for the care of the sick. Aye. Army logic!" He rolled his eyes and snapped the reins harder. "In any case, I wanted to warn you in case you should wish to change your mind."

"No, Addison, I won't change my mind. It sounds as though we nurses are sorely needed. In any event, it will be better than endless hours sitting and watching a sick man sleep." Beth smiled, alluding to her employment as a private nurse. "This, at least, will give me useful work."

"That's indeed the truth. Here we are." Addison stopped the carriage in front of a red-brick building and they exited. Addison went inside to find Major Owen, and Beth waited outside. She felt the chill in the air, a normal part of the summer weather, and fog still hung over the Bay. The main headquarters of the Presidio sat on a hill that gently sloped down to the shore. The post buildings were a fine red brick designed in the Georgian style, and across the water, the hills of Marin County were just beginning to take on the dull brown of summer. The sun was breaking through the fog that still floated over the Golden Gate strait.

Beth breathed deeply, taking in the grand scenery even though it was a backdrop to the bustle of an army post preparing for war. Troops marched in the distance, and the echo of gunfire in an open field created a strange dissonance in the beautiful surroundings. She pulled her jacket tightly around her. Farther to the south stretched row upon row of tents where the newly arrived soldiers lived—Camp Merritt—named for their commanding general.

Addison fetched Beth inside and into the office of a harried-looking middle-aged man in uniform.

He motioned her to a seat without rising to greet her. Beth guessed he was far too busy for such niceties.

"I am a recent graduate," she said in response to his question. "I was in a private posting for several weeks but I want a full-time post."

"This is full-time and then some, young lady. Dr. Grant says you're highly competent. I wonder, though, would the army life agree with you? We must keep strict discipline. No foolery and no fraternization with convalescent soldiers, young lady. That would not do."

"Major Owen…" she said.

He glared at her. "Address me as sir, young lady."

"Major Owen, sir. I don't think army discipline would be much more rigorous than nursing school. I would say that in many ways *we* were treated as soldiers. I can work through the night and the next day if I need to. My purpose is to follow the orders of the doctor and the dictates of good nursing procedure and not to deviate. I would make, I believe, a very good soldier." She lifted her chin a little and looked him right in the eye. He was quiet for a long moment.

"Very well, then. Contract is for three months, thirty a month. We have no facilities for you to live here. You're responsible for finding lodging as close to the post as possible. We may need you at a moment's notice."

Beth swallowed, thinking of the three miles' distance between the Mission District and the Presidio. It would take a long while to walk, and there was no cable car. She would have to find a way.

She put out her hand.

Major Owen stared at her in surprise but then shook it firmly. "Report for duty in three days at 0600, Nurse."

"I am prepared to start today, sir. Dr. Grant brought me and he is staying. Rather than make my way home, I would prefer to begin."

"Very well. I have no nursing supervisor as yet, nor do I have uniforms for you. Report to Dr. Grant. He will no doubt be at the hospital tents. That is all." With that, he turned back to the paperwork on his desk, leaving Beth to find her way.

Addison was still waiting out in the carriage, clearly admiring the view that had captivated Beth earlier. She climbed into the carriage and favored him with a brilliant smile.

"I shall have to go back to addressing you as Doctor," she said, "although it seems I must call Major Owen 'sir.'"

"Splendid! I was sure you would be accepted."

"I do have a small difficulty. They have no place on post for us to live."

"Ah. I'm aware of that and have a perfect solution. You'll come and stay with us for the duration. I assume you and Kerry won't mind sharing a room since you're such great friends."

Beth stared at him, then recovered herself and said, "That's very generous. Thank you."

She recalled Kerry's invitation from two months earlier. She had hesitated to agree since it wasn't really Kerry's place to extend it, but now, coming from Addison, she was happy to accept. It would mean more time spent with Kerry. She hoped their proximity would make them easier together, since they had some tension between them, even though they'd discussed the kiss. The visit to the Sutro Baths seemed to have opened up a new source of uneasiness. On the way home, Kerry had been uncharacteristically silent. Beth wanted to ask what was on her mind but felt that she couldn't. She very much wanted to know more about Kerry and understand what led her to wear men's clothes and work in a restaurant. Maybe living together would induce Kerry to be more forthcoming.

"Well, Nurse, shall we get to work?" Addison asked with a grin.

"By all means, Doctor. Let's begin. It's handy that I brought my nursing uniform. Now, do you suppose they have a private place where I may change?"

Addison stared at her, then laughed. "It's hard to tell either way but we'll improvise."

❖

Kerry walked into the bedroom where Beth was busily putting away her clothing. Kerry stopped to admire her neat economy of movement and to have the pleasure of watching Beth's sweet body without her knowledge.

"I hope I've cleared enough room in the dresser for you."

Beth must have been absorbed in her task because she jumped. "I apologize. I didn't mean to startle you."

"It's nothing." Beth turned back to her task, but not before Kerry noticed her frowning.

Relieved when Beth turned away to put on her nightgown, she quickly did the same, trying to ignore her growing agitation.

*I'll be damned if I'll say anything. It's up to her.* Her stomach was full of butterflies at the thought of how close Beth would be to her for this night and for many more to follow. She had many times imagined lying in bed with Beth in the night, but the reality clearly wouldn't fulfill her fantasy.

Beth knelt to say a prayer before she got into bed and Kerry watched her from lowered eyelids, her heart melting at the sight of such sweet purity. But she turned over as Beth climbed under the covers next to her.

Kerry pretended to sleep but it eluded her. Their combined body heat filled the space and Beth's scent filled her head. Every one of her nerves was on full alert. She tried to keep still since Beth had seemingly fallen asleep quickly and she didn't want to wake her and make her regret her decision to live in Addison's house. Sleep eventually took her, dreams full of soft skin and pink lips making her restless in her slumber.

❖

In the week Kerry had taken up her new position in the kitchen, she had continued to cook every lunch shift, and Chef gruffly informed the other cooks that Kerry had Danny's place at the grill. Chef was a practical man. Girl or not, Kerry was skilled and a reliable cook. He was not one, however, for any more coddling than necessary. He made no speeches of welcome nor did he instruct his staff to respect his female cook. His other cooks, therefore, felt free to make Kerry's life as miserable as possible. They hid her utensils and snickered as she searched for them. They tossed her *mise en place*—the setup of ingredients that she needed to cook—so that she spent precious time reorganizing it before beginning service.

Kerry cursed under her breath but didn't complain, which she knew would be futile. She would have to keep to herself, do her work, and hope the harassment would stop as they got bored with her lack of response.

With cheerful malice, Jim assigned her to the deep fryer as well as the grill.

"You know," he said, "you need to strain the oil to clear it." He looked around at the other cooks, who nodded sagely. "Or you can use egg white."

"Egg white?" Kerry asked, mystified.

"Of course. You clear consommé with egg white, do you not?" he asked loftily.

Kerry saw the other cooks smirking and knew something was wrong, but since she couldn't figure out what it was, she ignored it and went about her work.

A few days later, Jim ordered her to clean the oil for the deep fryer. She added egg white but the oil didn't seem any cleaner.

She built up the stove fires in preparation for luncheon service, noting that for once her cooking utensils were present and her *mise en place* undisturbed. She went downstairs to cold storage and was gone some minutes collecting all the fillets and steaks the prep cook had prepared earlier that morning. When she returned, Davey, the one cook who had taunted her least, said, "Kerry, somethin's amiss with the fryer!"

She looked and was horrified to see a mass of billowing, greasy white material boiling out of the fryer and dripping onto the floor. Seeing her expression, the cooks burst into laughter. Jim stood with his arms crossed. "You best clean up this mess quickly before someone slips on it. Luncheon service starts in fifteen minutes." She glared at him and went about cleaning it up, and Davey helped her when he saw Jim's back was turned.

After her shift, Kerry went to find Teddy and smoke a cigarette. She told him what had happened in the kitchen.

He said, "They're going to keep after you until you can show them."

"What can I do? Jim's the worst. The rest follow him."

"Then he's the one you have to deal with. Just think about what your dad would do."

Kerry thought. Lucky Jack wasn't especially vindictive, but no one ever got the better of him until big Moe. *I have to find Jim's weakness.*

Teddy encouraged her. "You're tougher than those boys. You're from the BC, remember?"

Kerry nodded grimly. She resolved to look for an opportunity. *Jack would have said the same thing as Teddy, and I won't let him down.*

❖

It was the first Saturday after the beginning of Beth's stay. They were having dinner and Addison said, "Kerry usually has her bath on Saturday night. Laura and I retire to the parlor and stay out of her way. Would you like to bathe tonight as well?"

Beth glanced at Kerry and saw that she was blushing. It unsettled her but she managed to reply, "Yes. I would. That is, if you don't mind, Kerry?"

"No. Not at all. That would be fine with me."

"Very good. That's settled." He went back to his enthusiastic consumption of the roast chicken Kerry had cooked for dinner, seemingly unaware of the tension at the table. After dinner, Kerry and Beth cleared away the dishes and went upstairs.

Kerry said, "I'll go down and heat the water for you."

Beth replied, "You don't have to do that. Just show me what to do and I can get started." As always around Kerry, she was feeling unaccountably uncomfortable but also excited at the prospect of this new task they would undertake together.

"I want to," Kerry said firmly, leaving Beth in their bedroom to prepare.

Kerry wrestled the biggest pot they owned onto the stove to boil and dragged the tin bathtub in from the backyard shed, setting it up in the Grants' kitchen. She scrubbed it out thoroughly while the water was boiling. She thought, as she went about her task, of how to ask Beth if she wanted any help. She argued with herself that it was too forward, but on the other hand, it seemed perfectly natural to offer to wash someone else's back. After she located the soap and towels and a suitable cloth for washing, she dragged two dining-room chairs into the kitchen to set things on and finally poured the boiling water into the tub and added enough cold water to produce a good temperature. She called upstairs to Beth that all was ready.

Beth came into the kitchen, tested the water, and pronounced it perfect. They looked at each other for a long awkward moment.

"I'll be right outside, if you need anything." The moment passed and Kerry left to sit in the parlor with Addison and Laura. Pretending to read, she tried to steady her hands and keep the images of Beth, naked and warm in the soapy water, out of her mind.

Beth removed her dressing gown and lowered herself into the tub carefully. *She is so dear and attentive to me. It makes me feel a little guilty.* It was Beth's nature to think she was the one who must do the caring; it was her work but it was beyond that. It was a novel but compelling feeling to be cared for.

She closed her eyes and soaked happily for a few moments. The tub was slightly warped and off balance. When Beth shifted, the tub tilted a little to one side. A large brown wood spider crawled up the side of the tub to the edge, and Beth opened her eyes, saw it, and emitted a deafening scream.

Kerry raced into the room and looked where Beth was pointing. "Just a moment, Beth. Don't be frightened. I'll get it." She seized a jar from the cabinet and, with its lid, swept the spider into it and then took it the backyard and dumped it. She returned to the kitchen.

Beth sat in the tub shivering, her arms pulled tight around her knees. Kerry knelt down beside her and asked, "Are you all right? I'm so sorry I didn't notice the thing when I brought in the bathtub."

"It has given me such a fright. Would you stay?"

"Of course." She kept her eyes focused on Beth's face and cleared her throat. "I could wash your back."

"Yes, please, that would be lovely."

Kerry moved behind Beth, trying desperately to keep her eyes above the waterline, where Beth's soft skin disappeared below the soapy suds. She thought with some amusement that Beth could cope with people in the depths of disease or suffering from terrible injuries and attend to their bodily needs without demure, but a simple spider threw her into terror. Her reaction was both odd and endearingly human. She was able at last to admire Beth's beauty. They had gone back several times to the Sutro Baths and had developed a way of avoiding to have to look at each other. But now, behind her, Kerry would indulge in the beautiful sight.

Kerry took more than a normal amount of time with soaping, washing, and rinsing. Beth had pinned up her hair, and strands of it escaped in the dampness curled against her moist skin. Her neck and back were warm and wet and slightly flushed. Kerry swallowed and tried some conversation to distract herself.

"I often saw those sorts of spider when I was growing up. They're not harmful, just ugly."

"Oh, and where was that then?"

Kerry's hand stilled. "Just around the neighborhood."

Beth turned and looked at her then. "You know, you never have said where you come from."

"San Francisco. We lived downtown." She was then entirely

discomfited both from trying to avoid Beth's question and by the sight suddenly, when she looked down, of Beth's shapely, rosy, heat-flushed breasts. Kerry hastily turned her head and Beth noticed.

"Are you embarrassed about something?" Beth asked, with a bit of a laugh in her voice.

Kerry cleared her throat. "No. Please lean forward so I can wash your lower back."

Beth complied and Kerry washed her quickly.

"Do you need anything else?" Kerry knew her tone was sharper than it should be, but her self-control was slipping quickly, the desire to touch Beth's soft breasts and pink nipples becoming overwhelming. With an effort she brought her feelings under control before she could make a mistake.

"No, I don't think so. Thank you."

"I'll be in the parlor then."

Kerry went back to the parlor to take up her book again, and both Addison and Laura looked at her questioningly.

"Is all well?" Addison asked.

"Oh, yes. I had to get rid of a spider that had taken up residence under the bathtub." Addison laughed and Laura clucked with alarm. Kerry tried to read her book but was unable to concentrate. The sight of Beth in the tub—naked, wet, so surpassingly lovely and alluring—was engraved on her memory.

Beth appeared at the doorway of the parlor. "Kerry, do you want me to heat the water for your bath?" she asked.

"Oh, no. I can do that. I don't mind. You should go to bed while you're still warm."

"But I'd be happy to. Please. Let me."

Addison and Laura turned and looked at Kerry. She suddenly felt churlish and ungrateful.

"All right."

Beth smiled brilliantly and went back to the kitchen. Kerry hastily left to prepare.

Beth was monitoring the pot of boiling water and had already dumped the tub off the back porch.

"You should've waited for me to do that." Kerry cocked her head at the empty bathtub.

"I can manage just fine. Remember, I have to handle sick people all the time. Dead weight."

"Still," Kerry said stubbornly.

"I'm happy to do for you what you've done for me."

"It's not necessary." Kerry, to her chagrin, was beginning to turn red. Beth was smiling at her in a tender, amused way.

"No. It's not, but it's what I wish," Beth said seriously. "I'd be happy to wash your back."

Kerry looked at her intently, searching for some hidden emotion, some of the desire she felt when she washed Beth's back. She could detect nothing.

"Very well."

Beth nodded crisply and they waited while the water boiled and finished preparing the bath together.

Kerry realized that she was going to have to take off her robe and get into the tub with Beth waiting beside her. She sternly told herself that she had no reason to be embarrassed.

She got into the tub and experienced the soothing, relaxing sensation of sinking into warm, clean water.

Beth sat on one of the kitchen chairs and regarded her companionably, questioning her about her work in the Palace Hotel kitchen. With Beth seemingly completely at ease, Kerry managed to relax as well, glad the sides of the high tub hid her hardened nipples.

It could be perfect, Kerry thought, her eyes closed as Beth slowly washed her back in small, tight circles. We're living together, sharing a bed. I'm able to cook for her every night. But it's not our house and we're not together as lovers. But she could think of no way to change the circumstances in which she found herself. Beth's feelings were a mystery. Beyond her friendliness and companionable affection, Kerry could discern nothing, and a sense of futility settled deep inside her.

❖

Beth and Addison came home from their labors at the Presidio late in the morning after an overnight shift, exhausted and barely able to eat. Laura fussed over Addison and Kerry attended to Beth.

Kerry was grateful Beth was able to get some rest and was only required to stay at work overnight every few days. On those nights, Kerry was able to sleep, unlike the nights when Beth lay at her side, utterly exhausted.

"That wouldn't be so bad, having so many patients, I mean," Beth said, "if the conditions were better." Major Owen had engaged an experienced nurse superintendent from the French Hospital, Marjorie

Reynolds, to direct the new six-member nursing force. She was, as most of her ilk, a formidable woman. She had been a nurse since the age of eighteen and was approaching twenty-eight. She informed Major Owen in no uncertain terms that the nurses were hers to direct in terms of their assignments and scheduling, and she made full use of every minute of the nurses' time. Beth, as energetic as she was, found it hard to keep up with Marjorie.

❖

Beth was attempting to make some patients who were ill with dysentery comfortable enough to be moved on litters. She was scrambling to keep up, as the corpsmen were keen to finish the backbreaking task of moving the patients to the new hospital building. She had been settling one patient when Nurse Moore called her over to help calm a delirious soldier so he could be strapped in. In her brief absence, two of the corpsmen had picked up her patient, who had just defecated again and was cursing and raving.

"Wait!"

"Eh. Miss. We must get on with the transport or Major Owen will have our hides."

"I have to clean this man up and calm him down. You cannot move him like this," she insisted.

The more senior of the two stared at her, a twitch in his jaw suggesting his irritation.

"Leave us do our jobs, Miss. It's not your place to question the major."

"*My* job, you stupid man, is to look after these patients. Yours is to move them from this spot to their new hospital. *I* say when it's time to move. Major Owen isn't here. And you will address me as Nurse instead of Miss."

The two soldiers gaped at her.

"Now return this patient to his tent."

Nurse Reynolds appeared just as Beth had made her last firm statement, and the two litter bearers turned away with their charge to put him back in his odorous tent.

"Nurse Hammond? Is all well?" Nurse Reynolds inquired.

"Yes, Nurse Reynolds, but I must go see to this man," Beth said politely but firmly.

"Very well, Nurse, report to me when you finish."

"You wanted to see me?" Beth stood in the doorway of Nurse Reynolds's small office after cleaning up the patient and allowing the soldiers to move him.

"Yes, Nurse, I wanted to hear from you the status of the patients' move to the barracks."

"We've got a few more truly ill men to move but essentially we're finished."

"Nurse Hammond, I'm quite impressed with your handling of the corpsmen."

"Thank you, Nurse." There was a pause. Beth asked, "Is there something else?"

"Yes. The major mentioned that if the medical unit is sent overseas, he expects me to pick my nurses. You're first on my list. In spite of your relative inexperience, I've found you entirely reliable. Your instincts and judgment are first-rate."

"Is it possible we'll go to the war theater, ma'am?"

"Possible. Nothing definite. Please think about it. We shall speak when and if there are more concrete plans."

"Yes, ma'am. I will. Thank you."

❖

Kerry awoke suddenly. Beth was tossing restlessly and moaning. She flung herself on her back. Kerry pulled herself up on one elbow and looked down at her face. She was muttering and suddenly screamed. Kerry pulled Beth into her arms and rocked her. She woke up and looked wildly into Kerry's face.

"You were dreaming. I think you were having a nightmare."

Beth slipped out of Kerry's arms and sat with her arms wrapped around her bent legs.

"Are you all right?" Kerry touched her shoulder gently.

"Yes, thanks. I'll be fine. Please go back to sleep."

Kerry lay down but continued to look at Beth with a worried expression.

"Truly, I'm well. It's over."

Beth closed her eyes and was softly snoring again. Kerry lightly rubbed her back and felt her muscles relax. Content that she would wake if Beth had another dream, she fell asleep with her hand pressed against Beth's back.

## Chapter Sixteen

It was a happy occasion in the Grant household when, in mid-September, both Addison and Beth were home for supper, and at an early hour. Kerry had made a crown roast of pork with a remoulade sauce she had lately learned to prepare at the restaurant, as well as new potatoes and apple pie for dessert. Even Laura was in a cheerful mood. They sat down to eat, and over their meal Addison announced that both he and Beth were to be sent out to the Philippines in October on the hospital ship, the *Golden Gate*, where they would remain for at least three months. Kerry and Laura sat in silence as Beth and Addison discussed the plans for their trip.

Kerry was grateful the Grants went to their bedroom soon after supper was over. Beth came to keep her company as she tidied up the kitchen.

"Is this what you want?" Kerry asked tentatively.

Beth looked into the distance and waited for a long time before answering. "Of course it is. It's a great honor to be asked, I can tell you. The army now admits it needs us. They're only sending the best civilians overseas. Nurse Reynolds had the pick of whom to take, and she chose me over more experienced nurses. She had to convince Major Owen that I was suitable. It will be much more difficult there." She went on at length about the challenges ahead. Kerry listened without comment and cleaned dishes.

Beth at last stopped talking and cleared her throat. "Are you happy for me?"

"I want to be. I want you to have what you want. I'm proud that Nurse Reynolds believes in you."

"There's something else, though."

"No, there's not."

"You're unhappy," Beth stated flatly. "You don't wish me to go."'
"It's not that simple."

"Explain it to me, then. Tell me what you're feeling. It's a worry to me when I can tell you're unhappy but you won't explain to me, just as you won't speak of your childhood."

*I'm in love with you and you don't know it and I can't tell you. I don't know how to tell you. I would like to show you but...* "I worry for your safety and I'll miss you very much, that's all."

"Is that all? Kerry, look at me, please."

Beth came up behind Kerry, who stood at the sink. Kerry slowly turned around and looked into her eyes. Beth's expression was concerned and tender, but still Kerry couldn't say what she wished to say: *I'm in love with you.*

Beth touched her cheek, and Kerry gazed at her longingly and covered Beth's hand with her own hand.

## CHAPTER SEVENTEEN

The *Golden Gate*'s voyage to Manila took three weeks. The medical staff's time was filled down to the second by Major Owen. He also took charge of their religious devotions in a fashion he wasn't able to when they were back at the Presidio. They all lived together on board, they had morning and evening prayers, and no one was granted leave to not attend, not even the several staff members who were seasick the first week. The prayer services were thus enlivened by doctors and nurses stumbling out of the salon to vomit over the guardrails of the ship, much to the amusement of the ship's seasoned navy crew.

To her relief, Beth wasn't affected, though she found the motion and sounds of the ship disturbed her sleep and also wished more than once for Kerry's soothing presence next to her in bed. She was indifferent to the religious exercise; her experience with Svenhard ensured that. It was just another duty she had to perform. She was content to attend meetings and lectures and spend a great deal of time stowing and organizing their vast supplies.

The *Golden Gate* was originally a passenger ship. It had been donated to the navy and refitted as a floating hospital in record time. The walls between the staterooms were knocked down and made into wards. Fore and aft were canopied decks for the convalescent soldiers to take fresh air, and the iron bedsteads were bolted to the deck to keep them in place. Each deck had a kitchen and two operating rooms and four wards. Three of the wards were for enlisted men and one was for officers. She had a full navy crew plus the medical staff and a steward and six hospital corpsmen. To Beth and the other staff fresh from the Presidio's makeshift hospital, it was both luxurious and efficient.

Due to the custom of doctors and nurses being separate most of the time, Beth found herself distanced from Addison, and she missed his gentle company more than she thought she would. He would give her discreet smiles whenever they were together with other staff, almost as though they were secret lovers. Beth was grateful for his silent notice and smiled to herself at the absurdity of the idea of their being lovers. She knew that would be the assumption of her fellow nurses, who noticed his quiet attention to her, and that also made her smile.

During her restless nights, her thoughts turned to Kerry more times than not. She recalled their jaunts to the park and to the Sutro Baths. Kerry's burning dark eyes stared into hers when she closed her eyes, and her low, slightly hoarse voice echoed in her ears. Between sleep and awakening, she floated on the waters of the Sutro Baths supported by Kerry's confident hands and strong arms. The memories were a pleasant and comforting refuge with an unexpected edge of bittersweet longing she couldn't quite understand. Her roommate was quiet and unobtrusive, so Beth was left largely with her own thoughts, which suited her fine She was once again in the midst of gossipy nurses; it reminded her very much of being back in nurses' training. They were told not to fraternize with the navy crew and could not, by custom, spend time with the doctors. She composed a letter to Kerry she hoped she could mail from Manila.

*Dearest Kerry,*

*We are still on our voyage to the East. Our arrival is expected in a few days. I was not seasick, unlike many others, for which I am grateful. We have had much organizing and unpacking to do. Chief Reynolds, predictably, wants it all done just so. We are cleaning everything yet again, although it was newly painted and clean when we boarded. No germ would dare take hold under Reynolds's nose, I dare say. The others are a good lot, mostly, but they chatter as all nurses do when they have leisure time, as if there is nothing else to discuss than the vagaries of their compatriots. I keep to myself.*

*I miss you and hope you are keeping well and enjoying your work at the Palace and the cooks are treating you well.*

*My fondest and most sincere regards,*
*Beth*

Beth reread the letter. She wanted to say so much more, but she couldn't find the words. She knew it sounded a bit overformal. She missed Kerry more than she would have predicted and knew she was looking forward to beginning the work for which they had been sent to perform, if only to take her mind off Kerry. They were to care for the casualties of war, and though Beth was only nominally patriotic and had no opinion on the rightness of the cause, she knew there would be people who were hurt or sick, and she wanted to care for them. All else was irrelevant.

Once the *Golden Gate* reached Manila it would be all hands on deck when the casualties started to arrive. Beth had faith in Nurse Reynolds who, during the months on base at the Presidio, had been an excellent chief who showed no favoritism, although Beth knew Reynolds trusted her. Trust she would work hard to merit.

Within a day of docking in Manila, they were overrun with patients. None of the soldiers had apparently received any but the most cursory care before the arrival of the *Golden Gate*. They were neglected, dirty, exhausted, and in some cases, quite ill—more than they needed to be. It was clear their officers had considered their illness a form of laziness.

Nurse Reynolds stood at the gangplank and performed triage as the corpsmen dragged up all the casualties. Beth was assigned, at her request, to the typhoid wards. They saw with grim satisfaction that disease took the greatest toll on the soldiers, not the enemy guns. Beth was again obliged to work two days straight without sleep before being relieved.

She staggered into the mess on the morning of the third day, convinced something to eat would somehow negate the effects of sleep deprivation.

A gray-haired cook fixed his sharp eye on her. "I'll give you some breakfast, Miss, but I think it's something else you need. How about a spot of grog?"

Beth was too exhausted to correct him and also didn't understand that he was referring to whiskey.

He gave her a glass. "Miss, this will help relax you. You're too tired to sleep, I reckon."

Beth absentmindedly took a huge gulp, which burned and made her cough. The old salt laughed and pounded her on the back. He brought her biscuits and gravy, which she managed to consume a little of before going back to her room.

The whiskey did relax her, but she fell into bed and tossed and turned in a state of semi-consciousness. Luckily, her stateroom mate was still on duty, else she might have been treated to hearing Beth mumble, "Kerry. Why did you kiss me? It's a strange thing to do but I do so wish you would again. You look at me with such longing." Beth played the kiss over and over. She didn't know what it meant and where it might lead, but her psyche had latched on to it.

❖

Chef Henri announced to his kitchen staff that the Palace Hotel was given the honor of hosting President McKinley for his visit to San Francisco. Further, he said, they would be preparing a huge banquet in honor of the occasion where the Mayor of San Francisco, the Commandant of the Presidio, General Merritt, and many other personages would dine with the President. Chef would plan the meal and all cooks' labors would be needed. He added that his sous-chef, Jim, would be assigned to make the demi-glace for the *boeuf bourguignon*, a task that Chef generally reserved for himself because it had to be absolutely perfect.

"This time, it will be up to *Monsieur* Jeem, because in him I have the utmost confidence, and I will be too busy with the rest of the meal."

Jim looked around at the other cooks with a superior smirk.

"I will, furthermore, entertain the idea of allowing one of you to prepare a special dish for *le Président*, but you will compete for the honor." The five line cooks looked around uneasily at one another. Only Kerry kept her eyes fixed on Chef Henri.

"Yes, Chef," they chorused.

After Chef left the kitchen, Jim leaned back against a table, crossed his arms, and said in a bored tone, "Which one of you no-accounts thinks he," and he aimed a spiteful glance at Kerry, "or she, or whatever you are, can impress Chef?"

No one said a word. They weren't only bored with Jim's single-minded harassment of Kerry, they were tired of his tyrannical ways with all of them.

"Hah. I thought not." He left the kitchen on some mysterious errand as usual. Kerry and Davey went out back to the garbage pit and, standing upwind of it, smoked a cigarette and conversed in whispers, sharing thoughts on what they might prepare.

"Do you want to get back at him?" Davey asked, clearly referring to the egg-white-in-the-fryer incident.

She looked at him suspiciously and nodded. Teddy's words about Lucky Jack resounded in her head. *Don't get mad, get even.* Davey had been the first one to stop the cruel teasing and had been friendly; the other cooks had followed suit, and they had become united in their common hatred of Jim. Together and separately they had played a variety of tricks on him. Since no one ratted on anyone, he was unable to exact punishment but had become meaner than ever. They had gelatined his tool drawer, frozen his jacket in the icebox, and pinned Kick Me to his back. Their crowning glory up to that point had been stuffing salmon heads into his pockets. His white jacket had stunk for a week and he raged around the kitchen throwing pots, but no one admitted to anything.

"He must not fail with the demi-glace," Davey said solemnly. "More than that, it must be perfect or Chef cannot use it. It takes forever to make."

Demi-glace took almost two days. The chef first had to prepare a brown sauce. That of itself was an arduous process of roasting veal and beef bones and reducing the sauce. Then the brown stock went into a sauce *espagnole*, which was mixed with more stock and simmered, seasoned, and strained. Like any French chef, Chef Henri was particular about all his recipes, especially his sauces, but the demi-glace was in a class all its own because of the complexity. It was a great honor for Jim to be asked to prepare it.

"If something should go wrong...?" Kerry asked, her eyebrows raised.

"I believe Chef would fire him if not kill him."

"What will you make for Chef?"

"Coq au vin," Davey said promptly. "You?"

"Salmon soufflé."

Davey rolled his eyes. "You're a caution, you are. I'll help you if you'll help me."

"Yes I will, but you have to help me with something else."

Davey looked at her and grinned. "We're going to take care of Jim once and for all.

"Ah." Davey put on an atrocious French accent, *"Le demi-glace, c'est fini?"*

*"Oui."*

"Chef will be most displeased."

*"Mais oui."*

"And Chef Jim? Is he too fini?"

"Fini." Kerry drew her hand across her throat.

❖

Two days before the great banquet, Chef ordered all cooks to report at six in the morning. He raced around the kitchen or, more accurately, he barreled, since he was a significantly large man who sampled too many of his pastry chef's desserts. His first order of business was the cooks' contest offerings. He went down the line and carefully tasted each dish. When he finished, he announced with a flourish, "The salmon soufflé—*magnifique*. It is the winner. You will make it for the banquet. Also, coq au vin, very good. *Très bien.*"

Davey and Kerry were ecstatic. Jim glared at them, and they hid their smiles and went back to work. They hoped that Chef would test the demi-glace soon. They were rewarded later in the afternoon when they heard Chef shout at the top of his lungs, "JEEEEEEEM!"

Jim came running and pulled up anxiously beside the stove where his sauce was cooking.

Chef didn't say a word, but he held out a spoon to him. Jim tasted the sauce and his face screwed up as he struggled not to spit it right back out in Chef's face.

"I…" He stuttered and looked entirely discomfited. It was a sight to behold.

"You! You *espèce de merde!*" Chef shouted. "This is ruined. You have destroyed me. Go! Out of my sight."

"But—"

"Now!" Chef bellowed.

On the other side of the kitchen, Davey and Kerry kept their mouths shut and their faces straight.

Kerry had obtained a jar of the hottest Mexican chili peppers available and dumped them into the demi-glace pot the night before. By morning, all had been well simmered and rendered the precious demi-glace an inedible, nausea-inducing mess.

Chef Henri called his cooks together. "It is fortunate I am able to cope with this disaster. I will instruct the hotel to reprint the menu today. We will have the salmon soufflé and, *Davide*, you will make four coq au vin. Sammy will grill the steak *poivre*. I will personally cook the sole meunière. Le Président will have a feast such as he would never get in Delmonico's—a great feast without *le boeuf. Oui.* It will be unprecedented. Now, *vite, nous allons!* We have much to do and little time."

Kerry and Davey cheerfully went back to cooking. Kerry helped Davey with his coq au vin and prepared some of the sauces Chef designed, including the meunière. It was another traditional sauce, like the demi-glace, though not nearly as complex, as it was based on simple brown butter, oil, and lemon. Chef Henri entrusted its preparation to Kerry, who in her short employment as a cook had shown herself reliable and competent. The cooks worked all night and all the next day to accomplish Chef's wishes and did it happily. Jim was no more. Fini.

President McKinley and the other distinguished guests, it was seen, did not miss their roast beef. The newspaper *Call Bulletin* printed the story along with the menu the next day and heaped praise upon the Palace Hotel and its restaurant staff. After the great presidential banquet, the Palace was famous for its fish and chicken dishes. It became a tradition for all the special banquets to serve fish and fowl. Davey was made sou*s*-chef. Chef told Kerry he could not, in good conscience, elevate her to such a position. She was naturally still too inexperienced, he reasoned, and no woman would ever be able to fulfill that responsibility.

## Chapter Eighteen

Kerry wiped a bit of sweat from her face and took another look at the cassoulet she was preparing. *What is Beth doing now? Giving an injection, writing a letter for some lonely soldier, or arguing with one of the military officers?*

Kerry had stood with her at the *Golden Gate* dock at the Ferry Building, and Beth had given her an ambiguous little hug and whispered, "I shall be home before you know it. I'll write when I can." At the top of the gangplank, she stopped and waved. Her smile was quick and friendly. *She was already thinking ahead to her future patients. Always it was her work.*

Kerry sighed and said under her breath, "It's certain she's not thinking of me." She stirred the vegetables more briskly than necessary and watched the prep boy out of the corner of her eye. The cassoulet was a savory stew of ham, pork, and white beans. It was a deceptively simple dish since it didn't have many ingredients. Chef had instructed Kerry meticulously on its seasoning. Kerry would always prefer to cook fish and other seafood, but she was keen to get ahead and impress Chef so she worked hard on the cassoulet. Cooking was her only source of pleasure now that Beth was gone.

She'd had several letters from Beth. They were short, cheerful, and full of news of her work. They were, Kerry knew, exactly like Beth herself. She had written, *Dearest Kerry* and *I miss you very much.* Those words, while pleasing, were to Kerry's mind indicative of friendship and nothing more. And she so desperately wanted more.

Kerry wrote back to Beth in a similar vein, for the most part, and detailed the daily trivia of the restaurant. On her last letter, the one she had posted the day before, she thought for a very long time about what she wanted to say and what she felt she could or should say.

*My Dear Beth,*

*It has been now two months since we last saw each other, and my sadness at your absence grows no less. It does, in fact, become worse over time. My days are truly without color and joy. As for my nights, I sleep poorly in spite of my fatigue. I worry for your safety and trust you are not being too overworked. You, who are so faithful and diligent, I know would scarcely ever refuse to perform a task set before you. As your letters describe, the tasks can be immense. I long for your safe return and for the time we can once again drive the promenade in Golden Gate Park or visit the Baths for a swim.*

*Kerry*

There was more, so much more she wanted to say but, just like when she was in Beth's presence, Kerry was unable to speak from her heart. She wasn't ready to commit the truth to paper and have to wonder how Beth would receive her thoughts when she was still so far away. *As though she isn't essentially far away when she's here. Now geography matches reality.* Kerry was more despondent than ever. She shook her head as though that would clear her unhappy musings and turned her attention back to the cooking tasks at hand. It was nearly time for luncheon service to start, and she would need to be alert.

About two thirty p.m., the orders were slowing down and Kerry was able once again to stop for a breath. She leaned against the prep table and swallowed some water. Behind her she heard her name called. It was Lambert, one of the older waiters, and he'd always made it clear to her how terrible it was that she, a mere woman, should be cooking in the august kitchen of the Palace Hotel. "Miss O'Shea. A customer wishes to speak to the chef."

"I'm not the chef, Lambert," Kerrie said. She looked around for Chef Henri or for Davey but didn't see them. She sighed. She supposed she would have to go. Lambert added, "Table twelve, Ladies Grill."

As Kerry approached the table, she saw that the single occupant was a very young woman with curly blond hair who, upon seeing Kerry approach, smiled in a slightly ingratiating but vacuous fashion. Kerry stopped by the table, but before she could say anything, the young lady spoke.

"I want to compliment you in person, Chef, on the excellent cassoulet."

Kerry was taken aback to be addressed as Chef, but she decided to have some fun on her own. The young lady had just mangled the pronunciation of cassoulet. Kerry controlled her smile and said in a low voice, *"Merci, mademoiselle."*

"Oh, goodness! You're French."

Kerry nearly rolled her eyes. The Palace Hotel had the most famous French restaurant in the United States after Delmonico's. This was a well-known fact. It shouldn't be a surprise the chef would be French too.

*"Oui, mademoiselle."* Kerry's knowledge of French outside of French cooking terms was limited and would be quickly exhausted. She said no more.

"What is your name?"

"Ker-rie." Kerry gave her good Irish name a French twist and smiled brilliantly.

"I see. Well, I shan't keep you. Thank you again for the delicious cassoulet."

Kerry bowed graciously and went back to the kitchen in a better mood. It wasn't much, but it was at least gratifying to have someone compliment her cooking. It also gave her a lift because it was clear the young lady didn't notice she was a woman. She was always thrilled to be mistaken for a young man.

## Chapter Nineteen

Omelet for Room 319, and she wishes Chef Ker-rie to bring it to her in person." Davey hung up the house phone after he had shouted his news loud enough for the entire kitchen to hear. "Ooo-la-la!" he added mischievously.

Kerry glared at Davey, even though she knew he was only teasing her in the usual way. Since Jim's departure, Kerry was treated exactly like all the other cooks. She had achieved a degree of acceptance from her peers, and she prided herself on taking as good as she could give.

Kerry frowned but said nothing. She recalled the curly haired, slightly vacuous young lady who had complimented her the day before. She cooked the omelet and prepared the service cart to the catcalls of the other cooks.

Kerry walked across the vast Garden Court, dodging between the carriages, which gathered to drop off their passengers. She could have collared a waiter to take care of delivery but figured she should make the customer happy, and since the customer had requested delivery by Kerry, she'd do what needed to be done. On her way upstairs, she admired the elevator. It was so large and so ornate, it was said that one could serve tea for four in it. She believed it.

She knocked briskly on the door and shouted, "Room service" and, when she heard a soft "Come in," entered the room and wheeled the cart toward the table.

"Mademoiselle, your omelet." She turned and saw the girl sitting in bed with an expectant expression.

"Chef. I do appreciate you bringing my breakfast in person. Could you perhaps stay and talk to me while I eat it?"

Kerry was astonished, mostly at the forwardness of the question but also at the small thought growing in her mind. It couldn't be.

"I can't. I'm needed in the kitchen just now," she said.

"You aren't French!" the girl exclaimed indignantly. "I should hardly think that chefs in the Palace Hotel believe it will foster good relations with the customers if they misrepresent themselves."

Kerry took a breath to quell her anger and ensure that what she said came out without an edge attached to it. "Ah, no. Please accept my apology for my small subterfuge. I'm not French, it's true. I am, however, a French chef." Kerry expected the difference between "cook" and "chef" wasn't an entirely necessary distinction to make for this girl, who didn't seem overly endowed with intelligence, although she was very pretty.

"I see, that much at least is true." She lowered her eyelashes and peered out from underneath them coquettishly. "I can expect then that you have prepared a superior omelet?"

"I can only pray that my efforts meet mademoiselle's approval." Kerry was enjoying herself now. An attractive young woman was flirting with her. "However, mademoiselle hasn't told me her name."

"It's Letty Stevenson." She put out a small hand and Kerry nearly kissed it but decided she need not overuse the French pose, so she shook it instead, but they both left their hands clasped for just a little longer than usual. "Well, then, in spite of the fact that you are *not* French and have tried to fool me into thinking you are, I'm disposed to forgive you." She tilted her head. "If you aren't too busy, would you stay and visit with me while I eat it?"

The question astonished Kerry, and she was more than ready to agree, but she couldn't abandon her post in the kitchen as the luncheon service was due to start in a few minutes.

"No, I regret to say I must return immediately to the kitchen." Part of her wondered why this girl would be so foolish as to not understand that, as a cook, she had her responsibilities. Kerry concluded that regular employment wasn't something Letty Stevenson had to bother herself about.

"Well, then, could you return later? Perhaps after lunch?" Letty raised her eyebrows suggestively.

Kerry couldn't quite believe what she was hearing nor what she sensed was behind Letty's question.

*She can't be seeming to want what she seems to want. This can't be what I think it is. She may not be a particularly virtuous girl but she isn't a...* Kerry wasn't sure what was the word for it, for herself, for what she fervently hoped Beth to be. A woman like many of the girls she'd grown up with in the dives and deadfalls of the Barbary Coast. A woman who preferred women. This girl surely couldn't be. *She has no idea what she's playing at. She wants attention and distraction, no more. Of course—she believes I'm a man.*

"I'm free at three o'clock," Kerry said, to her great surprise.

"You have no other engagements then?" Letty asked, and her tone was hopeful.

"No. I don't." Kerry knew she would only return home and perhaps take a carriage ride to Golden Gate Park and think back on the months with Beth when they went there together every Sunday and talked.

"It's settled, then," Letty said with finality.

Kerry nodded and left. She was occupied with luncheon service for the next several hours. Still, she mused, Is this girl inviting my attention because she believes me to be male? Is that what she's actually doing, or is she just a little lonely and wants conversation? That seems more likely. I'm not certain what I would do. I'm pining for Beth, who may never return my affections. If she does, then I shouldn't be considering a dalliance with another woman. That wouldn't do. But what if she doesn't, which seems more likely…

Kerry shook herself and said aloud, startling the cook next to her, "No. I'm dreaming, surely."

In the elevator on the way back to Letty's room, Kerry had entirely convinced herself Letty was just lonely and self-absorbed. When she walked in, Letty was in exactly the same state as she had left her hours before—sitting in bed, primly attired. This time, though, her eyes were shining and her complexion had taken on a slight glow. She watched as Kerry crossed the room.

"You're still dressed for the kitchen." Kerry heard the teasing in her voice.

"I'm sorry. I wasn't able to change. I didn't bring my street clothes today," Kerry said, humbly. She didn't add that it was easier to go about the city disguised as a young man while wearing her uniform.

Kerry sat down at the small table in the middle of the room, suddenly tongue-tied. Letty smiled at her patiently, and she finally summoned up a question to fill the yawning silence.

"Are you here for a holiday?"

"I—" she paused, curiously at a loss for words. But then she continued with more confidence. "Yes. I'm up from Sacramento for the week."

Kerry's ears picked up a false note somewhere in Letty's conventional sentence.

"It's rather odd, isn't it, to come to San Francisco by yourself? Not very enjoyable, I would imagine."

"My Aunt Grace lives here in the city," Letty said finally.

"But you're not staying with her?"

"You are interrogating me, Mr. Kerrie."

"Miss Letty," Kerry said, in a low firm tone. "What is it you want from me? You have invited me to come to your room. You're not dressed to go out. Are you ill? Shall I summon a doctor?"

"Nooo. No, indeed."

"Then what may I do for you?" Kerry asked, sitting next to Letty on the bed.

Letty tentatively ran her hand along Kerry's arm from her elbow to her wrist. Kerry felt the jolt of arousal and surprise at the same time. She had expected to be slapped, or at least told definitely to move back to her seat across the room. She froze. Letty was looking at her with a clear expression of desire in her hazel eyes. *Hazel eyes. Beth's eyes are hazel.* She dragged Letty into a close embrace and kissed her neck. Letty's arms wrapped around her shoulders. Kerry thought, Any moment, she is going to know whom she embraces. Then she will surely reject me.

Letty sagged in surrender in Kerry's arms and under Kerry's lips. She clasped her more tightly, her fingers dug into the smooth muscles next to Kerry's spine. Kerry moved away quickly, pulled the bed covers down, and pressed down on Letty's yielding body. She dared to push Letty's nightgown up a short way to stroke her bare leg.

She turned rigid where she had been yielding. Kerry propped herself up on her hands and looked into Letty's eyes searchingly. Then she rolled on her side but didn't break eye contact.

"You are…" Letty asked.

Kerry could see the shock of disbelief in her expression. "Yes, I am."

"Yet another subterfuge?" Letty asked, her fingers fluttering lightly over Kerry's sleeve.

"I again apologize. But do you wish me to leave?"

Letty slowly shook her head. Kerry kissed her very softly. Letty sighed and moaned and returned the kiss fervently.

It greatly aroused Kerry and she kissed Letty even more fervently. Suddenly, though, the thought of Beth leaped into her mind.

"Oh, Beth, I love you. I can't do this. I want to but I can't."

"Wha-wha did you say?" Letty gasped.

Kerry didn't realize she'd spoken out loud. She sat up and let Letty's limp body fall back on the bed.

"I'm sorry. This isn't what you really want. You *are* very lovely." Kerry tenderly brushed her hand over Letty's hair and then her cheek. "I once again need to apologize. I'm going to leave you now."

Letty partially sat up and propped her back against the pillows. "You are a disappointment all the way around then, aren't you?" She was clearly angry now.

"You would regret it and you would blame me." Kerry was suddenly feeling quite relieved. She had come close to doing something she would have regretted. "I must leave now." She left the room with Letty staring longingly at her as she gently shut the door.

❖

Kerry walked home from the hotel, although it took almost two hours from downtown at Second Street back to her home at the Grants' in the Western Addition. She had made no promises to Beth, nor had Beth made any to her, but it would have been a betrayal to make love to anyone else, even if Beth never knew. It was Beth and Beth alone she wanted, though the thought caused her nothing but despair. *None of this matters, for she doesn't love me and will never love me. So does this mean I'll never know love? Never touch a woman again? If Beth doesn't want me the way I want her, why shouldn't I be with someone else?*

That night, Kerry was restless and wakeful much as when Beth was sleeping with her. Touching Letty had aroused her awareness of her body's needs. She drifted between sleep and consciousness for a very long time. In her thoughts, Beth smiled at her tenderly and opened her arms, then her dress, in gentle invitation. Kerry's fantasy took flight and she helped Beth remove her clothes to allow her free access to her body. Kerry embraced and caressed her with wonder. Beth's eyes were closed but her lips were parted and her breathing quickened.

Kerry awakened, gasping, suddenly at the precise point where she would have begun to lead Beth to the final gratification her hand was seeking. She was shocked and then cruelly disappointed to find herself totally alone, her mind echoing the dreams and her body thrumming with unfulfilled lust.

## CHAPTER TWENTY

After the first frenzied week, life aboard the *Golden Gate* at anchor in Manila Bay was just as boring as the voyage over had been. The army had secured the city months before and they were now occupied elsewhere, mostly chasing the Filipino insurgents who, after throwing off their Spanish overlords, were not prepared to accept the Americans. When they weren't treating the minor mishaps of the army occupation forces, the medical staff occupied themselves exploring the city. Manila was a fascinating combination of Spanish and Oriental influences.

When the members of the medical staff were still home in the Presidio they were, in spite of the conditions, spared the horrendous epidemics that their counterparts back East had had to deal with, but they treated a few cases of pneumonia, measles, and typhoid. In the tropics, however, diseases multiplied. The soldiers were without defense in the alien environment. They ate all sorts of foods and indiscriminately drank dirty water. Thanks to Nurse Reynolds, Beth was able to observe a couple of surgeries: one for appendicitis and one for a gunshot. The *Golden Gate* was also equipped with the latest medical marvel—the X-ray machine. Nurses were not permitted to operate it, but they could, with the doctor, examine its results: the miraculously clear vista of the mysterious interior of the human body.

Beth was interested in the surgical aspects of nursing, but her real love was disease and its treatment. She followed Addison about the wards filled with soldiers suffering from typhoid, malaria, and yellow fever. She learned to use even more precautions. She had to take the quinine the soldiers were given to prevent becoming sickened by malaria. She washed her hands obsessively and harangued the hospital corpsmen to do the same. After observing a couple of their more careless counterparts grow ill because they ignored her, they were more obedient.

About three weeks after their arrival, Nurse Reynolds called the nurses together. "There has been an outbreak of typhoid at the fort at Cavite. The commander there will be evacuating all the sick troops, hundreds of them, and they will all be coming here."

Nurse Reynolds silenced the murmurs of dismay and issued orders to various people. Addison would be attending as the doctor in charge, which made the situation a little less frightening. Beth spared a quick thought for Kerry, wishing she could talk to her about this latest development. Kerry would have known exactly what to say, how to calm her.

❖

Beth was roused by the nurse she was to replace. It was dark already, and when she hurried from her stateroom along the outer deck up to the ward, the lights of the city were sparkling on Manila Bay. She hardly noticed; she was attempting to force her weary mind into some action.

*If I can at least think, I can work.* Her mouth was cottony; she hadn't taken time to clean her teeth. She'd slept in her clothes to save time. She stopped at the galley, however, and got a cup of the strong navy coffee from the cook, who grinned at her. She refused his offer of whiskey.

She went from bed to bed checking her patients. She read the notes listing their last measured temperatures and urine output. She set to work to bathe the most feverish and to give some light food to those who would take it. A very sleepy corpsman made a mixture of egg whites and whiskey in the little hospital kitchen. She finally sat down next the bed of a fair-haired young man who was especially restless. He was mostly out of his senses and gibbering in delirium, but when she touched his forehead, he quieted. She had to leave frequently to take temperatures or administer other baths or ointments, but she always returned to him.

She was dozing when Addison came at dawn to make his rounds. "Nurse?"

She heard a voice and felt a hand on her shoulder. She woke up abruptly. Addison looked at her sharply but not unkindly. She could see his hollow eyes and felt guilty she had dozed off.

"Report?" he asked abruptly. Beth took up the chart and read. They went to each bed on her side.

"Do you need relief?" Addison looked at her closely.

"No, Doctor. I apologize for falling asleep. If you'll allow me to obtain a coffee, I'll be back in just a moment."

"Very well," he said, giving her shoulder a soft squeeze before turning to the other side of the ward, which was under Nurse Trenton's care.

Beth gulped down a cup of coffee and hoped it would have some effect. She was in that stage of sleep deprivation where one is numb to nearly everything. The training helps, she thought. We learn the routines so well we don't have to be really awake to be able to perform them. She didn't remember the last time she'd slept a night through.

After a few days, the situation stabilized and the weary staff was able to rest some. Beth and Addison took a round of her patients. At each bed, they stopped and Beth reported. Along with the usual facts on each man's temperature, urine output, and whether he had managed to eat anything, Beth talked about the patients' responses to medicine and dosages. After they had come to the fourth man, Addison turned and looked at her curiously.

"You've a real feel for the treatment of disease. You absorb far more facts than any nurse, and you think, by God. It's not all rote to you, is it, Nurse Hammond?"

"I don't know, Doctor. It's my duty to be well informed on each man so I can help you."

"And you are, Nurse, but it's more than that. Have you ever thought of becoming a doctor?"

Beth stared at him. Such a thought had never crossed her mind. *Me? A doctor?*

"Do think about it, and if the thought appeals to you, we may discuss it further when this ghastly war is over." Addison and Beth completed their round and he went on to the other part of the ward.

When Beth was relieved, she went back to her quarters and lay down to try to sleep. It was impossible. Her body was exhausted but her mind refused to give up. Addison's suggestion that she go to medical school and become a doctor was almost more than she could absorb. She concluded that she had to think about it and to ask Kerry what she thought.

When she was back on duty the next day, she went around to each bed. They were strong young men and many of them were beginning to recover. Their fevers were lower and they had started to respond to the care. The night shift had obviously done a thorough cleaning. The smell of sickness, of vomit, sweat, and human waste had greatly lessened, and what was left was overlaid with disinfectant. Beth scarcely noticed it.

She reached the fair-haired soldier, who surprisingly opened his eyes and smiled at her.

"It wasn't a dream, then?" he asked in a whisper. "I believed I was dead and an angel was caring for me. But it appears I'm not dead, though you indeed are an angel."

"Soldier, you're not dead in the least, but I'm not an angel. I'm a nurse."

"Then you're the equal to any angel." He managed a slightly raffish grin.

"Please rest. You have typhoid and"—she reached for his chart—"your temperature was 104 two hours ago." She took his temperature again, and he eyed her solemnly like an obedient child.

"Very good." She smiled encouragingly. "It's now only 100. You will recover."

He sighed and said, "Lieutenant Roland Evers, ma'am. Pleased to meet…" Then he fell asleep. Beth shook her head and went on to the next bed.

Several days later, the typhoid patients who had survived were much better.

When Beth reached Lieutenant Evers's bed, his eyes lit up. He shyly asked if she would read to him. She agreed when she had the time. Surprisingly he had some books with him. Beth realized that, unlike many of the army men, the lieutenant was educated.

"I hope to return to my unit," he told her. "I'm not due home until January."

"We shall try and get you well enough," Beth said, amiably. "But if you go back to the front, do try to not get shot. The typhoid's quite enough."

"I shall do my best, Miss Hammond."

"It's Nurse—"

"I know that, but if you don't mind, I'd rather call you Miss." He cleared his throat.

She relented. "If you like." He was rather endearing. He was soft-spoken and very polite. "You are well enough now to read yourself, so I'll not be needed."

"But I so enjoy it! When you read to me, I mean," he said, lowering his eyelashes. He reached for her hand. She took it in what she hoped was a reassuring but non-romantic fashion, and he stared into her eyes.

"Miss Hammond, I can't tell you how much you have meant to me."

Beth's ears grew warm and she had a sinking feeling in her stomach. *They have warned us about this.*

"Lieutenant," she said, sternly. "Please do remember I have a professional obligation."

He dropped her hand rather swiftly. "I apologize," he said, "for overstepping bounds, Miss, but I'm quite certain of my feelings. When I'm released from duty, may I come to call on you before I return to Seattle?"

"Lieutenant, I'm flattered but it's not possible. Entirely impossible. I'm on duty and will be so for I don't know how long. You've been very ill and you mistake gratitude for a tenderer feeling. I assure you, you'll recover from that as you have from the typhoid."

"No, I will not." His eyes flashed. "Do you think I'm not serious? Please don't hide behind your profession. I've no wish to insult you. It is not the imaginings of a fevered mind, I assure you. I have quite fallen—"

"Lieutenant!" Beth said firmly. "Please say no more. You may not call on me. It's been my honor to care for you, but that is as far as my feelings go."

"Very well." He lay back against his pillows, looking wounded to the core. "I'll accept your wishes. But am I not an eligible suitor? I am intelligent, I am kind, I am patriotic!" He grinned, as did Beth.

"You're all of those things, Lieutenant, but I, I'm afraid, am not what you wish me to be."

"You could, perhaps with time, come to feeling for me?" He looked so bereft, Beth almost agreed with him, but held back. It would be no good to get his hopes up, only to dash them. Besides, what would Kerry think if a man came to call on her?

❖

Beth walked out onto the deck and stopped to gaze out over Manila Bay. The sun was shining and the reflections shimmered off the small waves. She thought suddenly of home and of another bay that caught the colors of the sky and reflected them back. It's November now and it may well be raining in San Francisco, she thought. I was very quick to dismiss Lieutenant Evers. Why is that? He certainly is as he says. If we were to see each other again, what harm would that do? It might do a great deal, Beth admitted to herself.

*I don't think I could fall in love with him. What does that say about me? I can try to pretend it's because of professional reasons, but that isn't the whole story. I can look at a handsome, educated, cultured young man and not feel a thing for him. I know it's true. I know that isn't normal. I just don't know why. Why can't I feel for him what I feel for Kerry when I look at her?*

❖

They didn't encounter any other crisis comparable to the typhoid outbreak. They received more casualties, and most of them were ill with various fevers. Few had wounds. Addison continued as before to discuss the infectious cases with Beth as though she were already a medical student. Beth began to offer her observations and opinions with more confidence.

Then out of the blue, in early December, their orders came to return to San Francisco. Another hospital ship had arrived, bringing fresh doctors and nurses, and taking the others home.

On the voyage home the *Golden Gate* crew and staff prepared to celebrate Christmas. They had a lovely dinner, and those on board with any modicum of talent endeavored to entertain the rest so there was some singing and a few poetic recitations. They prevailed upon Beth to play the piano, and she favored them with a few hymns and some of Mr. Stephen Foster's better-known compositions and a march or two by Mr. John Philip Sousa. The festivities were enlivened by the serving of wine. Beth, who was still unused to spirits, went outside into the warm tropical night to clear her head. One of the patients, who was a professional musician, had taken up the piano and was leading the rest in a sing-along.

Beth was once again staring across the water, and Kerry once more slipped into her thoughts. *She will be working. The hotel, no doubt, will host a big Christmas dinner. She would not be home with Laura.* Beth smiled to herself, imagining Kerry hard at work. She knew very well that Laura and Kerry only got along because of Addison. The sound of voices interrupted her reverie. She did not, just then, feel up to any company and so took refuge behind a stanchion and prayed whoever it was would walk on and leave her to her solitude.

"Oh, let's stop here." The voice Beth heard sounded familiar.

"Very well." A different voice, also familiar. Beth peeked out cautiously. It was Nurse Reynolds and Nurse Trenton. They stood at the rail, their backs to Beth, and they clearly had no idea anyone was nearby.

This is most inappropriate, Beth thought. I shouldn't lurk in the shadows undetected and intruding on their privacy. But as she was about to speak up she suddenly stopped, her curiosity getting the better of her.

"Please, Marjorie. Do say yes. Say we shall live together when we return to the city."

"It's not that I don't want to, Florence. Please try to understand."

"I do *not* understand. Your mother isn't ill and she can manage very well on her own. If she needs help, she can hire it, like anyone else!"

"Your mother is dead so you don't know how it would be if she were alive. My mother's health is very delicate."

"But you have the right to your own life, do you not?"

"My mother wants me to find a husband and settle down. That's what sort of life she envisions for me. She wants me to stay home until that occurs."

To Beth, Marjorie sounded resigned and hopeless.

Florence's voice took on a pleading note. From her hiding place, Beth could see she was facing Marjorie, who stared out over the water at the moon's reflection.

"When we first fell in love, you said you couldn't wait for the time we could live together. Then your mother took ill and you said we must delay. Now it's because she still needs your help or she expects you to get married. It's always something else."

Beth was frozen in place, only beginning to understand what she was hearing and seeing. The sadness in Florence's voice touched her deeply.

"But you know that you won't marry. You've said so. You wouldn't do that to me."

"Oh, Florence. I couldn't. I would never." Marjorie took Florence's face between her hands. "My mother wouldn't understand—about us."

They turned at the same time and faced each other. Their faces were in profile, backlit by reflected moonlight so that they looked ghostly.

"I love you. More than I can say. You must be patient. We will be together."

They kissed fervently, passionately, both of them groaning slightly. Beth was aghast, whether from longing or embarrassment she didn't know. She knew at that moment what had been transpiring between Kerry and herself. The pieces of the puzzle fell into place and the picture became complete. *Women can have these feelings for one another. They're real. Is this what Kerry feels for me? Is this why I can't return Lieutenant Evers's attentions? What about my feelings?*

Beth's mind started to work at a furious pace.

Marjorie stopped the kiss and said, "We mustn't. We better go back to the party."

Florence nodded and they left the deck. Beth was rooted to the spot where she stood trying to make sense of what she saw and what she thought.

*Of course Kerry was courting me. That's exactly how it felt. I've been so stupid and blind. How could I not have known? She hasn't said a word, but I know now why she looks at me as she does. That was why she kissed me!* Beth's face got hot. *She can't discern my feelings. I've confused her with my lackluster response. Poor Kerry, how she must be suffering. When I return home, I'll put this to rights. I will talk to her and ask her true feelings.*

Beth made up her mind with her customary decisiveness. She would talk to Kerry and they would be honest with one another. She was still unsure if what she felt for Kerry was love, but it seemed impossible that it could be anything else.

Through the long voyage back to San Francisco, Beth could think of nothing but the moment she and Kerry would at last meet again.

## Chapter Twenty-one

With Addison gone, Kerry and Laura coexisted in an uneasy truce. Kerry attempted as much as was practical to be out of the house, and that usually meant being at the restaurant. Luckily, that was quite possible, even welcomed by Chef, who was happy to exploit the labors of his unusual woman cook. Kerry was more than happy to be cooking, and if she wasn't busy with restaurant service, she was pestering Davey or Chef about learning new dishes.

Sleeping or eating a quick meal were her only reasons for being at home.

Laura's anxiety was evident even though Addison clearly wrote her quite often. Laura didn't share the contents of her letters with her. Kerry wished he would write her separately, but she imagined he was very busy and unable to manage more. She received a few letters from Beth. She read them over and over, folding and unfolding them until they were as soft as cotton. They were ambiguous at best and quite short, but it was all she had.

Kerry felt some regret over her encounter with Letty Stevenson. She was terribly lonely and missed Beth. She wavered between despair one day and hope the next. She was on the brink of trying to forget about her love for Beth as altogether hopeless. But she couldn't quite bring herself to do that, even while Beth was away. She thought of going back down to seek Sally out, but something held her back. There was no answer to any of it, really, except to keep busy at the Palace and try to stay out of Laura's way as much as possible.

*Perhaps when she returns, she'll realize how deeply she missed me. I hope so. That's my only hope. There are times when she's looked at me and I could swear...*

It was a rare evening that Kerry wasn't working and she and Laura were at home together for dinner. Laura had no shame about having Kerry cook for her. She felt it was only right; Kerry was as close to household help as she was likely to come.

She brought in the mail for them to look at during dinner, which eliminated the need for them to speak to one another.

Kerry didn't mind cooking at home. It gave her something to do. As she had grown older, she had become resigned to Laura's treatment of her when Addison wasn't around. She simply had no emotional investment in Laura liking her, and since it had always been that way, she figured it would always be that way. She was respectful of her because she respected Addison; that was the extent of it. She often wondered how they had come to be married, because in every matter but his choice of wife, Addison had always seemed to be sensible and intelligent.

Kerry finally concluded that it was a fluke based on her looks, which were, admittedly, very pretty, except for the perpetual pursing of her lips in distaste for anything outside her view of proper behavior. Kerry deduced she must have either caught Addison in a weak moment or she was very effective at concealing her true personality from him. Still, dealing with Laura wasn't easy when Addison wasn't present as a buffer. She had decided long ago that she wouldn't make it a burden to him if his wife was cross with her. She owed him for the roof over her head and the generosity he had always shown her.

Laura, as usual, didn't thank Kerry for preparing their supper of roast chicken and rutabagas—all expertly seasoned and tender. She handed over a letter to Kerry from Beth.

"She writes you so rarely. It must be a treat to get a letter."

Kerry glanced at her, looking for and finding the undercurrent of malice but deciding to ignore it as she always did. "They keep them quite busy, I expect. The hospital, I mean."

"Still…I would think she would make the time, being such a great friend of yours."

Kerry blinked. She wouldn't normally rise to Laura's bait, but the letters from Beth *had* been few and far between. That, along with her jumbled feelings for Beth and Laura's steady diet of nasty little comments and veiled digs at her for the past few months, caught up with her.

"What business is it of yours, then, how often and from whom I get letters?" she snapped.

"You be careful what you say to me, you little ingrate. You have no call to take that tone."

"I'll take this 'tone,' as you call it, if I want to. In spite of what you think, you've no control over me. Not now that I'm grown and can defend myself."

Laura looked away at the veiled reference to the slapping and beating she had subjected Kerry to when she had first come to live with them. "When Addison returns, I'm going to ask him to show you the door. You and your little friend. We've put up with you quite long enough," Laura said with a toss of her head. "I'm sure Addison will see that it's time."

"I doubt that even you can tell Addison what to think and what to do, Laura. He's his own man," Kerry said, now truly irritated that this fatuous, vindictive woman was presuming to speak for her husband.

"We'll just have to see, won't we?" Laura's eyes glittered and she smiled unpleasantly.

Kerry stood and threw down her napkin, picked up Beth's letter, and went upstairs, leaving Laura at the table. *I'll be damned if I go back down to help clear the dishes. She can damn well do them herself.* She knew, however, how stubborn Laura could be and that she would be forced to clean or else deal with the kitchen vermin after a few days of the food sitting out.

She slammed her door shut, fell on the bed, and opened the letter.

The beginning was the standard questions about Kerry's health and reporting that her own was well, then some details on the latest patients and the nurses' gossip. The last paragraph, however, caused Kerry to sit up, her stomach clenched and her palms moist. She read it twice with rising joy.

> *It seems our work here is nearly done, or as much as we can accomplish at the moment. I am to return to San Francisco in a month's time. It is my understanding that I will be given leave until the army decides if we are to be permanently posted at the Presidio or returned to the Philippines, or to have no employment at all. Keep well, dearest Kerry. I trust the month to pass quickly and we shall see each other very soon, as I promised you when we parted. I have very much missed you and our time together.*
> 
> *Yours as ever,*
> *Beth*

Kerry expected that Beth would return directly to the Grants as soon as she and Addison debarked, but she was quickly disappointed when she received another letter from Beth.

*Dearest Kerry,*
 *Since my return from the Philippines and my release from duty to the army, I fear I must stay close to home for a few days to care for my mother and help my father at the store. My mother has had a recurrence of her neuralgia. I am chagrined that our reunion has been delayed.*
 *As ever,*
 *Beth*

Kerry swallowed her disappointment and waited.
The next letter a week later was much better.

*Dearest Kerry,*
 *I believe I may die of boredom soon or at least slip into unconsciousness. I have passed the time when I needed a great deal of rest and now am confronted with my father's entreaties to help him at the store and my mother's requests to help him so that "he does not have a heart attack." Please plan to come and fetch me on your earliest free afternoon. I am anxious to see you again.*
 *Fondest regards,*
 *Beth*

Kerry prepared carefully and nervously for their outing. She wanted it to be special but also familiar and comforting. She wore a clean white shirt and had carefully washed and trimmed her hair. She took extra time to brush the horses up to their glossy best. She washed the carriage and cleaned the dirt from the inside and washed the blanket. She baked a pie and wrapped a few pieces to take along on their ride.

Now that Addison was back, Laura's attention was thankfully directed toward him and she was again ignoring Kerry. She fussed and fluttered and clucked and hovered over him until Kerry thought Addison might finally say something, but he appeared to soak it up. He was thin and worn-looking and seemed in no hurry to return to the county hospital.

On the ride to Beth's house, Kerry rehearsed their meeting over and over. Her anticipation was so keen it threatened to slide into despair were its conditions not met.

❖

While Beth was at home with her parents, she was absorbed in her own combination of anticipation and doubt. She hadn't wanted to see Kerry until they could be alone, because she was afraid of what they might say to one another and what someone else might overhear. That precluded inviting Kerry over to her home. Her parents' need for her attention was enormous when she had first returned, and it gave her a reason to put off the inevitable confrontation with her own feelings. She also felt guilty for not writing them more often, especially since she had taken the time to write to Kerry far more than she had written to her parents. After her long absence, she believed she should focus attention on them. That was possible for a few days, until the stultifying routine of their lives overtook Beth's relief at being at home and she longed to escape.

She also longed to see Kerry. On the trip home, she had thought of nothing but the scene between Nurse Reynolds and Nurse Trenton, Lieutenant Evers, and her consequent epiphany. The thought of seeing Kerry and confessing her feelings was almost more than she could contemplate because she had no idea what would happen next or even what she wanted to happen next.

For the first time in her life that she could recall, she was at the mercy of her feelings. Feelings that she couldn't control and feelings she felt equally compelled and terrified to express. *Is this what love feels like?* She wasn't sure she knew the answer. When she closed her eyes, she saw Kerry's soulful and wounded brown eyes and her tentative smile. Beth was sure that what she had to say was the right thing.

❖

At Kerry's knock, Beth flung the door open. After a moment staring at each other, they came together in a tight embrace and held it for a long time. Kerry thought she felt the tiniest relaxation of Beth's body into hers, but it came and went quickly. Then Beth was holding her at arm's length and smiling.

Kerry was torn between her joy at seeing Beth and her anxiety about their visit. She was rendered speechless, but her awkwardness was saved by Beth taking her arm and urging her forward inside the flat.

"Come quickly and say hello to Mother and Father, and then we shall be off."

Kerry followed her and politely greeted Mr. and Mrs. Hammond. They were distant, as usual, and seemed resigned to see Beth leave with Kerry.

## Chapter Twenty-two

They drove slowly through the streets. Kerry gave Beth an umbrella and tucked the carriage blanket around her securely to guard against the late-January chill. Their conversation was trivial and desultory as they rode through the quiet streets. They smiled at one another constantly. They hadn't even debated for a moment that they would go to Golden Gate Park. Kerry would turn and look at Beth when she was able to take her eyes off the street for an instant. Beth looked much like Addison—worn and weary—even though she had had a few weeks' rest. She was thinner. Kerry longed to cook her large amounts of food and even, God forbid, cluck and fuss over her like Laura did with Addison. Kerry had written of her promotion in the kitchen but now told Beth more about her constant battle to be taken seriously as a cook.

"I suppose," Beth said pensively, "it is easier if they think of you as just another man rather than a woman."

Kerry stared at her in surprise. "Do you think I want to be a man?"

Beth flinched at Kerry's tone. "No-no. It's not that. I meant that the other cooks—the men, I mean—would find it easier to think of you not as a woman, for you are in a man's job. That must make them very uncomfortable."

Kerry thought, Beth, love, you don't know the half of it. She had *not* written to Beth about her successful plot with Davey to undermine and finally get rid of Jim. She wasn't proud of her action. She fleetingly thought of Letty Stevenson and rapidly dismissed that as well.

There was another long pause. They finally arrived at the park and Kerry briskly set about tying up the horses and giving each a carrot and a pat before she turned to Beth. Again they looked at each other without speaking, until finally Kerry said, "Shall we go to the Conservatory of

Flowers? At least we shall be out of the rain." It had begun to drizzle in that sullen, constant way of San Francisco winters.

"Yes, I believe I'd like to be inside," she said softly. "I was in the tropics for only three months, but I'm feeling the cold much more than I expected."

She shivered and pulled her shawl about herself and nodded. Kerry longed to hug her and warm her up.

The gray, rainy day made the glass and white-painted wooden conservatory stand out in a stark fashion against the backdrop of bright-green plants that surrounded it. They went inside and the drastic change of temperature hit them. The conservatory was humid and hot. The silver-gray light filtering through the milky glass roof and walls seemed to highlight the green of the plants rather than dull it. Few other patrons were about. Most sensible people would be home warming themselves before their hearths. But not us, Kerry thought. Then she grasped they both felt the need to be away from their homes and families for this first meeting after so long a separation. Conscious of their awkwardness together, Kerry stared at a huge philodendron plant with a kind of wonder.

"Look, Beth," she said. "This plant is almost thirty years old!"

Beth stood beside her. "Oh, how marvelous!"

Kerry looked at Beth closely, trying to discern her mood. She was unusually quiet and uncharacteristically focused on the little plates bearing the plant names. Kerry longed to ask her how she felt about their seeing each other after their separation, but she seemed to be tongue-tied herself.

They wandered through the various rooms, and Beth slipped a hand under Kerry's arm as usual. Kerry turned to smile at her then.

Kerry felt the warmth of Beth's hand on her arm. The electricity of the touch sped along her nerve endings, but she endeavored to stay calm. She cleared her throat. "Are these plants like those in the Philippines?"

"Oh, very much so. *Quisqualis indica*, Rangoon creeper." Beth read from one of the nameplates. "I think I remember seeing these in Manila. In fact, the humidity comforts me. I don't think I was ready to come back to the winter. Even though it's milder than a mountain winter would ever be, I'm still cold."

Beth seemed to be babbling a bit about irrelevant topics, which was entirely unlike her. She seemed almost nervous. It mystified Kerry.

Their silence loomed, heavy with unspoken things. They stopped in a chamber with a large pond in the middle. Great hanging vines with large flowers dominated, but underneath a number of smaller plants and lily pads floated on the murky water. This room was even warmer than the others and the moist heat enveloped them. Kerry breathed it in. She was becoming a little light-headed from the heat or from anxiety, she couldn't tell which.

They both turned at the same time and stood face to face. Beth raised her hand to Kerry's cheek and laid her fingers there, lightly. Kerry waited for Beth to speak as the touch of her fingertips made its way straight to her heart. No one was in the chamber; they were utterly alone. They could hear the patter of rain on the glass roof, a steady accompaniment to their mutual silence.

"I learned a great deal about myself during this trip. Tour of duty, you might call it." Beth laughed a little.

Kerry was silent, holding her breath and trying to be patient.

"I found I was truly capable of far more than I could have ever imagined."

"Was it horrible?" Kerry asked. "I mean the men—the soldiers and their injuries?"

"No. They were mostly sick rather than injured. There were so many of them. That was hard until they were settled and recovered a bit. Then it was just like the hospital here at home. Except…"

"Except?" Kerry asked to bring Beth back to the moment. She had a distant look in her eyes.

"The soldiers could become quite emotional and could attach those emotions to us."

Kerry looked at her, uncomprehending.

"In their homesickness and physical sickness, they, er, sometimes made themselves believe they had fallen in love with us. There was one…"

Kerry's heart turned over. *It's happened. She met someone—a man. It was only a matter of time. I must surely die now.*

"Yes?" She asked the question with as even a tone as she could muster.

"Well, he was sweet and handsome. He was from up north. Seattle."

Kerry held her breath again, waiting for news of an impending engagement.

"His name was Roland Evers. He was a schoolteacher. He was quite charming but I refused him," Beth said with a sort of grim finality.

"Oh? Why?"

"I wasn't too sure why. Most sensible people would think me mad."

Beth's voice was light and teasing, but Kerry heard a note of something she'd never heard before. She waited, her despair ebbing away, but only a bit. That she refused the overtures of a young man was good news, but Beth's feelings toward her were still the same mystery.

"I wouldn't," Kerry said.

"You wouldn't? Why is that?"

Kerry cleared her throat nervously and looked away. "I'm sure not all women fall for the first man who asks them."

"Oh, no, I'm sure not. That would be inadvisable," Beth said with equal solemnity.

Kerry saw that a couple had entered. "Shall we walk around to the other side?" she asked abruptly.

She took Beth's arm and they went around to the other side of the pool to a bench. She drew Beth over to it and they sat down. She prayed the couple wouldn't follow them. Kerry was feeling even warmer; she could feel the sweat on her forehead, although it wasn't much hotter than the Palace kitchen during a busy service.

"It wasn't hard," Beth said, "for I didn't love him."

Kerry said nothing. Beth still had a distant pensive look, but she sounded decisive, as though her mind was made up about something.

"And something else. I saw something, heard something."

Kerry was looking at her closely. "Yes?" Kerry said, to encourage her.

"There were two nurses," Beth said, "part of our staff. They were very good friends. I heard them talking, saw them. They didn't know I was there."

She was speaking in a very low tone, forcing Kerry to strain to listen. Kerry was scarcely breathing and listening so intently she felt she might faint.

"They have a…a connection…they were, are, they…" Beth was clearly very close to tears. "They were in love with each other. I saw them kiss," she finally said.

Kerry swallowed, not wanting to interrupt Beth. But down in her heart, she began to hope. *She has finally realized. She knows. She knows!* Kerry didn't want to speak, even though she was desperate to hear what Beth would say next. She willed herself to be patient. Beth stared at the giant tropical plants for what seemed like a long, long time.

"Dearest Kerry?" Beth turned and looked her in the eye. "Are you in love with me?"

Beth's expression was tender and compassionate and Kerry relaxed a little bit, but the question hung in the humid, hot air of the greenhouse. Kerry realized that she had to answer truthfully. The chance she had been praying for had come at last, and she had to summon her courage and roll the dice.

"Yes, Beth. Yes, I'm in love with you."

"I thought so," Beth said simply. "I wasn't sure but now you have confirmed it." There was another long silence.

Kerry took a deep breath. "I fell in love with you the exact moment I looked into your eyes after you spilled the coffee at Addison's reception and I came to help you clean up."

"Oh, Kerry. These many months—you never said."

"I didn't want to offend you. I wanted to be your friend. I wanted you to like me."

"I do like you, very much," Beth said softly, absently tracing one of Kerry's fingers with her own.

"But you don't love me?" Kerry asked sadly.

"Oh, Kerry, I don't know. I don't know anything about love."

"Let me show you then." Kerry glanced around, and by some miracle they were alone.

Kerry put her arms around her and pulled her close. Beth tensed but didn't pull away, and Kerry pulled her even closer before kissing her, reveling in the sweet softness of Beth's perfect lips. Kerry didn't want to take advantage of Beth's acquiescence and press her too hard so she stopped the kiss, resting her forehead against Beth's. She swept her thumb over Beth's trembling lips.

"That is how much I love you."

"Yes?" Beth said, a little breathlessly. "I believe I'm in love with you but I don't know." She shook her head fretfully.

"Next week, Addison and Laura are going away for a month to see her family in Kansas City. Will you come and stay with me? We'll have a chance to be alone. Just us."

"Yes. I must think of what to tell my parents, but yes, I'll come stay with you."

Kerry was overjoyed but still fearful. She knew exactly what she wanted, but she was still terrified of offending Beth, who was, it seemed, in spite of her profession and all her time around sick people, a complete innocent. Nothing so far had indicated to Kerry that Beth understood all the implications of being in love or being physical with someone. Kerry had plenty of experience physically, but love was just as foreign to her as it was to Beth. She had never loved Sally. But she knew, with every fiber of her being, that she loved Beth and that they belonged together. If only Beth would give them a chance, they could become lovers.

❖

A few days later, Kerry drove Addison and Laura to the train station, who looked happier than she had ever seen them. Kerry was surprised Addison had agreed to a trip to Kansas so soon after he got back from the Philippines. Usually they took the trip to Kansas once a year, and Kerry had never noticed Addison being excited about seeing his in-laws. *Their reunion must have been successful.* She was not, however, disposed to question it because of the opportunity it presented her and Beth. Laura was dewy-eyed and clingy with Addison and had become much less inclined to bother with Kerry. Kerry was glad Addison had also come home safely and even more grateful that Laura was so taken up with him. He had been a wonderful guardian when she was truly lost, and all she wanted was to see him happy.

When she had dropped off Addison and Laura, she drove as quickly as she could to Beth's home to retrieve her and her luggage. George and Frieda, looking puzzled as well as resigned, stood outside the store to wave good-bye. Beth gave them each a quick hug and kiss.

She took her place next to Kerry in the carriage seat and gave her a smile of such brilliance and promise, Kerry laughed out loud as she clicked the reins to get the horses going. The day was one of the clear, cool ones that often brightened San Francisco's winter. To Kerry and Beth, the houses and streets of the city looked especially fine in the winter sun. They reached the Grant home on Fillmore Street, and Kerry helped Beth down from the carriage and took her suitcase from the back.

"Wait here a moment. I'll just take the horses down the street to the stable and I'll come right back."

Beth, who looked a little unsure and was blushing in very pretty fashion, nodded and watched as Kerry led the horses down the street.

## CHAPTER TWENTY-THREE

Kerry had cleaned the house top to bottom and planned and shopped for food. She didn't feel confident in or in control of many things, but she could at least make sure Beth was well fed. She had told Chef Henri point-blank she would only be coming in for luncheon service for a few weeks. Chef's mustaches twitched but he nodded. Kerry knew he wouldn't admit it out loud, but he considered her his best cook. She had heard him say a woman could never be sous-chef, but she had still become a favorite of his and she used that to her advantage.

"I don't want to rush you. We can sleep separately..." Kerry said shyly as they brought in Beth's suitcases.

"Oh, no. I couldn't sleep in Addison and Laura's bed." Beth's eyes flew open in alarm and Kerry winced. *She hasn't been here for five minutes and I've already put my foot in my mouth.*

"Rush me?" Beth asked, honestly confused.

"Never mind. Please forget what I said. It was silly."

"You're quite endearing when you're trying to be accommodating. I'm quite sure we'll be fine, as we always have been when sharing a bed," Beth said with a note of her old certainty.

Kerry thought, Perhaps you were fine but I was a mass of nerves and unsatisfied urges.

"Of course."

❖

They had a candlelight dinner. Beth was charmed and touched by the romance of it, and more so by Kerry's obvious efforts to make her feel cared for. Their togetherness had a feel of comfortable domesticity that made Beth think of the overheard conversations from the hospital ship and Florence's plaintive question, "When shall we be able to live together?" It was obvious this was what poor Florence longed for with Marjorie, and the lack of it hurt her.

During a lull in the conversation, Beth said, matter of factly, "Addison feels I might make a good doctor."

Kerry stopped with her fork midway to her mouth. "He does?"

"Yes. He does." Beth described the patients and what Addison had told her.

"Well, what do you think?" Kerry asked.

"I don't know, truly. It's an idea I've never entertained."

"Addison wouldn't be wrong about something like that. He wouldn't say so if he didn't believe it. I think you'd be a great doctor."

Beth acknowledged Kerry's compliment with a smile. "Because it's not something I've ever thought of, I must think of it longer."

Kerry nodded and went back to eating.

During another pause Beth could see Kerry was nervous and at a loss for words. "You've never yet told me about your childhood."

"I did indeed. I told you my mother died when I was born and my father raised me until he died and made Addison my guardian."

"Yes, but you've been a little short on detail, Kerry dearest. I've told you all about Mama and Papa."

Kerry took a gulp of wine. Stalling for time, she asked, "What do you think of the wine? I asked the sommelier for advice."

Beth's eyes narrowed. "It's very nice, I'm sure, but stop trying to divert me. We're here to get to know one another. I'd rather you answer my question."

"What is it you wish to know?"

"Where your people came from and where you lived and what your father's profession was. Things of that nature. Not unusual things."

"I have no wish to speak of it. It's too painful."

Beth had had a glass and a half of wine already, and Kerry could see she was clearly feeling it. Her color was high and her eyes bright. Kerry was hoping for that effect but she didn't expect to unleash a mass of curious questions.

"If I'm going to be in love with you, don't you think I deserve to know?"

"It's of no consequence to us now. There's only us and here and now," Kerry retorted. When she envisioned the time she would spend with Beth, she'd thought only of the sweet progress of physical intimacy. She didn't think she would be discussing her past.

"Why do you not wish to tell me anything? It has always been this way with you. Now you claim to love me and yet you don't trust me."

To Kerry's great astonishment, Beth flung her napkin down on the table and walked away.

Kerry caught up with Beth in the parlor and took her arm. "Please," she said, "I'm sorry. Come back to the table. I don't wish to anger you. Quite the opposite."

"Well?" Beth raised her eyebrows.

Kerry grasped then that Beth was just as anxious as she—maybe more so. She had never seen her be quick to anger.

"Come back to the table, please sit down. Let's finish supper."

Beth let herself be guided into the chair. "Thank you for making this wonderful supper. It's delicious."

"It's a pleasure to cook for you, Beth. I can see you're too thin," Kerry said.

"Oh, really? You've noticed my figure?"

"Yes. But it's more that I care about you."

"I see. Kerry dearest, I want us to know each other. That's why I ask you about yourself. Please don't be angry."

Kerry weighed Beth's words against her natural self-defense and decided it was worth the risk. "My mother was a whore. My father was a crimper and sometimes a gambler. They weren't married," she said abruptly, before taking a long drink of wine.

Beth paused with a fork halfway to her mouth. She put it down. "I see why you were so reluctant to tell me. What's a crimper though?"

"He kidnapped sailors for the ships. The captains paid him to drug them and deliver them."

Beth shuddered.

"There's more," Kerry said. She took another sip of wine.

Beth's eyes widened but she merely nodded for Kerry to continue.

"I helped him. I used to go down to the wharfs and get the sailors to the Grey Dog saloon, so's Jack could knock 'em out and tie 'em up for delivery to another ship's captain."

"How in the world did Addison ever meet your father?"

Kerry told her the story.

"Oh, that I can see. Addison thinking he could best everyone at cards." She grew serious again and asked, "But what happened to your father?"

"I can't talk about that, really. Don't try to make me." This time she took a very large gulp of wine and refilled her glass and Beth's as well. Under Beth's questioning, she was starting to remember what had happened.

"I won't. I'm just curious."

"Now you think I'm a horrible person." Kerry dropped her shoulders and absently traced the rim of the wineglass with her fingertip.

"No, I don't. It was the life you were given. You cannot be held responsible for it."

Kerry trembled violently and burst into tears. "I am though. It was all my fault."

"What was all your fault?" Beth demanded.

This time, Kerry got up and left the table and went outside. It wasn't past eight o'clock but was dark as midnight. She stared up at the sky, breathing deeply to stop the flood of tears. She felt a hand on her shoulder.

"Kerry?" Beth said very gently. "Tell me, darling. Tell me what it is."

Kerry turned and wept onto Beth's shoulder and neck. Then she haltingly told her the story about Big Moe, Sally, Teddy, and their plot. She left out the details of her relationship with Sally.

Beth listened and stroked her hair. "Kerry dearest. It's all in the past now. You're different. Besides, I couldn't care for someone who was a bad person. Therefore, you're good."

Kerry wiped her tears away and looked at Beth. "This isn't how I wanted our first evening to turn out. I envisioned something far different."

"Ah, yes, but you can't predict these things, can you? You've never told anyone, have you?"

"Addison knows," Kerry said.

"And he's an honorable man. He didn't reject you or send you away."

"No, but he had promised Jack—my father—to take me in."

"I'm not going to send you away either," Beth said seriously. "I think we're destined to be together."

Kerry wiped away more tears and smiled. "You do?"

"I do."

❖

In the end, Kerry didn't remember getting to bed or to sleep. She woke up next to Beth, both of them modestly clad in nightgowns. Her head hurt and her mouth tasted foul. She happily watched Beth sleep for a while until her urge to urinate was too powerful and she had to go out to the necessary.

When she came back, Beth was awake. Her smile was so loving Kerry thought for a fevered instant that they had made love. But she knew that wasn't true. In spite of the hangover, Kerry felt lighter. It hadn't been the end of the world, after all, to tell Beth the truth.

"Do you think you could teach me to handle the carriage and the horses?" Beth asked.

"I don't see why not, but I thought you liked me to drive?"

"I do, silly, but when you're at the restaurant, I don't want to be stuck here. I thought I might drive over to the Presidio and talk to Major Owen. Or go see my parents. Maybe." She made an unpleasant face that made Kerry laugh. "I'll get very bored here all by myself."

"Oh, of course. I know you're used to being busy all the time. I thought you might like to be idle for a bit. You can clean the house and shop and—"

"Oh? I can be like a housewife?" Beth asked with an edge. "Like Laura?" she added acidly.

"Um, no. Not exactly. And certainly not like Laura."

"Well, certainly not. Don't look so woebegone. I'm not angry."

They were easier with each other after Kerry's confession. It was a true pleasure to be together. Kerry thought constantly of how to approach the idea of their physical relationship but could find no solution. Sally had been the one in charge, and Kerry was young and easily led. She knew she must take the lead with Beth, but she was afraid.

It was more torture than ever to be together so much and so close but, in Kerry's mind, not nearly close enough. Beth was tender and affectionate, but she also was obviously unaware of the physical realities of love. Kerry knew that it was up to her and she was terrified.

❖

Kerry came home from the Palace luncheon service in the late afternoon, a few days after their tearful, wine-soaked supper, with a plan in mind. She rather reluctantly dismissed the idea of having any wine with dinner. It wasn't typical of their household, and its effect on her and Beth wasn't helpful.

"I wish Addison had a piano," she remarked, "so you could play for us in the evening."

"Yes, it's a pity. We would have to go and visit my parents."

"We could, I mean, if you wish." Kerry didn't relish the idea of unrelieved hours in the presence of George and Frieda, but she was willing to endure it for Beth's sake. She was both puzzled at and grateful for Beth's distant relationship with her parents. She didn't think they liked her very much. She was sure they didn't understand her or Beth's relationship with her. It was probably just as well.

"Yes, we could," Beth said, with little enthusiasm.

"Well, in the meantime, would you come sit next to me?" Kerry asked sweetly, but with a certain tone she hoped Beth would respond to.

"I would be charmed, I'm sure," Beth said, flirtatiously.

They sat next to one another, their hands in their laps and their eyes straight ahead. Kerry hesitantly put an arm around Beth's shoulders. Beth sat still for a moment, then nestled next to Kerry with a little sigh. Kerry rubbed her shoulder and turned to smell her hair. She nuzzled and inhaled deeply; it had been washed recently, Kerry noted, and wondered if that was for her or just a coincidence.

Beth put both arms around Kerry's waist and kissed her neck. Kerry's body temperature spiked and a shiver of pure physical craving shot through her. She lifted Beth's chin and kissed her. Their lips molded together and they broke the kiss to catch their breaths.

Beth was immersed in the sensations swirling through various parts of her body. Kerry's lips were incredibly soft and her kisses demanding in a not-unpleasant way. *Closer. More.* That was the message Kerry was sending, and Beth wanted to respond. She was surprised when Kerry scooped an arm under her legs and lifted her onto her lap.

"My dear, I'm too heavy for you." Beth was an inch or so taller than Kerry and solid from all the physical demands of nursing.

"No," Kerry said, between kisses, "you're not." Beth didn't know how long they sat that way, kissing until they were breathless, breaking off to hug tightly and begin again. Kerry's strong hands stroked her back and arms. Their combined body heat and rising desires made them both begin to loosen their clothes.

"Tell me." Kerry panted. "Tell me if you want me to stop. I don't want you to be afraid."

"I'm not afraid." It was true. Beth wanted to go on.

Kerry whispered, "Let's go to bed."

For some reason, those words and the tone in which they were uttered made Beth quiver. She nodded.

They staggered upstairs and fell on the bed, still kissing desperately. Beth closed her eyes and felt Kerry reach under her clothes, seeking bare skin.

Beth gasped at the touch. Her eyes were closed, and suddenly a jolt of fear and disgust shot through her. Suddenly, horribly, it wasn't Kerry touching her. It was Reverend Svenhard. Beth sat bolt upright, screaming, "No!" She pushed Kerry so hard, she fell off the bed onto the floor.

Kerry jumped up immediately and knelt on the bed next to Beth. "Beth!" she cried. "What happened? What's the matter?" She was obviously terrified she had hurt Beth in some way.

Beth had rolled over on her side and curled into a fetal position, sobs wracking her body.

"Leave me alone, I can't. I can't. Stop. Go away."

"If you want…I will," she said.

"Just don't touch me," Beth said, in a tight, hoarse whisper.

"No, not if you don't want me to."

Beth heard the door close softly and she sobbed that much harder.

## Chapter Twenty-four

L aura stared dreamily out the window of the train. They were on their way back home from Kansas City and the train, at that moment, was going through the Sierra Nevada Mountains. Laura barely registered the magnificent view of snow-capped peaks. She was thinking about the conversations with her father. She had primed him ahead of time so that their next-to-last day there he brought up an idea.

"Addison, what about you and Laura Jean moving back here? You can join my practice and then take over when I retire in a few years. I know it can be hard to build up a good practice from scratch—"

"Due respect, sir, but I must politely refuse your kind offer. I am very satisfied with my work in San Francisco City and County hospital and with the army," Addison had said. And since Dr. Matheson respected Addison, his only response was to compliment Addison's patriotism.

Laura, however, wasn't ready to let it go. She had been waiting for a moment to bring it up again. They were three days into the trip and Addison was sufficiently relaxed. For some reason Laura couldn't comprehend, visits to her parents usually set him on edge.

"Addison, darling?" Laura said, turning from the window to focus on him.

"Hmm?" he answered distractedly. He was reading a novel for once, *David Copperfield*.

"Addison!" she said more sharply when he didn't look up. "Please do stop reading. I wish to talk to you about something important."

He dutifully put a finger on his page and closed the book and looked at her expectantly.

"Why did you refuse Papa's offer?" she said, and couldn't quite keep the petulance out of her voice.

"I have no wish to go into private practice or live in Kansas City, my love. Is that hard to understand?"

"Yes, it is. I don't understand why you don't want to better yourself and improve our lives."

"Laura, you've said often enough how much you prefer San Francisco to the provincialism of Kansas City. What has changed your mind?"

"We could live in a nicer neighborhood. We could hire a servant. You wouldn't have to work such long hours. You know all the reasons! Papa has a very well-to-do clientele and they would adore you—"

"That all may be true, love, but I don't wish to move. I'm happy where I am. Let us please not pursue this. I ask you to adjust your thinking and accept things as they are."

"Very well, "she said gracelessly, and fell silent.

"Addison?" she said after an interval of perhaps five minutes. "Could you ask Kerry to find other housing when we return?"

This time, he brought his brows together. "Why ever would you ask me that? I have said she may reside with us as long as she wishes."

The memory of their argument before Addison came home was fresh in Laura's mind, but she feigned nonchalance. "Oh," she said, "I thought it might be time. She isn't a child any longer. She's employed."

"I promised her father," he said, but Laura broke in.

"Oh, surely you've discharged that debt. I don't see why—"

"No," Addison said. "She will have a home with us as long as she desires. I ask you to still your questions now and leave me to my book, my love."

He spoke neutrally but with a certain note of finality that left Laura simmering with resentment. *This is not the end of this discussion. I must persuade him. I'll think of something.*

❖

After Kerry and Beth's aborted attempted at lovemaking, they had both fallen into restless sleep. The next day, they said nothing beyond the necessary communications of everyday life. Kerry didn't know what to say and Beth was silent from guilt. Kerry made small fusses over making their meals and trying to get Beth to eat something. Beth would smile faintly and refuse. She had no idea what to say or what to do. So she chose to say nothing and do nothing. She thought she had made a mistake in coming to stay with Kerry. *I shall have to return to Mama and Papa and get back to work at the store until I can find another private post. This is too uncomfortable for both of us.*

On the second night, they got into bed without speaking. Beth lay still, trying to will herself to sleep.

Kerry leaned on one elbow and looked down into her eyes and touched her cheek. "Beth. Can you tell me what's wrong? Is it something I did?"

She spoke with so much patience and tenderness, Beth longed to tell her the truth. *I can't.* After a long pause, Beth sighed.

"No, it was nothing to do with you. I'm sorry that you're upset. Let's try to go to sleep." Beth turned over with her back to Kerry.

"What can I do?" Kerry pleaded.

"There's nothing. Please just let me be."

"But I'm worried. Are you ill? Are you hurt?"

"No. Nothing of that nature. Please don't worry. Now we must go to sleep."

Beth was aware that Kerry stared at her for a few more moments before lying down, and though her heart ached, she said nothing.

Beth lay awake with her mind racing. She was quite sure what ailed her. She was lying to Kerry. Something was wrong: the memory— sudden, sharp, and ghastly—of herself as a thirteen-year-old undergoing Svenhard's violation. It wasn't Kerry who had touched her. It had been him. The memory she had successfully buried roared back to life. In her rational mind, she knew that Kerry, not him, was touching her, yet it was like she was there, in that stuffy, horrible office, the smelly, sweaty stench of him surrounding her, the Bible open to some arbitrary page.

Kerry's touch, though, was something a part of her desperately craved. She was terrified, though, if Kerry touched her again, it would be exactly the same and she would recoil, thrust back to her victimized childhood. She wasn't able to decide which was worse—her feelings or their effect on Kerry, who looked so terribly wounded and confused. *It's impossible to disclose or discuss it. Once she knows, she may never even want to speak to me or even see me again. She will think me used and dirty. It's possible we'll never be as she wants us to be or as I want us to be with this standing between us. If I keep silent we can perhaps be friends, but that's all.*

Kerry watched her all the time, she knew. She was waiting for something different. The watchfulness was tempered with fear. But it was fear Beth couldn't do anything to relieve.

❖

Their time together sped by and they settled into a numb, uneasy routine. They still went to the park and downtown. They did not, by silent mutual agreement, return to the Sutro Baths. Just as she had when left alone with Laura, Kerry spent most of her time at work.

Beth stayed quiet and attempted to read and do needlepoint.

Not long after Addison and Laura's return from their trip, Beth had a letter requesting she come to the Presidio to interview with Major Dawson for a nursing post. She received this news with decidedly mixed feelings. She would be glad to get back to a working routine where she would have less time to think, her mind well-occupied with the demands of nursing rather than free to roam through the painful past and the despondent present. She knew vaguely that it wouldn't be possible to rid herself of this conundrum.

Kerry's presence in her life every day reminded her that she had changed. She needed to think of someone else's feelings. Someone for whom she cared very much, someone whom she had hurt deeply and was compounding that pain by staying silent. Someone whom she believed she was in love with. Yet Beth could neither bring herself to leave and return home to the Mission District, nor could she tell Kerry the reason for her frightened withdrawal, no matter how bereft Kerry looked or how many times she pleaded with her in the darkness of their bedroom.

❖

Kerry was at loss as to what to do about Beth's silence. She missed her so much during the day she asked Chef Henri for the rest of the day off. He was distracted and waved her away. She went to a bakery downtown and bought a tart. *It will be pleasant to sit outside and eat this and look at the bay and the Golden Gate. I hope she can risk stepping away from the ward for a few minutes.*

It was a clear, sunny day, as typical for San Francisco's winter as the gray rainy days were. It was cool but the sun made it pleasant. Kerry got off the California Street cable car about a half mile from the Presidio. She would need to walk the rest of the way but she didn't mind. It pleased her to be out of doors in the fresh air instead of in the hot, smoky, crowded kitchen. She trod a well-worn path from California

Street into the Presidio. Generations of soldiers had made their way from the fort into town to see their girls. Kerry made the trip in reverse to see *her* girl, who wasn't a soldier but wasn't far from being one. Kerry smiled a little thinking how much Beth took to and appreciated the military discipline of working at the post hospital.

Kerry stopped at the front desk and politely asked if Nurse Hammond was available. The nurse on duty, Marjorie Reynolds, contemplated her with her white cook's jacket and cropped hair and replied, coolly, "Wait one moment. I'll see."

"Kerry dearest! Whatever prompted you to come here to the hospital?"

"I wanted to surprise you. Wasn't this a welcome idea?"

"Yes, yes, of course. We're not busy at the moment. We have just a few boys who are really ill. The rest are ambulatory. Still, I can't stay away long."

"I understand, Bethy. I just wanted to see you for a few minutes. See? I brought a tart."

"When did you make this?" Beth asked, surprised.

"I didn't bake it. I bought it at Boudin's, along with the bread you like so much. The sourdough."

"Oh, you did? How wonderful." Leaving by a side door, they strolled along the pathway to a bench, where they sat and ate the raspberry tart together.

"I'll be going home straight away. Would you like me to bake a chicken stuffed with mushrooms and oysters for supper? I'll stop at the butcher on my way and get a fresh hen, not too big." Beth watched Kerry's face as she planned their dinner. She felt guilty that, instead of being angry, Kerry seemed to take ever more care of her and cook more and more elaborate meals.

"With the bread too, of course," Kerry added, and smiled rather sadly.

After Kerry left, Beth went back to her task of washing and folding linen. She usually didn't mind it when she had little else to do. It was one of those rote tasks she could perform without thought. Now, it left room for the endless circular guilty thoughts and the questions to which she had no answers.

"Do you need any help?" Marjorie asked, startling Beth out of her reverie.

"Oh, by all means, if you wish."

"Stephen asks me about you every time I see him. He's most taken with you, I think. It is a sadness to him that you wouldn't allow him to call on you," Marjorie said in a conversational tone.

Beth sensed something behind her words. She had met Marjorie's brother Stephen when they resumed working at the Presidio Hospital. He was a dashing captain and had asked to court her, but she had refused. *Does she suspect something about Kerry now that she has seen her?*

"I'm simply not in a position just now to make any new friends," Beth said, in what she hoped was a pleasant tone. "We have such demanding work," she added, knowing Marjorie couldn't argue with that, though many nurses managed to be courted by young men or by doctors, and to marry, though a number of them didn't.

"I met your friend, Kerry," Marjorie said, in a seeming non sequitur, but Beth instantly knew she wasn't making idle conversation.

Thinking of the scene she had witnessed on the *Golden Gate*, Beth took a breath, then took a giant chance. "Yes. She brought me a raspberry tart. She had left work early to come and have a short visit with me." Beth paused, but Marjorie said nothing.

Beth continued. "Do you and Florence have a house?"

Marjorie's eyes widened. During the long pause Beth could almost hear the sequence of Marjorie's thoughts as they clicked into place.

"Ah. We would like to very much, but my mother's health is still poor," Marjorie said after a moment. "I must stay with her. Florence wouldn't be, er, comfortable at my mother's home." Their eyes met.

Beth nodded. "Yes, that's very difficult." She thought of poor Florence's entreaties of Marjorie during the Christmas party aboard the *Golden Gate*. She held Marjorie's gaze and Marjorie gave her a tiny sad smile and nodded back.

"So, Nurse Hammond, what are your future plans? Do you want to continue working here for the army or return to a civilian hospital?" Beth saw that the subject of Florence was clearly closed for the moment, but they had taken a small step forward. She thought for a moment—considering if it was a good idea to tell Marjorie about Addison's suggestion.

But before she could decide, Marjorie said, "The army may soon make us nurses permanent employees. That is why I ask you of your plans. I would hope you would give serious thought to staying on. Dr. McGee is currently lobbying the war office in Washington to create a special corps for nurses."

"I suppose so," Beth said carefully. "I do love the work and am fond of all the soldier boys and you and the others, of course." She was rewarded by a rare smile from Marjorie.

"Well. I'd consider it an honor to have you remain under me. I would hope to be given an army rank, and all of us would benefit. You're an excellent nurse, one of the best I've ever seen."

Beth cleared her throat.

Marjorie looked at her keenly. "Speak up, Nurse. Do you wish to say something?"

"No. I would be honored to work with you as well. It's just that, well, I'm not sure what I want to do."

"I find it hard to believe you don't consider nursing your life's work. You have a gift, Elizabeth. It would be a shame not to use it." Beth was startled that Marjorie used her first name. It was the first time she had ever done so.

"It's not that, Nurse Reynolds."

"Then what is it? I'm not in need of your final decision, but I would like to know your thoughts."

"Dr. Grant thinks I should apply to medical school and become a doctor."

During the long silence, Marjorie looked away, then down at her hands, which had been neatly folding a sheet but were still.

"That is kind of him to say, but it would be inadvisable for you to take him up on his recommendation. Dr. Grant means well but…"

Now Beth was even more confused and taken aback that Marjorie would feel that way.

"Please tell me why you think so. You and he both agree that I am very, very good at nursing. He says I have a knack for medicine, for discerning symptoms, for—"

"It's not your intelligence or ability I question, Nurse," Marjorie said sharply.

Beth stayed quiet, waiting for Marjorie to explain herself.

"Men are doctors, women are nurses. It's the natural way of things. You would have a very difficult time with the men in medical school and after, trying to work with them at the same level. It's not a suitable profession for a woman. I do hope you aren't seriously considering trying this?"

"I don't know yet. I have been thinking about it but I've reached no conclusion. Your opinion matters to me, of course, but so does Doctor Grant's." Beth was hurt that Marjorie had reacted to her news in such a negative fashion.

"Well. I have expressed my opinion. I can only hope you take it to heart," Marjorie said stiffly. She was obviously unhappy and ill at ease. She went back to folding and stowing linen.

Beth was sorry; she had hoped their friendship would prosper from their shared understanding. It occurred to her suddenly how ironic it was that Marjorie spoke of the "natural order of things" when the love of her life was another woman. How does one reconcile those two opposite ideas? Beth thought. Well, it's a discussion we may have at some future time.

## Chapter Twenty-five

Addison had decided not to accept the army's offer to return to service, and he offered Kerry and Beth the use of the carriage.

"I have performed my patriotic duty and I want to go back to the hospital, where they have thoughtfully not replaced me."

"I'll drive you to work and come and fetch you in the evening," Kerry said to Beth, as though there was nothing more to discuss.

Beth objected. "Nonsense. You'll be working until after midnight. I'll be on the usual twelve-hour shift—six to six."

"You've no other way to travel to the post, Bethy."

"I shall have to find another way. I'll walk."

"You can't walk. It's too far and your work is entirely too hard. I'll take you. Now please don't argue anymore. I'm not one of your patients whom you can bully."

Beth's eyes blazed but she bit off her response. "Very well."

Every day, Kerry took Beth to work and then came home, slept for a couple hours, then went to work herself. Beth found a colleague to bring her home. Kerry came home at midnight and crawled into bed next to Beth. They woke up at five a.m. and started all over again.

After a few weeks, Beth was alarmed at how tired Kerry looked and said so. Kerry wouldn't admit to exhaustion, but she decided to come home rather than work the dinner service. After dinner with Addison and Laura, they had retired to their bedroom.

"I'll apply for quarters at the post, then you won't have to endure this."

"No. If you do so, we'll never see each other."

"Kerry dearest, you must get some rest, or you'll damage your health."

"Beth, it's not me I worry about. It's you."

"Me?" Beth asked. In spite of her fatigue, Kerry got out of bed and paced. Beth sat on the side of the bed and watched her.

"Do you love me?" Kerry asked after a time.

"Well, yes, of course. I—" Beth stopped. *It's true. I do love her.*

"Then tell me what's wrong. Three weeks ago, you couldn't let me touch you. Since then, we've been living under this terrible tension. If this is something to do with me, tell me. If it isn't, please tell me so I can help. Please, Beth. Please."

Beth stayed silent, tracing the pattern on the quilt with her fingertip.

"Beth. Look at me." Beth turned her face to the side and looked down. Kerry knelt on the floor in front of her, holding Beth's face between her hands as she looked her in the eye.

"They will have some housing ready for us soon. I'll move. It's better that way," Beth said, dully.

"No. That isn't what you want, it's not what I want. We are to be together."

"Kerry, I can't be to you what you want me be. It's not fair to you."

"No. Beth, I love you. Don't speak to me about fairness. Please tell me what's troubling you."

"I can't. Please don't ask me anymore."

Exhaustion and frustration overcame Kerry and she could no longer rein in her emotions.

"You don't care for me as you claim to." She stood up and went to the window that overlooked the yard.

"Oh, but I do. Kerry, that's why I want you to be well and happy."

"My wellness and happiness depend on you. You love me, I know you do. I love you and I want to show you how much. Don't you want me, too? I think you do." Kerry touched her arm and Beth shivered.

"Yes, I do, but—"

"But what?"

Beth started to cry and looked away. Kerry was torn between sympathy and anger. She wanted to comfort Beth but she knew the moment she touched her, comfort would turn to desire. She couldn't bear the thought of another rejection.

"I'm leaving, Beth. I need to get away from you. I can't stand it.

You won't tell me what's wrong, you push me away at every turn, but you claim to love me. I can't live this way."

"Kerry, please. Don't go."

"You can offer nothing to keep me here, Beth," she said angrily. "You won't be honest with me and tell me what's wrong. You won't touch me. You can barely look at me."

"I can't give you what you want. I can't...do things with you. I'm sorry."

"Do you think that's all I want?" Kerry demanded. "Do you?"

Beth cried harder and put her hands over her eyes. She whispered, "You are the best and most loyal and loving person, and you have no idea about me."

"Then tell me."

"I can't."

"Tell me. I swear it will make no difference. If it does then I'll tell you and I'll go away and there will never be anything between us. If you don't tell me why you can't be my love, then I'll leave you." There it was. Kerry knew there would be no turning back now. *Roll the dice. Win or lose.*

"I can't. It will kill you. The shame would kill me."

"Beth. How can anything about you be more horrible than what I already know? I know about Chinese girls just eleven years old made to be the toys of old men for money. Drug addicts who sell themselves for the opium and the men who would use their bodies. You know very well where I came from. My mother was a whore who died of an infection when she had me. My father was a criminal. He kidnapped and sold defenseless sailors like slaves. Is what you have to tell me really so much worse than that?"

Beth kept on crying, but it was clear she wouldn't say anything more.

Kerry turned and left the bedroom, slamming the door behind her. Without a word, she walked past Addison and Laura, who sat in the living room. She took her coat from the rack and stomped out the front door. She'd be dammed if she'd spend another minute begging a woman to love her who wouldn't even speak to her truthfully. She was tired of feeling like a top, spinning endlessly with nowhere to go.

❖

Addison and Laura stared at the front door in surprise. Addison was genuinely concerned. Kerry hadn't lost her temper like that since she'd first come to live with them.

"Whatever's wrong, do you suppose?" he asked.

"I am sure it's nothing," Laura said airily. "Young women can be so moody." She went back to her embroidery.

Addison was quiet and thoughtful for a moment but then jumped up abruptly and went upstairs.

Addison knocked softly on the door, but before Beth could say anything he opened it a crack and peeked in. "Beth, is something wrong? Kerry just left and it seems she was quite upset."

Beth clearly tried to stem her crying and sound normal, but she failed miserably.

"No, nothing's wrong, thank you."

Addison drew a chair to the side of the bed and sat down. He touched her shoulder gently, handing her his kerchief. "I'm concerned. Kerry hasn't left this way since she was newly here and had an upset with…" He was about to say with Laura, but thought better of it. "I see you're distressed." He made it a statement that invited a confession.

"It's nothing. We had an argument. I'll recover my composure soon. Thank you."

He sat quietly looking at her for another moment. "As you wish, but please feel free to confide in me if you're inclined." He returned the chair to its corner. "I've become quite fond of you, and I think of Kerry as a daughter I never had. I hope you both know you can come to me with anything at all."

He smiled gently at her, hoping she would take him up on his offer as he closed the door softly behind him, sighing as he heard Beth start weeping once again.

## Chapter Twenty-six

When Kerry walked through the door of the Grey Dog, she saw Sally at the bar. Her back was turned and she was chatting up a natty-looking gentleman standing next to her.

Sally had on a fine green damask frock and her face paint was perfect. She had an apparently happy grin on her face. Her long eyelashes lowered seductively as the gentleman said something to her. It was Leo who tapped her shoulder and pointed to Kerry, who stood a few feet away. Sally turned and rested her elbows on the bar. Her eyebrows went up.

"Well, look what the cat drug in. I knew you'd be back, girl. You finally tired of them swells, eh?"

"Yes, Sal, I believe I am. May I buy you a drink?"

"My good man, please give me a moment," Sally said smoothly to the gentleman. He nodded, obediently turning back to the bar and calling on Leo for another drink.

Kerry took Sally's elbow and steered her to a table. She was relieved, in a way. The familiar sights and sounds of the Barbary Coast washed over her. She was home.

Sally called over her shoulder, "Whiskey, Leo. A bottle of W.A. Lacey, if you please." She named one of the better brands sold at the Grey Dog.

"I'm not really disposed to be nice to you after the last time you left me," Sally said, looking at Kerry closely.

"I'm sorry about that, Sal. I was a lot younger then. I was stupid and didn't know what I wanted."

"Yeah. You're all grown up now, I see." Sally climbed into Kerry's lap, wrapped her arms around her neck, and buried Kerry's face in her cleavage. "You came back to me. I've missed you so, honey."

"I've missed you too, Sal. More than I can say, but let me breathe a little, please."

Sally frowned but she let Kerry loose. Kerry gently lifted her onto the other chair, and Leo slapped the bottle and two glasses on the table.

"Come on, Kerry-o. Let's have us a drink." Sally poured the whiskey to the top of the glasses. They picked them up and, smiling broadly, clinked them together. Kerry drained hers, coughed, and then grabbed Sally and gave her a long sloppy kiss.

Kerry broke their kiss and looked at Sally. She needed some diversion and here it was, such as it was. Sally had put on more than a little weight in the intervening years, and she looked tired. *Tired and ill used. But at least she wants me.*

"Good to see you, Sal. I've been missing you too."

Beth didn't know how much time had passed. She usually knew exactly what action she would take next every moment of her life, without exception. Now she was immobilized and indecisive. *I don't know what to do.*

Beth's head ached from crying and from despair. She sat up and took the glass of water by the bedside and drank it. It was warm and stale. *She's out in the dark somewhere. She's distraught.* Beth was suddenly afraid of something happening to Kerry. *At least I can go find her.* She went to the dresser, poured some water into the basin, and washed her face and tidied her hair. She ignored the puffy red swelling of her eyes and the paleness of her cheeks. It didn't matter. Kerry mattered, and she had to find her.

She went downstairs and into the living room. Addison and Laura looked up as she entered.

"Addison? I fear that Kerry has gone off somewhere." She bowed her head, but not before she glimpsed Laura's triumphant expression and Addison's sympathetic look.

"Well. When she's had bad moments before, she has gone back to the Barbary Coast, where she grew up. Much like a homing pigeon."

"And where exactly is that?" Beth asked.

"It's down at the wharf, on Jackson Street. It's very dangerous, though. It's…You can't go there yourself. I'll take you."

"No, Addison, thank you, but no. I must go by myself." She lifted her chin. Laura was looking at her oddly.

"I see. Well, come to my office and I'll write the address down for you."

Once at his desk, he looked into a battered book. He wrote it out on a scrap of paper.

"The cable car will get you to within a few blocks. Beth, it's a very rough neighborhood. A young woman alone…I should go with you."

"I'll be careful, I promise. Thank you for this." She held up the scrap of paper.

"Yes. Please do try and get her to come home. It's not a safe place for the reasons you think and for some reasons you may not know."

"I do know, Addison. I know because she told me." Addison looked at her closely and nodded and then did something that surprised her. He kissed her cheek. She pressed her lips together and nodded, squaring her shoulders as she left the house in search of the one person who might truly love her.

❖

If Kerry squinted, she could see Sally standing at the bar. Sally was starting to look better than she had an hour before. *God, I can't drink. I'm getting so drunk this ugly old whore is starting to look good to me.* She peered through the smoke of the saloon. *She must be ready to go. I think she said to wait for a half hour.* Kerry sighed. *I must be mad.*

A half hour previously, Sally had once again been sitting in her lap and kissing her and whispering in her ear. Sally's face hovered close to hers. Kerry could smell her—the odor of sweat and booze and cigarette smoke. Sally was sitting on her lap again and her legs were beginning to go numb. Kerry shuddered inwardly and stopped Sally's babble with a kiss.

"Kerry, honey, I have to go. Don't move. I'll be back. Have another drink," she added. "Just you wait for a little bit. I have to turn one more trick then I'm all yours, Kerry-o."

"Just make sure you clean up good or I ain't doing it with you," Kerry mumbled.

"Oh, don't worry, honey," Sally crooned in her ear. "I'll be fresh as a daisy. I can't wait until we get together and I can feel your tongue in my cunt." She slipped away and went back to the gentleman waiting at the bar. He grinned hugely and put an arm around her and called Leo for another drink.

Kerry wanted to be much drunker before even thinking about what she was going to do. She sat sipping the whiskey and thinking, *A half hour? I can't really tell time.*

*I'm going to sleep with a fat, over-the-hill whore because I can't have the woman I love. Well, it don't make sense but there you are. Oh, Beth, and you think you're not worthy of me.*

Kerry sipped her whiskey. *I want to be drunk but not too drunk.* Not having Sally as a distraction was hard. She kept thinking of Beth. Beth dressed for work. Beth swimming in the pool at Sutro Baths. She pictured Beth asleep, her face at rest. She thought about how her breasts felt in that brief moment when she could finally touch them. She shook her head and rubbed her eyes.

She heard a voice. "Hey. You don't look so good." Kerry looked up. There was Minny, dressed up, painted, and regarding her seriously with a hand on her hip.

"Minny. Don't tell me—"

"What do *you* think?" Minny's voice was brittle and angry.

"I guess you're working," Kerry conceded tiredly.

"What are you doing here? You don't live here no more."

"I don't know, to tell you the truth."

"You came for Ma, didn't you?"

"Yeah, I suppose." Kerry sat back in her chair and poured another glass of whiskey. "You don't need to be a whore, Minny. You could do something else." Kerry was feeling a little sentimental about her childhood friend.

"What else would I do?" Minny sounded a little sad now instead of angry.

"I don't know."

"I got to get back to work. You oughta leave, you don't belong here no more."

Kerry couldn't read Minny's tone. She could have been sympathetic or dismissive. It was hard to say. Kerry continued to drink and wait for Sally to transact her business. Her mind kept returning to Beth and her abrupt departure during their argument, and she was starting to regret it.

❖

The trip downtown had taken far longer than Beth imagined it would, and that fed her anxiety. She got off the cable car near the Ferry Building and walked along the Embarcadero to the north. Within two blocks past the Ferry Building, she felt distinctly unsafe. The genteel passersby coming and going to and from on ferries gave way to slightly threatening figures. Men with glittering eyes leered and muttered at her. Groups of toughs drifted by and catcalled to her.

She held her head up with her eyes forward, clutched her handbag, and marched on. She stopped under a lamp to check the address. She shivered in the cold breeze blowing off the Bay. She asked someone for Jackson Street. It was two more blocks away. She wasn't at all certain that she would find Kerry, let alone induce her to return home. She had no idea what she would say or how she would explain her predicament.

Finally, she made it to Jackson Street and peered into the Grey Dog. It was so crowded, smoky, and dark she had to wait for her eyes to adjust. She peered into the gloom for quite a while and was beginning to despair of ever finding Kerry. Then she spotted her at a table in the back, hunched over a bottle, her head drooping so low it was nearly on the table.

## CHAPTER TWENTY-SEVEN

B eth smoothed her dress distractedly and squared her shoulders. She walked over to the table, feeling as though half the room was watching her. *It's likely they never see a respectable-looking woman in this place.* She was nearly to the table when a plump, blond woman came out of nowhere and plopped down in the chair next to Kerry. Beth stopped. She watched as the woman scooted her chair close to Kerry and practically smothered her with kisses. Beth's heart sank. *I let her go. She doesn't know I'm here. I have to at least try. If she won't come home with me, then so be it.*

She had walked through the bar, paying no attention to the comments and stares of the patrons. She saw only one person, Kerry, who didn't notice her approach because she was so absorbed by her companion. She broke off from kissing Sally to swig something.

Kerry was attempting to get herself excited by kissing Sally with a lot of tongue. It wasn't working. Sally was moaning and writhing with what might have been real excitement. Kerry stopped for a breath and happened to look up and see Beth. Sally grabbed her face and tried to turn her so they could kiss some more. When she couldn't move Kerry's head, she followed her gaze and saw the somberly dressed young woman with her dark blond hair neatly pulled back.

Beth stood next to the table, her eyes fixed on Kerry, but she said nothing.

Kerry was astonished and suddenly ashamed. She sat up a little straighter and tried to pull herself together. "Hello, Beth," she said, coolly. "What are you doing here?" She had an inkling of why Beth might have come, and a tiny spark of hope penetrated her darkness of anger, drunkenness, and shame.

"Kerry. I want to talk to you," Beth said evenly. "I want you to come home."

"Who's this?" Sally demanded. Both Kerry and Beth ignored her, however, their eyes fixed on each other.

"Beth, I think we've talked enough. There's nothing more to say."

Sally glared at Beth. "Honey, you ain't got what she wants. You better go on back where you came from."

As if Beth hadn't heard a word either of them said, she repeated, "Kerry, I want to talk to you. I *need* to talk to you. To explain."

"I don't believe you." Kerry didn't want to say what she was saying but she seemed powerless to stop. "I'm stayin' here," she said defiantly.

Beth stood composed, just looking at her. She seemed about to say something else, but, instead, she turned and walked out of the Grey Dog.

Kerry slumped in the chair and stared moodily at the glass of whiskey in front of her. Sally started kissing her and feeling her breasts. She crooned in Kerry's ear, "I'll just be off to the outhouse, and then I'll be right back and we'll go upstairs and I'll get cleaned up and we can…" She paused and grinned and batted her eyes. "Don't you go getting too drunk."

Kerry finally looked at her. Ugh, she thought. I don't want to do it. I can't do it. Beth. She came all the way down here to find me. I need to know what she wants to tell me, no matter what it may be. Sally homed in for another sloppy kiss, but Kerry put her arm out and stopped her.

"I'm goin', Sal. I'm sorry. Another time." She stood up and walked toward the door, waving good-bye to Leo.

"Kerry-o! Wait. Come back here, you no-good tease. You think you're too good for me? You ain't nothin'. You're just another piece of Barbary Coast trash like what the tide brings up. That high-class bitch isn't going to want you and she can't do nothing for you. Not like me. Come back here!"

But Kerry didn't stop to listen; she was already out the door and walking swiftly down Jackson Street to the Embarcadero. She searched around wildly for Beth. *She can't have gone very far.*

The gaslights were few and far between, and they cast a dim glow in the fog. *She'd go up Market to catch the cable car. That's got to be it.* Kerry walked faster. The cold air was starting to sober her up.

She made a sharp right turn by the Ferry Building and looked toward the cable car stop. She spotted Beth standing under the streetlight. Kerry could see that a big lout was making his way over to her so she took off running. It seemed to take forever; her legs wouldn't move. She got close enough that she could hear the man's deep threatening voice and Beth's softer replies. The man was pushing too close to Beth, who bravely but foolishly stood her ground.

She ran between them and turned and faced down the man. He was drunk as a skunk and three times her size.

"Sorry, pardner. She's with me."

"Be gone, you little shit. She don't want you," he growled.

He lunged and Kerry dipped her head and butted him in the gut. He staggered back, choking. She gave him a smart blow to the back of the neck and down he went.

"Beth," Kerry panted. "Let's head up the street before he comes to."

Beth let Kerry grab her arm and drag her along Market Street. They couldn't see any cable cars coming. Kerry looked back and saw the drunk pulling himself up from the pavement. He would recover his senses in a moment and they'd be in trouble.

"Here," Kerry said, as she spotted a cab and waved him over. They climbed in.

"Howdy, folks. What's your pleasure?"

Beth looked at Kerry and Kerry gazed back at her. They laughed as they tried to catch their breaths.

"Golden Gate Park," Beth said suddenly.

Kerry said, "You're out of your senses, love, but let's go."

"I may be out of my senses but I am glad to see you, though I'm surprised." Beth settled her handbag on her lap. "You were somewhat occupied when I left," she remarked acidly.

"I didn't know what to do. When I left you, I mean. I was angry. I knew I could have a few drinks and a few laughs with old Sally."

"It seems as though you had more than a few drinks," Beth said, a slight edge in her voice. "And Sally seems to know you very well."

"Uh…" Kerry was completely at a loss. She knew she should explain but she couldn't. "How did you find me?"

"Addison told me. He gave me the address of the Grey Dog Saloon. He was right. It's a bad part of town."

"Beth, you don't know the half of it. But you came to find me. Because you came to find me, I think you want to tell me what you wouldn't tell me before."

"You're right, I have to tell you but I've never told anyone." Beth took a deep breath. "But let's wait until we get to the park." She took Kerry's hand in her both of hers and they rode in silence across town to the park.

The cab let them out at McLaren Lodge on the eastern end of Golden Gate Park, near the Conservatory of Flowers. It was nearly pitch dark, but a slight glow from the moon filtered through the nightly fog and clouds and reflected off the Conservatory, giving it a ghostly white glow. They walked down the promenade and sat down on the nearest bench. Kerry turned to Beth, trying to divine her expression in the dark.

"It seems to me, it's time you tell me what has happened to you and why you react as you do when I…touch you. I promise you. I'll listen and I won't judge you. I'm in love with you. Nothing will change that. Ever. You saw tonight where I come from. That was where I spent my childhood, Beth. That was my home." Kerry squeezed Beth's hands.

"Your breath is still filled with drink."

"I'll try not to breathe on you then. You talk and I'll listen."

Beth took a deep breath and told her about Reverend Svenhard and his "Bible lessons." She left little out, describing her parents' betrayal, her love for the young Italian girl whom she had never spoken to again, and the feeling that everything had been her fault. Somehow, saying everything out loud took some of the bitterness with it, and when she was done, she suddenly felt room in her soul for the first time, as though the darkness embedded there had escaped with the words.

"So it was when you touched me," Beth paused, "there. It's as though it wasn't you. I *know* that it's you and I love you, but my body or my psyche rebels without my being able to control it."

Kerry was silent a long time. Beth worried it was from disgust. Finally she spoke and her voice had the rough Irish accent that Beth had noticed before, the same one she'd heard with the whore in the bar. Beth knew she must be greatly moved.

"Him a preacher and he treated you worse than he would treat a pretty waiter girl. At least with them on the Coast it's an honest thing. If it's not clean or good, at least they make the choice. I never heard of a preacher man doing that."

"Come, Kerry dearest. How many preacher men have you *really* known?" Beth was so relieved she was laughing a little.

"Well, none, maybe. But still that seems too fantastic to think of. A man of God going after a little girl. There's men for sure that want the youngest they can find. But not their own friends' daughters. You were innocent, Beth."

"No. He said it was my fault."

"Never mind what he said. He was lower than a reptile, he was," Kerry said. "If I'd been there, I would have got someone to kill him or done it myself."

"Well, now you know," Beth whispered, amazed at Kerry's vehemence.

"I'm glad you told me."

"You are?"

"Surely. It explains so much. It doesn't matter. It's over. No one can use you or hurt you again. I love you. You're a good woman, and that bastard was wrong. It wasn't your fault, it was his."

"My parents are ashamed of me," Beth said, sadly. "We can barely speak."

"It could explain why you'd never want to marry. Your parents couldn't argue with that." Kerry was smiling. "You can keep on doing your nursing work and stay with me."

"After all, women who work—no man would want one." Beth rolled her eyes but grinned a little.

"That's so, isn't it? Then it's all settled."

They sat still, huddling together without speaking.

"Kerry?"

"Yes, Beth, love."

Beth cleared her throat. "Who was that woman—the one sitting on your lap?"

"Just someone I used to know," Kerry said evasively.

"Kerry, if I'm to be honest with you, you must be honest with me." Beth didn't sound angry exactly, but she was grave.

"I, er. She was…"

"Please don't try to protect me," Beth said. "Who is she?"

"She was my sweetheart when I was younger."

"Sweetheart? Do you mean like me?"

Not exactly like you, Kerry thought grimly.

Beth tried hard to see Kerry's expression in the shadows.

"You and she?" Beth asked.

"Yes. We did. But I don't love her, and it all started when I was real young." The sentence came out all in a rush and then Kerry fell silent again.

"I want to be the only one," Beth said simply.

"You are, I swear!" Kerry cried fervently and kissed her to prove it. Their kiss got heated and Kerry swore quietly at the feeling of Beth's body pressed against her own.

Beth shivered and snuggled closer to Kerry. "Oh, Kerry dearest, I want to be with you as she was. I want that more than anything!"

"We will, Beth, we will."

"I'm freezing! I have to get indoors before I get the frostbite," Beth complained with a smile.

"Oh, you. It is not *that* cold, you silly."

They turned and looked into each other's eyes and smiled and kissed again.

"It's a ways back to Addison's house and there are no cabs out here. We better start walking."

Beth clung close to Kerry, hanging on her arm. The trees were swathed in fog; the moonlight gave them a mysterious glow. It was spooky and compelling.

Kerry pulled Beth close to her and they walked home quickly.

❖

Addison was attempting to mask his worry by concentrating on a medical journal. He stole a glance at Laura. She was embroidering with an odd smile, as though she was harboring an especially delightful secret. It was nearly midnight when the front door opened and Addison heard their voices. He threw his journal aside and strode into the hall.

They were removing their coats and looked flushed, likely from the chilly night, but they were smiling.

"Ah. Beth, Kerry. I'm quite relieved to see you both."

"Hello, Addison," Beth said.

He was astounded at the contrast in her mood before she left and her quite obvious happiness.

He turned to Kerry, who was unwinding a scarf with her gaze fixed on Beth. The intensity of her expression surprised him. "Kerry. I'm so glad you've returned home," he said, meaningfully.

"Addison. Sorry to have made you fret. I'll try not to do that again." She turned once again toward Beth, who returned her smile.

"We're very tired. We'll retire now," Beth said, with a contrived yawn.

"Of course, naturally," Addison said. "Kerry, will you need the carriage tomorrow to drive Beth to work?"

"Yes, please," Kerry called over her shoulder. She was already running up the stairs after Beth.

He watched them for a moment, an idea slowly coalescing in his mind. He turned and went back to the parlor.

Laura sat with her hands folded and an unreadable expression on her face. Addison wondered that she hadn't said a word to them upon their safe return.

"Ready to turn in?" she asked.

He nodded.

# Chapter Twenty-eight

Addison sat behind his desk regarding Kerry and Beth, who sat before him. *What have they come to tell me? I believe I know. How shall I react? It's not as though it's a great surprise. I've suspected since Kerry came to us at age fifteen. They fell in together so naturally and so easily. Now they're together. They've come to tell me so.*

He cleared his throat. "Well," he said, just a little too heartily, "how are you two and why so formal?"

They glanced at one another and Kerry nodded slightly. Beth looked down. She appeared to be about to jump out of her chair and run from the room. Kerry looked at her anxiously and squeezed her hand.

"I..." Beth said, then faltered.

Addison nodded benevolently.

"I need your advice," Beth said hesitantly. "I...I have spells."

Addison raised his eyebrows. This was altogether not what he expected. "Spells? What sort of spells, Elizabeth?"

He rarely called her by her whole name. It unnerved her even more. "Well, they come. They happen. I remember things."

"How shall I say it?" Beth had asked Kerry earlier. "I can't tell him it's when we want to make love."

Kerry had said, "No, you don't have to tell him that. Just say what happens."

"Things?"

"When I was ten years old, the minister of my church put his hands on me."

Now Addison frowned and his eyes grew hard. "How do you mean? As a healing gesture?"

"No." Beth looked down, embarrassed.

"Then what do you mean exactly?" Addison kept his voice even, but Beth could hear the anger in it.

"He touched me. He used me to..."

She couldn't say it. She could scarcely bear to think of it.

"I understand. Say no more," Addison said. "Did you tell your parents?"

Beth told him about Mama Rocco's futile effort.

"I see. That is despicable, disgusting. I can scarcely credit it. However, I know you're an honorable young woman and would never lie about something so vile. What can I do? Do you wish me to call the police?"

"Oh, no!" Beth said hastily. "He's dead. He has been for many years."

"Well, then, you may dismiss it from your mind. It's over, thank goodness. It's brave of you to tell me."

"But it's not over," Beth said, miserable. "I have these memories or spells—I don't know what to call them—when it seems I'm back with him again."

"Are you hallucinating? What brings them on?" Addison was now writing notes down.

"Um..." Beth hesitated. She looked at Kerry, needing help. Kerry looked alarmed, obviously unable to speak.

"No, not hallucinations. Memories. At odd times."

"What times?" Addison was now fully engaged in his professional mode and treating her as a patient from whom he must elicit information in order to make a diagnosis. He threw his pen down and fixed his eye on them, and they stared at each other.

"Come, Beth. You're a nurse. You know we can't treat the patient without knowing all the particulars of the symptoms."

Kerry suddenly burst out. "She can't tell you because it's too private. It's not important when. It's just that these memories affect her terribly. She's very unhappy. Can you help her?"

"Have you been witness to these 'spells,' as she calls them?" Addison asked.

"Yes," Kerry said, firmly.

"Well, then, perhaps you would care to explain."

Kerry took a breath and said, "They're like nightmares. They come upon her and she can only cry and babble. It's very distressing. It's like she's lost her mind."

Beth silently breathed a sigh of relief. She was afraid Kerry would tell all. She didn't know why she thought so, but she knew that the facts of their relationship were unusual enough they both didn't wish to reveal them. They hadn't even discussed it ahead of time.

Addison listened without comment. Then at last he said, "Your faith in me is gratifying, but I am very much afraid I can't help you. The mind is mysterious. I am well versed in the diseases of the body, but I know nothing of the ills of the mind. It doesn't seem as though you must be committed to an asylum."

Both Beth and Kerry regarded him with genuine terror.

"Don't be afraid," he said reassuringly. "I'm only trying to say that I'm unable to be of direct assistance in helping you. You may find, Beth, that having spoken of these things, the burden will ease with time, the emotions attached to this terrible part of your life disappearing now you have released them into the open, so to speak. I can find someone who deals with the ills of the mind, if you like, should these spells continue. Hopefully, however, that won't be the case. I suggest you just give it time."

Beth and Kerry both looked relieved, and Addison warmed at their clear affection for one another. He cared deeply for them, and the nature of their relationship was none of his business as long as they were happy and healthy.

❖

"Are you sure?" Kerry asked Beth. It was a Saturday evening a couple of weeks later. They had agreed to wait until Addison and Laura weren't in the house. The wait was long and arduous. Even their frequent stolen kisses didn't help much. Addison and Laura had gone to attend a band concert, which Kerry and Beth had politely begged out of, citing fatigue. In reality, both were brimming with anticipation.

Beth's confession to Kerry and her reaction to it had freed something within her. *I don't have to be afraid or ashamed. She understands. She loves me. She* loves *me.* That release in her fueled another, deeper longing to be as close as she could be to Kerry. She wasn't afraid of that intimacy anymore; she wanted it more than she'd ever wanted anything, even her nursing certificate.

"Yes," Beth exclaimed. "I'm sure! I'm very, very sure. It's what I want more than anything."

They had changed into nightgowns, together, in the same room with no hiding. It still made them a little shy, but they were able to laugh at themselves. They sat next to one another on the bed and looked into each other's eyes. As they did, their breaths quickened. It was Beth who took Kerry's face and kissed her on the mouth soulfully and tenderly.

Kerry thought she would melt, that they both would melt. They slid down on the bed together, kissing and clinging together, letting their feelings direct their movements. Hands explored, thighs crisscrossed. Kerry was desperate to touch Beth's naked flesh, and Beth seemed equally desperate to be touched. They were perfectly in tune.

"Tell me," Kerry breathed, "if I must stop."

"Don't stop," Beth said. "I don't want you to stop. I want everything. I'm not afraid. I want you so very much."

Kerry slid her hand under Beth's nightgown along her smooth thigh and past her hip to her side and finally to her breast. She moved slowly, still a little hesitant, holding back.

Beth closed her eyes in an involuntary response to so much stimulation and the feelings it invoked. Kerry's hands were warm and firm and moved slowly but surely over her body. They made her tingle all over. She was basking, she was reveling in the feelings. Kerry kissed her with such adoration and tenderness, she wanted to weep with joy. Her body seemed to know the ultimate purpose of the kisses and touches as it moved and opened and relaxed in preparation. She felt no fear.

Kerry lifted up Beth's nightgown and looked for one long moment. The movement caused Beth to open her eyes and see Kerry gazing at her naked body. She felt exposed but not ashamed by it. Kerry's expression was grave with love and something like hunger. Beth was still too shy and she closed her eyes again. The next thing she felt was warmth and wetness on her nipple, and she understood it was Kerry's mouth. A monumental wave of pleasure coursed down her spine and settled between her legs. She groaned and her hips jerked. Kerry lay down on her, pushing her body into the mattress. They heard the front door close downstairs and Addison and Laura's voices. Kerry looked at Beth with alarm.

Beth pushed her away and pulled her nightgown down. "They're home. We can't."

"But Beth—"

"No! Not when they're in the house. It's not possible."

Kerry lay back, glum and more frustrated than ever. She was going to have to think of something. It was clear this was an even more delicate proposition than she realized.

Later, after Beth had fallen into a restless sleep, Kerry lay awake looking at her. Her brow was furrowed and she murmured a little in her sleep. Kerry's anguish was tempered by compassion. She knew how Beth must have suffered at the hands of the vile old preacher. Kerry suddenly thought about Minny after Sally had set her to whoring when she was only thirteen. She was never the same. Kerry resolved to give Beth as much time as she needed and wanted. *She'll know when she's ready.*

❖

"Laura, my dear, please put your mind at ease. There's nothing to worry about. They're adults and can do as they wish."

Laura had again brought up her displeasure and unease with Kerry and Beth's seemingly odd behavior. She was attempting to engage Addison's attention and get him in agreement with her so she could proceed with what she wished to do. He was, as usual, being obtuse and stubborn.

"They are young women! Young women are flighty and impetuous. Surely that must concern you?" She pleaded with him. She pouted prettily and looked at him from under her eyelashes. She used a concerned tone of voice rather than angry one. Nothing was working very well. Addison remained infuriatingly indifferent.

The latest item to bother Laura was that Kerry had asked to borrow the carriage overnight. She couldn't say why; something was hovering just under her consciousness, though she couldn't say what it was. Whatever she sensed, it prompted her to want to intercede or, in this case, get Addison to intercede if possible. Any objections would have to come from him.

Kerry always had been and probably always would be steadfastly unresponsive to Laura's feelings. Laura had a glimmer of awareness that her treatment of Kerry, starting from the day Kerry walked into her house, was guaranteed to not produce any sort of emotional attachment on Kerry's part. But it didn't concern her. Kerry was an object in her orbit she couldn't control. Laura knew Beth and Kerry were conspiring and were up to no good, but she couldn't articulate what exactly put her so on edge. The secret conversations she listened to late at night only fueled her imagination. Kerry told Laura they would be away until late Sunday evening but hadn't told her why or where they were going, and Kerry wouldn't respond to her questions. Hence she was appealing to Addison as head of the house, but he wasn't cooperating.

"Kerry is capable of looking out for herself. And Beth as well, I dare say. They haven't indicated they're off to illicit rendezvous with young men, so I see no cause to worry," he said.

"That is where you're wrong, James Addison. I worry about Beth. Kerry is a bad influence."

Addison sighed. "Laura. Kerry may not behave how you wish she would, but, morally, she is above reproach. She works. She helps around the house. She has done nothing to warrant your distrust. As I said, this is her home for as long as she desires, and Beth's as well. They may come and go as they please. We aren't their parents, in any case."

"Oh, you're blind, Addison and you're wrong. We must serve as their parents. It's only right." She felt this was the only basis upon which to appeal to him, but so far it was ineffective. She was going to have to take matters into her own hands.

"Laura, I fail to see—"

She uttered a groan of frustration and strode out of the room. She was determined to find out the truth. *He will see and he will act as I wish him to.*

## Chapter Twenty-nine

"But why won't you tell me?" Beth asked. They were on their way downtown, but Kerry wouldn't tell her where they were going. She'd only said, "I don't wish to stay at home. We need privacy and Addison and Laura will be there."

She didn't need to elaborate. Beth knew very well. She couldn't say how she knew they must be secretive, but she knew it as she knew in her heart that she loved Kerry and wanted to be with her forever and in every way possible. It seemed as though that was possible. *I am free now. I no longer need to fear my reaction when she touches me. I want her to touch me as much as she wants to.* That thought made Beth shiver, not from cold but in an utterly pleasant way.

Whenever Beth thought of Kerry and Kerry touching her, she got a flutter in her stomach. It was a pleasant frisson of anticipation, as though for a party or present, but something more as well. As they had discussed their plans and gathered their things and packed a small suitcase, she had smiled at Kerry and was rewarded with a blazing smile and a look of such love it made her faint. She was a bit weary, as usual, from the long day on the wards at the Presidio General Hospital, but she scarcely noticed it, so caught up in the anticipation of their night together.

They set off in the carriage. It seemed to Beth like a holiday as they made their way downtown. It had been a few years since she had actually been on Market Street. It was early evening, the sun hadn't set. Downtown San Francisco bustled all around them. The street was filled with vehicles of every type; cable cars crisscrossed the main street. Wooden carts hauled goods of all types. Pedestrians walked in between the various vehicles, some slowly, as though they were on a country lane instead of a city street. Some darted and dodged the traffic.

Beth took it all in with a sense of exhilaration. She watched Kerry deftly navigate through the chaos, her face set in concentration but clearly enjoying herself. Beth thought how good it was to be a citizen of the great city. She spotted a large open vehicle filled with several severe-looking gentlemen in suits, but no horses were pulling it. It moved on its own power.

"Kerry, look! What is that? How does it go without horses?"

Kerry followed Beth's pointing finger. "Ah. That's one of those horseless carriages. The au-to-mo-bile." She pronounced it carefully. "It's the new thing. Teddy told me that it runs on gasoline, which must be refilled." She laughed. "He's obsessed with getting one but they're so costly, he can't afford it."

Beth smiled. "Well, horses are a great deal more pleasant, but still you must care for them and feed them. The au-to-mo-bile will not tire, I expect." Beth thought of how that vehicle might be used for patients.

"I want to show you something, two things, really," Kerry said. "Look here. It's the Palace Hotel." They had reached the corner of New Montgomery Street and Market, and on their right stood the gigantic seven-story hotel. Beth craned her neck upward to the top.

"I knew your hotel was large, but I never dreamed it was this big. Are we going to stay there?"

"No. I don't wish to be noticed and become the subject of gossip. I have enough trouble as it is."

"I see," Beth said, somberly. "Well? Where *are* we going?"

"You'll see momentarily. I want to show you another place."

They drove a few more blocks down Market Street. Beth quelled her curiosity; it was so lovely just to be out together. Kerry stopped in front of a building fronted by huge white Romanesque columns even more grand than the front of the Sutro Baths.

"What is this?" Beth asked.

"The Bank of California. I have a savings account there my father started for me and Addison looks after. It's for me whenever I want it. I add to it now since I'm paid as a cook. I never knew what I would do with it, but I know now. I want to buy a house."

Beth looked at Kerry, who had stopped the carriage in front of the bank and was gazing at the white columns with a pensive air.

Beth cleared her throat. "This house you speak of, would I live there with you?"

"Yes. You would. Of course. We can't afford it yet, but someday."

"You've thought a great deal about this, haven't you?"

"Beth, I think of nothing but you. And me. And of us together. I want to give you something." Kerry reached inside her jacket and produced a plain gold ring.

She took Beth's left hand and carefully placed it on her third finger. She sat back and smiled. "Now you will be an honest married woman. We couldn't check into a hotel otherwise. I must preserve your reputation."

Beth gazed at the ring then at Kerry's tender expression, then back again. She nearly wept she was so touched, but another little butterfly flutter inside closely followed that feeling, and her cheeks grew warm.

To cover up her reaction, which unnerved her, she spoke briskly. "I hope a supper of some sort is coming up before too long. I'm positively famished."

Kerry grinned at her with eyebrows raised and Beth knew that she had been caught out. The thought didn't disturb her though. Kerry clucked the horses back into motion and merely said, "Certainly, love. Coming right up."

❖

Kerry had dressed from head to toe in fine men's clothes she'd left in the carriage. Beth was taken aback both by how wonderful she looked and by her daring. She wore a wool jacket and vest and striped trousers and boots. She also wore a hat. Beth ventured to ask her why.

"Because, my love, I don't want to attract attention. As a husband and wife, we will be invisible—and no source of curiosity."

They drove past the mighty Palace Hotel once more, which took up an entire city block.

"It's the largest and most luxurious hotel in the West," Kerry pointed out proudly.

"And to think you work there and cook in their restaurant. It's a marvel. I'm so proud of you!"

Beth squeezed Kerry's arm and smiled at her lovingly.

Kerry's heart turned over and she had hold to back her tears. None of the abuse by the boys in the kitchen had ever made her cry, but a smile and a compliment from Beth undid her as nothing else could.

"Your work is more important than mine," she said seriously. "You must take care of the wounded and sick soldiers."

"There. We won't argue about this. We both have our purpose."

They found a restaurant to have a quiet dinner. Beth teased Kerry. "Don't you want to criticize the food, since you're a cook in such a fancy restaurant?"

"No. It pleases me to eat a dinner that someone else has prepared. It's a relief to not think about it. I'm enjoying it."

"It's true. We're always our own worst critics." Beth said.

After dinner they turned north on Sansome Street and stopped in front of a modest building. It was a hotel—not nearly as fancy as the Palace, but it was genteel and comfortable. They were shown to a modest but comfortable room.

"Should we retire now?" Kerry asked, full of anticipation.

Beth, suddenly shy and apprehensive as they faced each other across the bed, said, "Oh, I saw a piano downstairs in the sitting room. What do you say we go downstairs and I'll play awhile."

Kerry started to frown but stopped in time to arrange her features in a sweet smile. "Of course," she said, gesturing gallantly to Beth to exit the room first.

No one else was about in the public area of the hotel. Most of the guests were still at dinner or otherwise out for the evening; it was only eight p.m.

The piano, surprisingly, was a good one; it was an upright and seemed new. "It's even in tune!" Beth exclaimed. She opened the bench and pulled out a handful of sheet music. "Let's see what they have."

Kerry stood by; she didn't wish to say much. She had deepened her voice to accomplish their checking in but staying in that register was a strain. More than that, she was churning inside with a mixture of desire, terror, and impatience. She was taken aback that Beth wished to go slowly. She had assumed that Beth was as eager as she was.

Beth sat down on the bench and motioned Kerry to sit next to her. Then she launched into the *Moonlight Sonata*. Its melancholy elegiac notes brought both of them into the present. Kerry watched Beth's face and waited for that dreaminess to appear, that otherworldly glow Beth seemed to get when she was playing. Then she looked down at Beth's hands. They were strong but delicate; they moved over the keys with assurance. Kerry thought of how it would feel when Beth put her hands on her. She shivered again. Beth caught her movement and smiled at her, and this time her smile was mischievous, and a little lascivious. Kerry smiled back meaningfully and patted her shoulder. The piece ended and they were quiet a moment, communicating with their eyes. Beth looked away when their gazes held and became heated.

"What else do we have?" she asked, riffling through the music. "Ah." She set up another music pamphlet on the stand.

Kerry read the title: "Beautiful Dreamer."

"Mr. Stephen Foster," Beth said, somewhat primly. "He's a fine songwriter. I enjoy most of his pieces, especially this one." She turned and gave Kerry a smile of such radiance, Kerry's insides grew warm and liquid. *Beth. Beth. I do love you. And astonishingly, you have fallen in love with me.* She tore her eyes away from Beth long enough to read some of the words to the song as Beth played.

> *Beautiful dreamer, wake unto me*
> *Starlight and dewdrops are waiting for thee*
> *Sounds of the rude world, Heard in the day*
> *Lull'd by the moonlight have all pass'd away*
>
> *Beautiful dreamer, queen of my song*
> *List while I woo thee with soft melody*
> *Gone are the cares of life's busy throng*
> *Beautiful dreamer awake unto me*
> *Beautiful dreamer awake unto me*
>
> *Beautiful dreamer, out on the sea*
> *Mermaids are chanting the wild Lorelie*
> *Over the streamlet vapors are borne*
> *Waiting to fade at the bright coming morn*
>
> *Beautiful dreamer, beam on my heart*
> *E'en as the morn on the streamlet and sea*
> *Then will all clouds of sorrow depart*
> *Beautiful dreamer, awake unto me*
> *Beautiful dreamer, awake unto me*

She watched Beth play through the song and spoke the words to herself. She saw that Beth caught their meaning as well, because her face grew still and her eyelids lowered. At the end, Beth left her hands on the piano keys for a long moment, then turned and said, "Shall we go upstairs?"

## Chapter Thirty

Beth saw Kerry's hand shake as she lit the oil lamp and it filled the small room with an orange glow. Beth came in and shut the door, turned the key, and leaned back against the doorframe.

Kerry whispered, "Shall I leave the lamp on or would you prefer darkness?"

Beth held her eyes. "We've shared a room and a bed for these many months. I'm surprised at how shy I feel again."

"I feel the same."

Kerry crossed the room and stood in front of Beth, who put her hand on Kerry's chest, right over her heart. Beth could feel it beating rapidly, making her glad she wasn't alone in her nervousness.

"Let's leave the lamp on. For now," Beth said.

Kerry gathered Beth in her arms and kissed her. Beth said a silent prayer that all would be well. They kissed for a long time, both to prolong the moment and because it was such a pleasure. Their privacy was a gift.

Beth found it hard to breathe as Kerry unbuttoned her dress and helped her out of it. "It's good that I'm not a corset wearer. That would surely defeat you." Her words made Kerry laugh for a moment.

"It's well that you're not. I can hardly imagine how you'd be able to do your work on the wards." She slipped the dress off Beth's shoulders and it dropped to the floor. Beth locked her gaze to Kerry's and carefully stepped out of the dress one foot at a time. They bent simultaneously to pick it up and knocked their heads together. They both groaned, rubbing their heads.

"We are a pair, aren't we?" Beth said.

"A pair of what? Fools?" Kerry asked, but she was laughing. "Clumsy oafs?"

"Let me take care of that." Beth picked up the dress and took it to the armoire. As she folded it, she saw her own hands shaking. She stood in front of the armoire for an extra moment.

Kerry came up behind Beth as Beth closed the armoire and put her hand on her bare shoulder. "You're cold," she whispered.

Beth turned around and they embraced again. Beth reached up to take the pins out of her hair.

"Let me," Kerry said. She pulled out the hairpins and Beth's hair fell over her shoulders. Kerry moved her hands into Beth's hair, tugging gently. Beth shivered.

"Warm me up," Beth breathed. They moved toward the bed kissing and sat down.

"Aren't you going to take your clothes off?" Beth asked.

"Oh. Yes. I guess I must." Kerry removed her shirt and shoes and pants.

To Beth she seemed to be moving in slow motion. Though she had seen Kerry naked briefly during their personal moments, seeing her like this was exceptional. Together they pulled the bedspread down and got under it. As they kissed, Beth warmed up, and as she warmed, her blood heated; it was almost enough to quell her nervousness. Kerry moved tentatively, seeming reluctant to remove Beth's underclothes.

Beth took Kerry's hand and slid it around her breast. She fondled it and Beth gasped as her nipple hardened against Kerry's palm. She reverently unbuttoned Beth's chemise and pulled it off. She dropped the garment over the side of the bed and turned to gaze at Beth's nude body as she had before.

Beth looked up at her face, her eyes so dark they looked completely black, and Beth heard her sharp intake of breath. Kerry lay down and, for the first time, they touched from head to foot, legs entwined with no barriers between them. Kerry kissed Beth ardently from her forehead to her cheeks to ears and neck and back to her lips. They kissed for such a long time, Beth was breathless and the place between her legs was throbbing. She wanted more but didn't know what to ask for or how to ask for it. She slid her hand around the back of Kerry's neck, which was warm and a little damp.

"Kerry, dearest?"

Kerry stopped kissing her and looked at her quizzically. "Yes, love?"

"You promised you would show me how much you love me. Back at the conservatory—the second time you kissed me."

Kerry rolled over on her side but kept a hand on Beth's stomach, making slow circles that maddened her.

"Yes, I did and I do love you."

"Well, I feel that, but you're driving me mad."

"Oh? Well, that's all to the good."

"You!" Beth slapped Kerry's chest and they laughed.

Then Kerry grew serious. "I didn't want to go too swiftly for you, in case…"

Beth understood what she meant.

"Oh, love. That's over. Since that night in the park when we talked and I made my confession, I feel in my soul that I'm free. You've freed me. Your love has freed me. Please don't be frightened."

Kerry looked at her for a long moment, then began kissing her again, this time her hands moving over Beth restlessly, insistently. Her palms were very warm but dry. Her touch was light and firm. The sensations captivated Beth. It seemed her body was no longer under her control. She gave herself over to it and to Kerry completely, without reservation or fear. Kerry parted her legs—not roughly but with purpose. Beth gasped and her hips jerked. Kerry's fingers probed her, seeking, teasing, exquisitely torturous. Kerry took one of her nipples into her mouth once again and flicked her tongue over it again and again.

Beth's nervous system was overwhelmed. A pressure of immense pleasure began to build. Her thighs and abdomen tightened and relaxed and then tightened again. She thrashed involuntarily until the feeling coalesced into one intense wave and she cried out. Kerry wouldn't release her but kept hold of her, stroking her gently until it happened again. Beth lay panting, her strength gone. Kerry kissed her face, her eyes, her cheeks, murmuring, "I love you" over and over.

❖

Afterward, they lay quietly. Kerry propped herself up on one elbow and with her other hand stroked Beth's face and neck lightly.

"I've never felt this way," Beth said finally. Her eyes were closed but she smiled slightly.

"It's wonderful, isn't it?"

"There is truly nothing else like it." Beth had never given any thought to the idea of her body as an instrument of pleasure. She had scarcely ever entertained the idea of pleasure in any form. She knew of bodies as mechanical entities: they absorbed food and excreted waste;

they breathed and slept; they grew diseased or got hurt; they died. That was what she knew of the human body, her own and everyone else's. Kerry showed her things about herself she'd never imagined. She had known, of course, about the sexual relations of men and women; it was just that she hadn't associated anything like that with herself. Kerry called forth sensations from her flesh that left her breathless, craving, and at last satisfied. She understood what it meant for someone to make love. She embraced the paradox of arousal and release. *You want desperately for the feeling to never stop yet you fear you might die of it. But you don't die. That sensation reaches its delightful crescendo and then explodes.*

"Show me how to do it. Show me how to give you what you just gave me."

"Oh, that's easy, my love. We start like this." Kerry kissed Beth and their lips molded together and opened. She moved Beth's hand to her breast and then between her legs.

"Oh, my," Beth said, astonished at what she felt. Kerry was soft, so very soft, and so warm.

"Is that how I felt to you?" she asked. Kerry merely nodded, her breath coming in short gasps as her hips pushed against Beth's hand. Beth watched her face as she moved her fingers the same way Kerry had. She was full of wonder at how Kerry looked and how she felt. She was humbled by her ability to give the same profound pleasure to Kerry that Kerry gave to her. Everything felt so natural.

❖

It was late that night before they slept and late in the morning when they woke up. A sharp knock on the door awakened them. Kerry said in an urgent whisper, "Answer! Tell them we'll be out presently."

Beth cleared her throat and said, "Who is it?"

"Sorry to bother you, madam. Breakfast service will be over soon."

"Ah, thank you for letting us know," Beth said pleasantly. She started to giggle. Kerry giggled as well and they snuggled under the quilt. They looked at each other in the light coming from the window.

"I can scarcely believe we're here together. I can never remember feeling like this," Beth said. "I'm so in love with you, Kerry dearest. I knew I loved you before, but now we're so much closer. It is, it is…" She opened her eyes wide and sighed. "It is more than—It is a miracle."

Kerry smiled. "I wanted to tell you but it was better to show you."

"You have shown me and I'm a changed woman." They clung together and their bodies moved against each other. They kissed over and over.

Beth broke off to say, "We must get up and put our clothes on and leave. I can scarcely bear to be parted from you, although I know we aren't parted exactly, but only must go back to the world outside."

"We must."

"You don't suppose they'd let us stay in the room a while longer?" Beth asked, suddenly.

"I don't know. It's Sunday. I could ask, I suppose."

"Oh, do!" Beth said enthusiastically. "And ask if we may have some food brought in."

Kerry dutifully dressed and went down to the lobby. She talked to the desk clerk solemnly man to man.

"Newlyweds, are you?" He winked.

"Yes. If you could leave us until the evening, I will make it worth your while," Kerry said. "And if you would send out for some food. Let us say some turtle soup, some bread, and a jug of drinking water."

"Consider it done," the young man said.

Kerry went back upstairs to their room. Beth was sitting in bed with the covers pulled up to her armpits but her hair was flowing over her shoulders, and when Kerry opened the door, she smiled so lovingly, Kerry nearly wept again with joy.

"It is all arranged, love. I asked them to bring us something to eat in an hour."

"Well. I *am* hungry and I believe I should be very tired, as we got so little sleep, but…" Kerry was methodically removing her clothes and Beth was becoming distracted watching her. "I'm less concerned with my hunger or need for sleep than I am with other things."

"Is that right?" Kerry had taken off her shirt and was just then unbuckling the leather belt she wore. Beth stared at her, momentarily speechless.

"My only need right now is you," Beth said, finally.

When Kerry finally finished disrobing, she walked to the bed, completely naked. Beth could scarcely breathe, the sight affected her in so many ways.

She said nothing but turned the covers back.

# Chapter Thirty-one

B eth floated through her days on the wards. She was especially nice to the patients and extraordinarily cheerful and companionable with the other nurses. Beth's coworkers noted she had never said much beyond what was necessary information, but now she actually spoke before being asked a question. They remarked upon it and teased her. But Beth only smiled and said nothing.

Marjorie Reynolds was perhaps her closest friend, and they chatted and occasionally ate together when they had the time. She asked Beth directly, "You have an air. Is it someone special?"

"I'm just in a good mood." That was certainly true, if vague. She was supremely contented carrying out her duties and thinking about Kerry. In the back of her mind always was the memory of their love the night before and the anticipation of what would come when they could finally be alone and in bed together in the dark. It was not as it was at the hotel. They tried to be quiet so as not to wake Addison and Laura. They didn't discuss, however, the idea that they would do nothing but sleep. They were far too enamored of each other to consider not making love.

It was difficult at times, since Kerry didn't often return home until after midnight if she was working during dinner service. Beth would return home at six thirty, have supper with Addison and Laura, then retire to bed and fall into an exhausted sleep, only to wake to Kerry's kisses and caresses. They would make love until they slept from sheer exhaustion. To make up sleep they often didn't get out of bed until noon on Sunday.

"Are you sure that's what you wish to do?" Beth asked doubtfully, stretching beneath the covers. It was their first Sunday off in several weeks. Kerry proposed that they go back to the Sutro Baths, but Beth was tired from the workweek and wanted to stay home.

"Yes, I'm quite sure. Think how enjoyable it will be now." Kerry's dark eyes danced with mischief. She grinned and raised her eyebrows.

Beth laughed. "You're a devil. I'm not sure I should agree to this."

"Oh, please say you will, Bethy," Kerry said. "We must practice your swimming or you'll forget."

"Very well."

Sutro's Land's End train wound around the cliffs above the Pacific Ocean. It passed near the Cliff House, which hung precariously off the side of a giant cliff. Up above was Adolph Sutro's huge mansion. Beth and Kerry used the cover of Beth's dress to hold hands discreetly. It was a trial for them to keep straight faces as they obtained their dressing-room key and clothes baskets. The bored attendant glanced at them curiously but made no comment.

Kerry was dressed as usual in trousers and a shirt, but she was jacketless, for the day was warm. It was clear to even a casual observer that she was a young woman. Kerry went into the tiny room first and Beth followed. Beth threw the deadbolt lock and turned. The moment she turned, Kerry pushed her against the door and kissed her fervently. Beth instinctively returned the kiss but put a hand on Kerry's chest and pushed her back gently.

"Kerry, dearest, we're here to go bathing. Let's make use of the time." The corners of Kerry's mouth turned down but she said nothing. They silently removed their clothes and put on the bedraggled bathing costumes, never taking their eyes from one another.

I could touch her breast right this moment, Kerry thought. What would she say? What would she do? But she refrained.

They found themselves once again in the large saltwater pool and surrounded by hundreds of Sunday holidaymakers. The local ministers had complained of Mr. Sutro's godlessness of having his business open on Sunday, but to no avail. The San Francisco citizenry were overjoyed to have the diversion and flocked to the Sutro Baths in record numbers.

"Let me see you swim," Kerry said, liking the way the swim costume hugged Beth's curves.

"Oh, I think I must have another lesson," Beth responded, much to Kerry's surprise. It was a sunny day and the sunlight filtered through the glass roof and walls of the Baths, rendering the pools of water bright blue. Beth's eyes were more green than hazel in the light, and to Kerry they seemed to glitter with joy.

"Very well," Kerry said, and bent in the water and stretched out her arms. Beth lay down on her back. She looked up at Kerry and went limp. Their eyes locked together, and Kerry kept her face still and grave. Beth didn't move. Kerry was hard pressed to not kiss her at that moment. Her expression was one of perfect trust and love.

Kerry cleared her throat. "Would you like to practice your stroke?" she said softly.

"Yes, I believe I should," Beth said, though she could scarcely breathe. She tore her eyes from Kerry's and turned on her side and began to move her arms languidly and kick her feet. She fell into a rhythm and Kerry walked with her for a moment before releasing her. Beth glided away under her own power, staying on the surface easily. Kerry swam after her and they swam side by side to the other side of the pool. The many other swimmers were invisible to them and they were deaf to their shouts and splashes. They might as well have been completely alone. They swam back and forth for a while. Beth was still a bit tentative in the water. She watched Kerry play on the ropes and with the rings and the slides very much as she did during their first visit. *She is so at home in the water, so graceful and sure.* As she watched Kerry, she mentally removed the ugly faded bathing dress she wore. In her mind she thought of Kerry in bed or in the bathtub.

When Beth was twelve, she discovered and devoured *Bullfinch's Mythology.* One of the stories that had struck her forcefully at the time, though she had no idea why, was the story of the Pleiades. That myth came back to her as she watched Kerry. To the twelve-year-old Beth, Artemis the huntress was a figure of awe. Her companions were the dozen beautiful girls called the Pleiades. Beth read that they would often stop at a clear forest pool to bathe.

In Beth's mind, the Sutro Baths was transformed into a tree-shaded pond where the sunlight floated. She and Kerry swam and cavorted with a crowd of lovely, nude young women. Their girlish laughter rang as they splashed about and chased each other. Beth caught up with Kerry in the water and, grabbing her shoulder, spun her around so they could embrace, and their wet bodies came together deliciously as they kissed.

"Beth?"

Beth came back to the present with a start. She was sitting on the side of the pool, her feet dangling in the water, and Kerry lay at her knees grinning up at her.

"Are you all right, love?" Kerry asked. "You look odd. What are you thinking?"

"Yes. I'm fine." She smiled to prove it. "Are you ready to leave?"

Kerry smiled even more widely. "Yes. I most certainly am."

## CHAPTER THIRTY-TWO

Kerry playfully stuck her tongue in Beth's navel, making her jump. She laughed when Beth lightly slapped the side of her head.

"That tickles," Beth said.

"Does it?" Kerry asked, laughing. "Perhaps I should do it again." It was Sunday morning, and though the sun was bright outside, neither felt especially compelled to rise and put her clothes on.

Kerry kissed Beth's stomach and abdomen instead and laughed as she jerked. She moved back up and pulled Beth into her arms, thinking it was a good time for what she had in mind. She had wanted to wait a bit and also to have more privacy than they could manage at the Grants' for what she intended. They moved together kissing. Kerry moved her hand lower, touching Beth gently but insistently. She was rewarded with a light groan. She kissed her way down Beth's body and finally parted her legs.

Beth's eyes were closed and she was luxuriating in Kerry's kisses and caresses. She had wanted to complain when Kerry stopped touching her on her most sensitive area to resume kissing her, but she felt it was hardly fair. She felt well loved and well taken care of. She had, however, become delightedly used to a certain progression, a certain order that was most gratifying. The change confused her.

Then she felt Kerry's tongue; it made her jump. It was such an unusual feeling she wasn't sure at first if she liked it. She propped herself up on her elbows and opened her eyes and watched Kerry for a moment. But the sensations were too much and she closed them and lay back down. *Oh. My God.* Kerry's tongue moved over her most sensitive parts, delving inside her only to move back to her clitoris. The world spun and she held onto Kerry's shoulders to keep from falling off.

"I hope you didn't mind," Kerry said some time later.

"No. Not at all. It was just—overwhelming," Beth said. Her breathing was finally slowing down. Her limbs were heavy and she felt relaxed but not sleepy.

"I couldn't have imagined a feeling such as that. The other way—that's wonderful too."

"How would you like to try it?" Kerry grinned.

"Oh, I fear I wouldn't be any good," Beth said, "but I want to, very much." She gazed at Kerry with adoration, and Kerry kissed her again.

They kept on kissing for some time and Beth continued to press her fingers against Kerry's warm flesh. *If I can't do this properly will she stop loving me? I hope not.* Kerry's body stiffened and surged against her.

"Now?" Beth asked.

"Yes. Please. Now." Kerry gasped, her eyes huge and dark.

She kissed Kerry's sharp hipbones and her flat smooth stomach and carefully lowered herself between her legs. *This is certainly amazing. I never dreamed of such intimacy. It's truly a miracle.* Her efforts were rewarded quickly. Kerry cried out and twisted convulsively. She clutched at Beth's hair. To Beth's surprise, Kerry pushed her away, and she looked up, alarmed.

"My love? Is something wrong?"

Kerry gasped for breath. "No, not at all. It's too much for me. The pleasure. Stop a moment."

They lay close together, not speaking for a time. Beth was feeling unaccountably pleased with herself except for a tiny part of her mind—the evil, jealous part that thought, against her will, Everything she has done with me, she has already done. In a moment that should be one of her happiest and most loving, Beth was appalled to find herself thinking of Kerry with other women. She made a sound, a sigh—nearly a grunt. Kerry propped herself on her elbow and peered into her face, looking concerned.

"Beth, love? What is it? What's the matter?"

Beth was startled at Kerry's perception and ashamed of her thoughts. "It's nothing."

"It's not," Kerry said firmly. "I know you and that wasn't the sigh you make when you're satisfied. It was different altogether. Please tell me. I won't be angry."

"No, truly, it was nothing. Don't worry."

"I see." Kerry clearly wasn't mollified, but she was graciously willing to cease her questions. Beth felt even worse. She didn't know how she should feel. *I couldn't really expect her to be virginal like me, considering what her life has been like. Why do I feel that what we have together isn't as good somehow, or not unique? I'm being childish and ungrateful.*

❖

"I have an idea," Kerry said, some weeks after Beth's withdrawal after lovemaking. "You must think my childhood was appalling with what I did with Sally and the crimping I carried on with Jack, but it wasn't all like that. I want to show you something. Would you come with me?"

Beth spun around, again astounded at Kerry's insight. *Has she become a mind reader then? She has the ability to understand my body as though it were her own.*

"Come with you where, Kerry?" Beth asked somewhat suspiciously.

"Oh, my dear, don't be frightened." Kerry laughed, upsetting Beth a little. "I'm not proposing we go back to the Grey Dog and visit Sally."

"I should say not," Beth said, indignantly. "I have no desire to ever speak to that woman. Once was quite enough. If I saw her again, I'd be tempted to shoot her."

"My goodness, Bethy. I had no idea your feelings were so strong."

Kerry was still smiling and her tone indicated she considered Beth's reaction highly amusing. This angered Beth more.

"What has happened to you, love? You're in a healing profession and you wish to inflict harm on the likes of Sally."

"Oh, it's all very well for you to make fun of me. It's an enormously amusing situation to you then. You have no idea how I feel."

Kerry turned serious in an instant. "I'm sorry, Beth, if I've upset you. Would you tell me please what disturbs you so?"

Beth's anger died down and again she was ashamed of herself for her unreasonable response.

"Kerry, dearest, it's just that—these many months since we've been together—I've felt so… Oh, I'm not saying this well."

"Bethy, it's fine. Just tell me. I promise you I'll listen."

It was those words, almost exactly, that had finally reached her on that night in Golden Gate Park, when her reserve had finally cracked and she confessed about her abuse by Svenhard.

She looked into Kerry's warm brown eyes and became teary. "Oh, it's so silly. I'm such a fool. You'll think me so ridiculous."

Kerry put an arm around her and wiped a tear from her cheek. She smiled. "No, I won't. I want you to tell me."

Beth sniffed and took a breath, gathering her thoughts. She looked at Kerry. "I love you so much. I'm so in love with you. I love what we are with each other, what we do together." Beth blushed inadvertently. "It's just that I know that you've been with other women and done the same things with—" She stopped, embarrassed, but she wanted to say it, she wanted to tell Kerry the truth.

"I can't forget that you touched other women the same way you touch me. And they have touched you."

Kerry put a finger on her lips and said, softly, "Beth. I know what your trouble is. You're jealous."

Beth's eyes widened. "Yes, I suppose so. Isn't it the height of girlish silliness?"

Kerry laughed again but it wasn't an unkind laugh. "Well, Elizabeth," she said solemnly, "you *are* a girl, after all."

"Yes, but I'm grown up now and it's not becoming and it's terribly immature—"

"Beth? I may have done things with another girl. I have. I can't change the past. Nor can you."

That gave Beth pause, for it reminded her again of what had been done to her. She waited to hear the rest.

"Nonetheless, I tell you this with all my heart. My body, my hands, my lips may have touched her body and given her pleasure. That's true. But there has never been, nor will there ever be, anyone other than you who has touched my heart, my soul, or my spirit as you have. And that makes the same touches I exchanged with Sally trivial. With you they're entirely new. I'm new again with you. You came to me a virgin, and I tell you I came to you that way. I was virgin in love. Only you will ever have that part of me." Kerry lifted Beth's hand to her lips and kissed her palm.

"Oh, my God, Kerry, I know that. I'm sorry. I know how much you love me."

"I do. And since I love you, I want to know all about you and I want you to know all about me. So come with me, please. I want to show you something."

❖

It was still there. The sign was the same.

"What is this place?" Beth asked with some anxiety. She took in the sign, Oddities of Interest.

"This is the Cobweb Palace. Now, I know you have no love of spiders." Kerry was teasing her. "But spiders aside, oddities aside, I saw something here when I was only ten, and I didn't know then what I was seeing, but now I do."

"You're being mysterious again. Please tell me I won't have a thousand spiderwebs sticking to me and nasty spiders all over me."

Kerry took her hand. "Trust me, Bethy. Once you see what I have to show you, spiders will disappear like the fog every morning."

Beth still looked skeptical.

They walked through the front door and blinked and peered in the dimness until they could see. Many of the animals were gone, long dead, even the raucous obscenity-spewing parrot.

Old Pop Warner still stood behind the bar, but he was getting on in years. The wags said spiders would soon be spinning their webs over him as though he were one of his own oddities of interest.

He nodded an indifferent greeting to them.

Kerry slowly led Beth around the Cobweb Palace and they stared for a good amount of time at each of the many portraits of women.

"I came here as a youngster," Kerry whispered. "The animals and the other things amused me, but these pictures drew me as nothing else did. I came to see them over and over. I didn't know why then, but I understand now. My younger self was drawn to these women because I knew they would be my destiny. I didn't know it would be one in particular." Kerry smiled lovingly at Beth. "So now you know that my childhood held some innocence, some wonder, some love. It wasn't as depraved as you might imagine."

Beth took her hand. "I do know that. Something good must have made you what you are. I'm sure Addison had much to do with that, but still you were already fifteen when you went to him and so much had happened to you before that. We truly cannot change the past and can gain nothing by regret."

Kerry knew Beth was speaking of her but thinking of herself. She took Beth's hand and led her back outside.

"There's certainly nothing in my present or in my future that will ever cause me any regret." She looked Beth in the eye, and Beth's eyes answered her. They smiled at one another and took a nice stroll along the waterfront. Even on the wicked Barbary Coast, the sparkling San Francisco Bay reflected the sky, and its sun lit them with its own air of innocence.

# Chapter Thirty-three

Addison and Laura returned home from church and Addison helped Laura out of the carriage.

"I shall be home in an hour or so," he told her. He was off to the hospital for a short while.

"As you wish," Laura said, bored.

She put her coat and hat away in the armoire and went into the hallway. It was clear Kerry and Beth weren't about. *They aren't awake yet. It's disgraceful laziness.*

When she reached the top of the stairs, she stopped. She heard their voices. They were muffled, indistinct. The door was still closed.

*Do I dare?* Laura was consumed with curiosity. She couldn't resist the compulsion.

She crept to the door on her hands and knees and put her eye to the keyhole. Her mouth dropped open.

Beth's back was turned toward her; she could tell by her long swath of dark blond hair falling across her back. She focused, however, on a hand moving over that back from shoulder blade down to—Laura couldn't bring herself to say the word even to herself. The hand disappeared under the cover, then moved back up and then back down. She couldn't quite make out what they were saying, but it was clear what they were doing.

❖

Laura sat in the armchair, pretending to knit. Beth and Kerry came through the front door, their laughter bouncing off the walls and into her ears.

"Good afternoon!" they caroled on their way to the kitchen. Laura glared in the direction of their retreating backs. Their high spirits infuriated her, and her inability to confront them without revealing her subterfuge frustrated her. *It is the same with Addison. He would demand to know how I came to form my conclusions, and then if I tell him, he will be angry. He would never notice their behavior; he's entirely unaware of anything except his work.* Laura's multiple resentments coalesced into one very large black cloud, and she fumed silently.

*There must be some way, something I can do.* Then she had a moment of clarity. *Beth's parents. That's the key. They'll want to remove her from a degrading situation. I can explain it so it doesn't reflect badly on Addison and me. That is what I shall do. I can separate them. Beth's parents will see to that. When Beth has to leave and Addison finds out why, then surely he will understand and agree with me. He will tell Kerry to leave.* She was satisfied. She felt better than she had in weeks.

❖

It was a pleasantly warm July afternoon. Laura stood outside Hammond's Dry Goods Store, suddenly hesitant. How would she frame what she'd come to say? She squared her shoulders, straightened her hat, and marched through the front door. She recognized Mr. Hammond, who stood behind the counter adding up a customer's purchases.

Laura waited until the transaction was complete and the customer had departed, then she smiled.

"Mr. Hammond?" she asked.

He nodded, with a quizzical expression. "Madam. May I assist you?"

"Ah, you don't recognize me, perhaps," she said in her most pleasant social voice.

"Er. I'm not sure."

"I am Dr. Grant's wife. We met at the hospital at your daughter's graduation from nursing school last year. Oh, I think it must be a year and four months ago."

"Oh. Yes, I believe I do."

"Mr. Hammond, I wish to speak to you and to your wife."

"I beg your pardon, Mrs. Grant. It's the middle of a workday and…" He looked as though he might refuse.

Laura thought impatiently, Oh, deliver me from small-time

shopkeepers. "It is important. It concerns your daughter, Beth. Please indulge me. I beg you."

"Very well." He reluctantly put the Closed for Lunch sign on his door and they went upstairs to the flat.

Mrs. Hammond offered a cup of tea, which Laura refused, and they settled uneasily around the kitchen table. The Hammonds gazed curiously at her, and she had a brief moment of doubt before she steeled herself. She abruptly said, "It concerns your daughter, Elizabeth."

George raised his eyebrows and glanced quickly at his wife, whose expression was blank, impassive. He said nothing, however, and waited for Laura to continue.

"I feel I must tell you something extremely painful and difficult to say. I only say this for her sake and for yours," Laura added. She was gaining confidence; she knew her motives were pure. "She has fallen in with bad company. I do regret to say that the company is Dr. Grant's foster daughter, Kerry."

Now the Hammonds looked deeply confused. "I beg your pardon, Mrs. Grant, but I'm not at all clear what your concern is."

Laura, having stated what she considered sufficient cause for alarm, was at a loss what to say further. In her mind, the only course of action for the Hammonds was clear: they must fetch Beth home without delay.

"I, um, wish to say that Beth has come under evil influence and—"

George said, abruptly, "This would be your foster daughter, Kerry? She is the evil influence?" The tone with which George uttered "foster daughter" indicated clearly that he felt that Laura was definitely at fault for whatever had happened. It was irksome, since Laura never used the term "foster daughter" in regard to Kerry and herself, but it seemed she couldn't attempt to explain that now.

"Well, yes. I have reason to believe she harbors unnatural tendencies." She was uncomfortably aware that she had inadvertently implicated herself and Addison as possessing some guilt for allowing such a situation to develop, but she forced herself to ignore that thought and soldier on.

George looked angry. "You have a great deal of gall to come here and tell us this when she has been living in your house these many months."

"George—" Frieda said, but he waved away her protest.

"You must leave now, Mrs. Grant. You have said what you came to say. I scarcely think the three of us have anything more to discuss." He stood up and Laura followed, uncharacteristically at a loss for words. She had expected a *little* gratitude, at least. She walked stiffly to the cable car stop, angry at having a mere shopkeeper dismiss her, one whose daughter was living under her roof, at that. She could only hope some of what she had said had gotten through their thick skulls.

## Chapter Thirty-four

Addison was irritated when Nurse Bennett called him off the ward to speak with George Hammond, who had appeared and demanded an audience with him, immediately.

Addison protested that he had a full load of patients to examine. When Nurse Bennett told him the name of the caller, it took him a moment to understand who it was. He then grew worried that something was amiss with Beth. When he saw Mr. Hammond's expression, he invited him to come to his office where they could have some privacy.

"What is it?" he asked anxiously. "Has something happened to Beth?"

George looked at Addison contemptuously. "I think you might be able to tell me that."

Addison raised his eyebrows. "Please, sir. I have no time for foolishness. State the reason for your visit," he said impatiently, hoping to convince the man to get to his point. Thinking of George's complicity in Beth's childhood torture filled him with fury.

"Your wife came to see us, Frieda and me. She wanted to let us know that Beth was in some trouble."

"Good grief, man. What is it? Has she had some accident?"

"Naw. Nothing like that. Your missus, she said Beth was in some trouble."

"What sort of trouble?" Addison demanded, completely out of patience.

"She said Beth's come under a bad influence and the bad influence was your girl Kerry."

"What do you mean exactly by 'bad influence'?"

George cleared his throat, then swallowed convulsively. "Uh. She and Kerry. They—you know—Kerry's gone and turned her head, and now she won't know how to behave."

"Could you be a little plainer in your speech, sir? I'm still not following you." Addison was beginning to think that his barely conscious awareness of the nature of Beth and Kerry's relationship was in fact correct.

George turned bright red. His hat was bent entirely out of shape from his restless hands.

"It's Kerry. Doctor, she isn't a natural woman. She's gotten our Beth turned on the wrong path. That's what Mrs. Grant said," he said, a little defiantly.

Addison didn't know whom he was more incensed at: his meddling wife or this self-righteous fool. He wasn't sure a man who let the family pastor abuse his daughter had any right to the moral high ground. He knew, however, that George was finally asserting his paternal prerogative. *I can understand even if it's far too late.* He was, however, even more angry that Laura had taken it upon herself to interfere. Her belated spate of maternal worry about Kerry and Beth was deeply suspect. *I'll have the whole story out of her, but in the meantime, I must deal with Hammond.*

"I am sure we will sort this all out, Mr. Hammond. I will be in touch with you soon."

George was clearly surprised at his abrupt dismissal, but he scuttled from the office, his hat still mangled in his hands. After Hammond left, Addison sat in his office for a while. *Laura has truly crossed a line this time. I always knew she was self-absorbed and rigid in her thinking, but I never thought she would be such a terrific busybody. There surely is something afoot with Beth and Kerry, but that's none of our business.* Then he shook his head and returned to the ward and to his patients. He would deal with the situation when his workday was over.

Beth was called to the charge nurse's desk at midmorning. Her father stood there with his hat in hand.

"Papa, I'm surprised to see you," she said in a neutral tone of voice.

"Elizabeth, I must speak with you."

Beth glanced at the charge nurse, who was bent over a chart. "I cannot speak to you. I am at work now, Father. You don't wish me to abandon my work, do you?"

"Ah, I thought because I asked you to, you would."

"Papa. I can't." It was typical of him to assume she would just drop everything and go with him.

"Your mama and I must speak to you as soon as possible."

"What? Is Mama ill? What's the matter?" The charge nurse had noticed the tenseness of their interaction and had left discreetly. They were alone.

"No, nothing like that." He looked embarrassed then. "But we must see you."

"But what is this about, Papa? Can you not give me a small hint?"

George mauled his hat and wouldn't meet her eyes. "I can't say. Not here. Please, Elizabeth. It is important."

Beth felt a little sorry for him. He'd never quite grasped that when she was seventeen years old, she decided that her parents would no longer have a say over anything to do with her. She saw that her papa still wanted to play the *paterfamilias* and expected her obedience.

"Very well. I'll come directly after work."

Laura was unusually quiet. She wouldn't meet Addison's eyes. Beth wouldn't be home for another hour, Addison knew. Kerry would be cooking at the Palace and not return home until much later. It was time. Addison thought of the visit from George Hammond.

"Laura," he said, quietly, "we must speak." She was looking down at the table and she raised her eyes to meet his. He saw a look of guilt. He dreaded the conversation they would have, but he knew they couldn't avoid it this time.

They ate in silence for a while as Addison gathered his thoughts. In a neutral tone, he remarked, "Beth must have had an emergency at the hospital. She wouldn't wish us to wait upon her."

"I'll leave a plate for her on the stove."

He put his fork down and looked at her for what seemed to her an eternity. "I had an unexpected visitor today," he said.

Laura looked back at him, apparently not comprehending.

"George Hammond. Beth's father."

She blanched slightly.

"Why don't you tell me why he said he wanted his daughter back home again. Immediately. He expected me to take care of it. He was polite, but it was clear he considered me guilty of some sort of oversight. I pretended to understand what he was referring to, but in truth I didn't. He told me of the visit from you." Addison stopped speaking and looked at Laura.

"I'm waiting, Laura. What did you tell Mr. and Mrs. Hammond?"

She raised her eyes, which were flashing and defiant. "I had to do it, Addison. They had a right to know."

"A right to know what?"

"About their daughter."

"*What* about their daughter? Speak plainly, Laura. I'm losing patience."

"I told you a long time ago and you wouldn't listen to me."

He opened his mouth but waited for her to say more.

"It's Kerry. She has—"

"What about Kerry?" he asked, harshly.

"She has caused Beth to—" Laura hesitated. "Oh, I don't know how to say this, Addison."

"What are you talking about, Laura?"

"She's no good, as I told you from the beginning. She is, well, she isn't a real woman."

"What does that mean, Laura?" He kept his voice quiet, dangerously quiet.

"She has seduced Beth into unnatural acts. I saw them. I…" Laura was speaking very hurriedly.

Addison raised an eyebrow. He knew what she was trying to say, but he wanted her to own it. He wanted her to be honest.

"You saw them? What?"

"Oh, Addison, you're just being cruel. You know what I mean. You do! Through the keyhole of the bedroom door. They were touching, they were…" She faltered again, her hands moving distractedly in the air as though that would explain it.

He stared at her. "You spied on them?"

"I had to know! I had my suspicions and I had to know the truth. Addison, you must send Beth back to her parents. You must tell Kerry to leave this house. I will not have such a person in my home. What she's doing is despicable. It's time you admitted she is a horrible person. I don't know what she is, but she doesn't belong in a respectable home and we must save Beth. You must see that."

❖

After saying good-bye to Captain Reynolds, Beth walked into her parents' flat, kissed them each perfunctorily, and sat down at the kitchen table. Her mother and her father were in their usual chairs. *Nothing much has changed with them, nor will it ever.*

"Well, Papa. What caused you to come seek me at the hospital?"

"We needed to see you," Frieda said abruptly. "We want you to come home."

"I see no—"

"You are to come back here to live with us immediately. I am ordering you to," George said, but his voice betrayed his lack of confidence in his own authority.

She looked at him with a mixture of contempt and defiance. "Papa. Why are you saying this now?" she asked calmly.

"We have a duty to you. We are your parents," George said with a tiny bit more conviction. "Mrs. Grant has informed us you are in danger. You have come under the influence of a bad person and she is greatly concerned."

Now Beth was genuinely confused. "Who? What?"

Frieda interceded. "Mrs. Grant thinks your friendship with Kerry isn't good for you."

"She's mistaken," Beth said coldly. She was pleased that her voice didn't show any of her sudden fear. *Laura knows about us. How? We've been careful.*

"No, she is not. Why would she have come to us? You're entirely too sure of yourself, girl. It's time you paid more attention to your elders and time you returned to live with us. We should be looking after you. I'm ready to agree that your head may have been turned by this young—this person, but enough. You will come home."

"You'll look after me?" Beth asked George. "As you looked after me when the right Reverend Svenhard was molesting me?" She spoke in a conversational tone, but the effect on George and Frieda was remarkable. They both flinched.

"Oh, you know exactly of what I speak, do you not? Mama? Papa?" She looked at each of them in turn. "You abandoned me to that monster. You were complicit. Mrs. Rocco tried to tell you but you wouldn't listen. Neither of you would listen. Instead you forbade me to see the Rocco family."

She stood up. "You long ago forfeited the right to tell me what to do or where to go or who to love. I'm in love with Kerry O'Shea. If you try to stop me, I promise the entire neighborhood, the entire city of San Francisco, will know what happened to me. I thought for the longest time it was my fault. I believed Svenhard when he told me no one would listen to me. He was right. The two people who should have listened to me did not. You abandoned me when I was ten years old. I am twenty now, and it's too late to want me back. I'm leaving." They stared at her. She collected her purse and went out the door.

Frieda caught up with her. "Beth, darling. Try to understand. He could do nothing. He would have lost the store. *We* could do nothing. We couldn't help you. I'm sorry."

"Spare me your excuses, Mama. He may have made the decision but you did nothing as well."

"Please forgive me, Beth. I'm so sorry. It was wrong. You were mistreated and it has come back to haunt all of us. If you're to have a normal life, you must forgive us and you must come home. We can be a family again."

"I am not going to forgive you. I am not coming home. This is not my home. I will do as I please. Nothing you can say will change my mind. I don't care what you think."

She left her mother weeping at the doorstep and walked down Guerrero Street. She was not thinking of where she was going, or of her parents, but was rather concerned about the larger question of what would happen to her and to Kerry now that Laura had found them out.

When she'd first come to stay with the Grants, Kerry was quite candid with her. "You have to watch out for Laura. She's never liked me. She used to beat me but Addison made her stop." Beth had always been especially polite to Laura, but Laura seemed to shun her because of Kerry. *What has she discovered and what will she tell Addison?* It suddenly occurred to Beth that the consequence she feared the most was the loss of Addison's respect and friendship. *It'll destroy Kerry. She loves him even if she doesn't say so. He saved her life, gave her a home, educated her. If he ceases to care for her, she'll be devastated.*

Beth was so absorbed in her thoughts, she didn't hear her name at first.

"Beth!" someone called. She looked around and then she saw that she was in front of Rocco's Produce Store and the voice belonged to her long-ago friend, Theresa.

❖

"So," Addison said to Laura. "Let me be clear. You think I'm going to have to show Kerry the door because she has led Beth astray."

"It's your responsibility. I am sure Beth's parents will want her home as soon as possible." His long silence had encouraged Laura. She'd recovered her confidence though his anger had momentarily shaken her.

"If you don't, I'll leave you. I've had enough, Addison. This is my home and I believe that I have a say in what goes on in my home. I believe I have a right to expect my husband to agree with me."

He was silent again for a long time. "Very well, Laura. You've made your wishes clear. I'll speak to them. I'll give them a month to find a new home."

Laura opened her mouth to speak but fell silent when she saw the hard coldness of his eyes. Suddenly her victory didn't seem quite as sweet as she had anticipated.

## CHAPTER THIRTY-FIVE

Beth blinked and with effort focused on her surroundings. Theresa laughed. The sound of her laughter called up many complicated feelings in Beth. Coming on the heels of her recent encounter with her parents, the day had a strangely dreamlike feel.

"You're in another world, as usual," Theresa said. They hadn't spoken in many years, but Beth sensed that the length of time didn't matter to Theresa.

"Hello, Theresa. Yes, I was lost in thought."

"How long has it been?"

"Truthfully, I don't know. Perhaps ten years?" The thought saddened Beth. "It's good to see you."

"You could've seen me before now."

"Yes, I suppose that's true. But I—I was distracted. My parents forbade it and then I went to nursing school and…oh, never mind. I am sorry."

"When you left, my mother wouldn't tell me why." Theresa was arranging oranges. "But she told me you weren't to blame. When I was sixteen she explained to me what had happened."

Theresa's dark eyes were very calm and clear. Beth saw no censure in them. She nodded.

Theresa said quietly, "My mama's inside. Do you want to see her?"

Beth nodded.

Theresa was very pregnant. She no longer skipped as she had when they were young, but her step was still light, considering her size.

Mama Rocco presided over the cash register. She looked exactly as Beth remembered her.

"Mama! Look who's here!" Theresa called as they walked through the store among the bins of vegetables that Beth recalled had fascinated her so much. Now, after having been to the Philippines, it seemed strange that something so normal should have seemed so exotic.

"Lizbetta!" Mama said, and promptly kissed both of her cheeks. "It's lovely to see you. Theresa, put the sign on the door and we'll go in the back for a coffee and talk."

In a moment, Beth was seated in a cramped office in the very back of the store. Theresa made espresso and Mama Rocco scrutinized Beth for a moment before she spoke. Beth had noticed that her English, though still heavily accented, was now fluent.

"So, Lizbetta, you're well?" Mama asked, and Beth sensed the feeling behind the question.

"Yes, Mama Rocco. Thank you, I am. And you?"

"Ah," Mama said. "We are as ever. Theresa will soon have her first and our fourth grandchild. Papa's at the farm. He is always working still."

Theresa brought their coffees and sat down with some difficulty.

"We have missed seeing you," Mama said, as though it had been weeks rather than years since their last encounter. She didn't seem angry in the least. Beth's thoughts inevitably roamed back in time to when she went to the Roccos and Mama had induced her to confess about Reverend Svenhard.

"You tried to tell my mother," she said suddenly.

Mama's eyes opened wide. "Tut. Lizbetta. That is all over." Beth glanced at Theresa, who was sipping her coffee and looking into the distance.

"You must respect your parents," Mama said, seemingly apropos of nothing.

"Yes, but I'm sorry she didn't treat you very well."

Mama Rocco took a big gulp of coffee and waved her hand in a gesture of Italian dismissal. "It's of no consequence. Now we sit and have a coffee, eh? Tell us about yourself, Lizbetta."

So Beth talked about nursing and the Philippines war and Addison. She heard about all the Rocco kids, the grandchildren, and Theresa's husband Aldo. She left an hour later and made her way back to the Grants feeling as though a circle had closed.

## Chapter Thirty-six

The four of them sat through a silent, tense dinner the next evening. Beth had explained her day to Kerry when she came home from the restaurant, and together they spent a sleepless night wondering about their future. Addison had left a note the next morning asking them to meet with him after dinner that evening.

Addison asked Beth and Kerry to his study. Laura, for once, tidied up the supper dishes by herself. It seemed to Kerry that she had an infuriating air of satisfaction.

Beth and Kerry sat in front of Addison's desk waiting for him to speak. They couldn't discern from his expression what he was thinking; they purposefully didn't look at one another. He sighed deeply as though his thoughts pained him.

"I don't want to say what I must say nor do what I'm about to do." He put his fingers together and looked into a corner of the room. "It is with deep regret that I must ask you to leave my home. Both of you."

"Why?" Kerry asked, the barest hint of challenge in her voice.

"Laura isn't comfortable with your..." He hesitated, uncharacteristically at a loss for words. "With the two of you." They said nothing so he continued. "It's necessary for me to concede this to my wife."

Beth said, abruptly, "I saw my parents yesterday. I know Laura went to speak to them."

"Ah, yes. I would rather she hadn't done that but, believe me, she thinks she had your best interests in mind," Addison said neutrally.

"That's not true!" Kerry burst out, ignoring Beth's restraining hand on her arm. "You know it's not true. She—"

"Please try to understand, Kerry. I think you can, even if this situation is past Laura's understanding."

"What of you, Addison?" Kerry asked desperately.

He closed his eyes for a moment, then looked from her to Beth.

"When I was a boy in Boston, I often spent part of the summers with my father's sister Lucy. She lived near the Boston Common. My parents took a holiday together without me every year for a month." He smiled at what was clearly a happy memory.

"For as long as I could remember, Aunt Lucy lived with a companion, Amy. I called her aunt as well. For the longest time I thought they were sisters. They both had taught at the same school for many years. Amy was more fond of children, I think. She spent much time with me, flying kites and sailing my model boat. Aunt Lucy was more reserved. She thought children should be seen and not heard, but she was very kind to me in her way. I looked forward to my month's visit with them every year. I heard my father refer once to a 'Boston Marriage.' My mother shushed him since I was in the room. Later, I heard of other women like Lucy and Amy. People always spoke of them with condescension—little shrugs and winks. Somehow, I knew they were a kind of a couple." He stopped speaking and let the meaning of his words sink in. Beth and Kerry sat very still.

Addison said, "I know Kerry's childhood was unusual, unconventional. She grew up to be an unconventional woman. When you two became friends, it seemed right to me, and I knew in my heart that it was with you as it was with Lucy and Amy, although I didn't recognize it for a long time. And when I did, I still didn't want to consciously think it." He stopped and smoothed the papers on his desk.

"What I am saying is, I don't exactly understand why, but I accept without understanding." His voice became sad. "Laura doesn't understand and will never accept."

"She's never liked me!" Kerry cried, the pain of Laura's betrayal bringing out her Irish accent. "From the moment you brought me to your home, she's never once had a kind word to say. I've kept silent because I didn't wish to hurt you and…" She closed her eyes and took a breath. "But, now, why are you letting her do this to us?" Beth put her hand back on Kerry's arm and squeezed gently.

"I'm chagrined that I must treat you this way. I always will be grateful to your father, but I must think of my wife first. I apologize to you as profoundly as I can but see no other way. I must keep peace in my home, and the two of you are old enough now to be on your own, without her anger in your way."

Kerry scowled. "I see that. Well, she's finally gotten her way. So we'll leave." Beth only looked at Addison in dismay and with a hint of compassion.

They stood up and walked out the door, and before Kerry closed it she saw Addison still sitting at his desk, his hands folded across his waistcoat, staring into space.

❖

"It's outrageous what she has made him do. He promised me I would always have a home. She's a witch. I shoulda known she'd finally get her way. She's horrible to him. I want to kill her. This is all her fault. Addison is the only person outside of Jack I ever trusted. I never thought he'd betray me like this."

Beth let Kerry rant on for a while but said, finally, "There is nothing we can do. You can't avenge yourself without hurting Addison."

"He would understand." Kerry bit off her words. "He knows now what sort of person she is. You know she must have spied on us somehow. It wouldn't be beneath her. She's turned Addison against us." She clenched her fists.

"Kerry, dear, you heard what Addison said. He understands, but he has to live with Laura."

"Can't he just tell her we're staying?" Kerry asked. "It's his house. He's the man. He can demand that she follow his orders."

"I think he cannot."

"I can't believe you're taking this so quietly. But then you haven't lived here that long. You haven't known Addison as long as I have. I'll never forgive him for this."

"Kerry. I know you're hurt. Addison is your best friend, isn't he?"

Kerry stopped pacing and stared at her. She looked away and said, quietly, "I once believed he was."

"Then you must forgive him. You can see how much this hurts him."

"Well, I blame Laura the most, but..."

Beth waited for a moment, then put her arm around Kerry's shoulders and lifted her chin up so their eyes could meet. "It's time we find our own place. I wouldn't have wanted this to happen but it's for the best. I was angry that Laura went to my parents, but it was better that we finally had it out. Let's get our own home, Kerry."

❖

"It's done, Laura. I've done what you asked. I wish to give them some time to make arrangements."

"Oh, but of course, Addison dear. They may have that. I'm so very happy." Laura was magnanimous in her victory. Addison saw that and was even angrier at her. His self-loathing transformed his anger at himself into anger with Laura. He thought, I am no longer in love with her. I can barely stand to look at her.

She put her arms around him. "It shall just be us now, and the peace and quiet will be glorious. I do think it will be good for us, don't you?"

He looked down at her and disengaged her arms. "You may think so, if you wish. I no longer find I have much feeling for you at all."

She stepped back, looking surprised and searching his face for his meaning.

"We will continue to be married. Like you, I've no wish for scandal. Rest assured, no one will know anything is wrong."

"Addison—"

"No. Don't say a thing. You've said quite enough already. You have my name. You and I will continue to occupy this house as usual. You no longer may expect any tenderness or affection from me. You're a meddling, mean, vain, and unhappy woman."

Laura paled. "Addison, please. I thought—"

"Laura, I no longer care what you think or what you feel or what you want. I've given you your wish. Your treatment of Beth and Kerry convinces me you are a woman completely lacking in empathy, understanding, or generosity. To keep you happy, I have turned away a friend's child whom I have come to think of as my own and broken a promise. But you're happy. And, of course, that is what matters most."

Addison walked out, his heart heavier than his footsteps.

❖

"I think that what I want, aside from a comfortable room in a place that is convenient for both of us, is a piano."

It took some searching but they finally found a room to rent in a house on upper Divisadero owned by a widow. It wasn't far from the Presidio but also on the cable car route and only a mile and a half from the Grants' home, although they wouldn't be visiting often, if at all. It had a view of the San Francisco Bay. Beth joked that the uphill walk back home from the hospital would prevent her from becoming too fat from Kerry's cooking. Kerry would be able to ride the California Street cable car downtown to the Palace Hotel. The widow was distinctly disinterested in her two tenants other than that they paid their rent on time and didn't make noise. In her downstairs parlor was a reasonably good piano and the widow, Mrs. Thompson, said, "No one has ever had an interest. Please feel free to play as often as you like."

"We must save money," Beth said, ever the practical one. "With what you have saved, some day we can buy a house, even while paying rent here."

Kerry agreed. She could think of nothing better than that she and Beth would share a home together rather than merely a room. But she still hadn't quite forgiven Addison.

Beth said, "If you look at it from his perspective, he had to do it for his wife. You'd do anything for me, wouldn't you?"

"I would, you know I would."

"Then you understand why Addison had to do what he did."

Kerry was still sore, but she had no wish to quarrel with Beth. She had to admit it was a relief to be away from Laura's constant aura of distaste and distrust, even if it came at the price of losing her attachment to Addison.

## Chapter Thirty-seven

It was January first, 1900, and San Francisco citizens welcomed the New Year, the new decade, and the new century. Though the papers said the new century wouldn't officially begin until 1901, the common folk thought it still began at midnight, 1899. On New Year's Day, Beth and Kerry walked to the hill behind their new home. The houses were sparse this far up Divisadero Street. Less than a mile away were dairy farms with herds of milk cattle grazing quietly on the dune scrub. And always, in the distance, they could see the crystal-blue expanse of the San Francisco Bay. Across the Bay, the hills of Marin County were bright green from the winter rain. A steamer glided through the Golden Gate, and Kerry wondered where she would dock and if a crimper was waiting to steal her sailors for another captain. *It has no more to do with me. Thank God. I'll never go back to that life.*

They sat and ate a little bit of lunch as they admired the scenery. They were subdued. Their Christmas dinner had been two days before. They had, in fact, shared it with Mrs. Thompson, but without Addison or Beth's family, the holiday had seemed far lonelier than they had anticipated.

With her high color and windblown hair, Beth had never looked better to Kerry. She was quietly looking off in the distance, seeming contemplative, and Kerry was suddenly afraid.

"Will you go to medical school? Like Addison thinks you should?"

Beth didn't reply for a moment. She kept staring at the sea. Finally, she said, "I don't know. It would mean great sacrifice for us both." She turned and looked at her and put a hand on Kerry's cheek.

"I want you to have what you want," Kerry whispered. They

kissed, gently at first but then with increasing fervor. Then they broke apart.

Beth said, "Now that I know you love me and I love you, now that I know what that means, anything seems possible."

They kissed again, and as Beth felt of her cheeks, she said, "You're crying."

"Happy." Kerry gasped, wiping at her cheeks. "That's all."

"But still," Beth teased her, "it's wonderful."

Kerry wiped her eyes and grimaced at the teasing, then smiled at Beth. "I never thought you'd fall in love with me," she said. She took Beth's hand and squeezed it. Beth squeezed back.

"Stand up for a moment," Beth said, as she stood and reached her hand down to Kerry. She turned to face toward the sea.

Kerry looked at her as she gazed off in the distance, memorizing the way the sunlight touched her face, the way her eyes showed her every thought, the way her lips curved in a gentle smile.

"Well, I never thought I'd fall in love with you either. Yet here we are."

"Yes. Here we are. Here we stay? Always together, no matter what?" Kerry asked meaningfully.

Beth laid her head on Kerry's shoulder and wrapped an arm tightly around her waist. "Always. No matter what."

Their hands clasped, they turned and once again looked out over the Golden Gate and beyond to the horizon.

# About the Author

Kathleen Knowles grew up in Pittsburgh, Pennsylvania, but has lived in San Francisco for more than thirty years. She finds the city's combination of history, natural beauty, and multicultural diversity inspiring and endlessly fascinating.

Other than writing, she loves music of all kinds, walking, bicycling, and stamp collecting. LGBT history and politics have commanded her attention for many years, starting with her first Pride march in Cleveland, Ohio, in 1978. She and her partner were married in July 2008 and live atop one of San Francisco's many hills with their cats. She works as a health and safety specialist at the University of California, San Francisco.

She has written short stories, essays, and fan fiction. *Awake Unto Me* is her first published work.

# Books Available From Bold Strokes Books

**Initiation by Desire** by MJ Williamz. Jaded Sue and innocent Tulley find forbidden love and passion within the inhibiting confines of a sorority house filled with nosy sisters. (978-160282-590-1)

**Toughskins** by William Masswa. John and Bret are two twenty-something athletes who find that love can begin in the most unlikely of places, including a "mom-and-pop shop" wrestling league. (978-1-60282-591-8)

**Worth the Risk** by Karis Walsh. Investment analyst Jamie Callahan and Grand Prix show jumper Kaitlyn Brown are willing to risk it all in their careers—can they face a greater challenge and take a chance on love? (978-1-60282-587-1)

**me@you.com** by KE Payne. Is it possible to fall in love with someone you've never met? Imogen Summers thinks so because it's happened to her. (978-1-60282-592-5)

**Bloody Claws** by Winter Pennington. In the midst of aiding the police, Preternatural Private Investigator Kassandra Lyall finally finds herself at serious odds with Sheila Morris, the local werewolf pack's Alpha female, when Sheila abuses someone Kassandra has sworn to protect. (978-1-60282-588-8)

**Awake Unto Me** by Kathleen Knowles. In turn of the century San Francisco, two young women fight for love in a world where women are often invisible and passion is the privilege of the powerful. (978-1-60282-589-5)

**Franky Gets Real** by Mel Bossa. A four-day getaway. Five childhood friends. Five shattering confessions...and a forgotten love unearthed. (978-1-60282-585-7)

**Riding the Rails: Locomotive Lust and Carnal Cabooses**, edited by Jerry Wheeler. Some of the hottest writers of gay erotica spin tales of *Riding the Rails*. (978-1-60282-586-4)

**Rescue Me** by Julie Cannon. Tyler Logan reluctantly agrees to pose as the girlfriend of her in-the-closet gay BFF at his company's annual retreat, but she didn't count on falling for Kristin, the boss's wife. (978-1-60282-582-6)

**Snowbound** by Cari Hunter. *"The policewoman got shot and she's bleeding everywhere. Get someone here in one hour or I'm going to put her out of her misery."* It's an ultimatum that will forever change the lives of police officer Sam Lucas and Dr. Kate Myles. (978-1-60282-581-9)

**High Impact by Kim Baldwin.** Thrill seeker Emery Lawson and Adventure Outfitter Pasha Dunn learn you can never truly appreciate what's important and what you're capable of until faced with a sudden and stark reminder of your own mortality. (978-1-60282-580-2)

**Murder in the Irish Channel** by Greg Herren. Chanse MacLeod investigates the disappearance of a female activist fighting the Archdiocese of New Orleans and a powerful real estate syndicate. (978-1-60282-584-0)

**Sheltering Dunes** by Radclyffe. The seventh in the award-winning Provincetown Tales. The pasts, presents, and futures of three women collide in a single moment that will alter all their lives forever. (978-1-60282-573-4)

**Holy Rollers** by Rob Byrnes. Partners in life and crime Grant Lambert and Chase LaMarca assemble a team of gay and lesbian criminals to steal millions from a right-wing mega-church, but the gang's plans are complicated by an "ex-gay" conference, the FBI, and a corrupt reverend with his own plans for the cash. (978-1-60282-578-9)

**History's Passion: Stories of Sex Before Stonewall**, edited by Richard Labonté. Four acclaimed erotic authors re-imagine the past…Welcome to the hidden queer history of men loving men not so very long—and centuries—ago. (978-1-60282-576-5)

**Lucky Loser** by Yolanda Wallace. Top tennis pros Sinjin Smythe and Laure Fortescue reach Wimbledon desperate to claim tennis's crown jewel, but will their feelings for each other get in the way? (978-1-60282-575-8)

**Mystery of The Tempest: A Fisher Key Adventure** by Sam Cameron. Twin brothers Denny and Steven Anderson love helping people and fighting crime alongside their sheriff dad on sun-drenched Fisher Key, Florida, but Denny doesn't dare tell anyone he's gay, and Steven has secrets of his own to keep. (978-1-60282-579-6)

**Better Off Red: Vampire Sorority Sisters Book 1** by Rebekah Weatherspoon. Every sorority has its secrets, and college freshman Ginger Carmichael soon discovers that her pledge is more than a bond of sisterhood—it's a lifelong pact to serve six bloodthirsty demons with a lot more than nutritional needs. (978-1-60282-574-1)

**Detours** by Jeffrey Ricker. Joel Patterson is heading to Maine for his mother's funeral, and his high school friend Lincoln has invited himself along on the ride—and into Joel's bed—but when the ghost of Joel's mother joins the trip, the route is likely to be anything but straight. (978-1-60282-577-2)

**Three Days** by L.T. Marie. In a town like Vegas where anything can happen, Shawn and Dakota find that the stakes are love at all costs, and it's a gamble neither can afford to lose. (978-1-60282-569-7)

**Swimming to Chicago** by David-Matthew Barnes. As the lives of the adults around them unravel, high school students Alex and Robby form an unbreakable bond, vowing to do anything to stay together—even if it means leaving everything behind. (978-1-60282-572-7)

**Hostage Moon** by AJ Quinn. Hunter Roswell thought she had left her past behind, until a serial killer begins stalking her. Can FBI profiler Sara Wilder help her find her connection to the killer before he strikes on blood moon? (978-1-60282-568-0)

**Erotica Exotica: Tales of Sex, Magic, and the Supernatural**, edited by Richard Labonté. Today's top gay erotica authors offer sexual thrills and perverse arousal, spooky chills, and magical orgasms in these stories exploring arcane mystery, supernatural seduction, and sex that haunts in a manner both weird and wondrous. (978-1-60282-570-3)

**Blue** by Russ Gregory. Matt and Thatcher find themselves in the crosshairs of a psychotic killer stalking gay men in the streets of Austin, and only a 103-year-old nursing home resident holds the key to solving the murders—but can she give up her secrets in time to save them? (978-1-60282-571-0)

**Balance of Forces: Toujours Ici** by Ali Vali. Immortal Kendal Richoux's life began during the reign of Egypt's only female pharaoh, and history has taught her the dangers of getting too close to anyone who hasn't harnessed the power of time, but as she prepares for the most important battle of her long life, can she resist her attraction to Piper Marmande? (978-1-60282-567-3)

**Wings: Subversive Gay Angel Erotica**, edited by Todd Gregory. A collection of powerfully written tales of passion and desire centered on the aching beauty of angels. (978-1-60282-565-9)

**Contemporary Gay Romances** by Felice Picano. This collection of short fiction from legendary novelist and memoirist Felice Picano are as different from any standard "romances" as you can get, but they will linger in the mind and memory. (978-1-60282-639-7)

**Sex and Skateboards** by Ashley Bartlett. Sex and skateboards and surfing on the California coast. What more could anyone want? Alden McKenna thinks that's all she needs, until she meets Weston Duvall. (978-1-60282-562-8)

**Waiting in the Wings** by Melissa Brayden. Jenna has spent her whole life training for the stage, but the one thing she didn't prepare for was Adrienne. Is she ready to sacrifice what she's worked so hard for in exchange for a shot at something much deeper? (978-1-60282-561-1)